THE TR

Brian Callison was
He was educated at
before entering the .... navy in 1950 as a
midshipman with the Blue Funnel Line, sailing
mainly on cargo liners to the Far East and
Australia. On leaving the sea he studied at
Dundee College of Art. He has held several
administrative posts, including those of managing
director of a construction company and general
manager of a large entertainment centre.

He also served several years in the territorial
army with the 51st Highland Division Provost
Company, Royal Military Police, and now main-
tains an active connection with the sea as an
officer of the Royal Naval Auxiliary Service.

His first, phenomenally successful novel, *A
Flock of Ships*, was published in 1970 and has
been translated into nine foreign languages. His
most recent novels have been *The Bone Collectors*,
A Thunder of Crude and *Trapp and World War
Three*.

BRIAN CALLISON

THE TROJAN HEARSE

Fontana
An Imprint of HarperCollinsPublishers

First published in 1990 by HarperCollins Publishers,
77–85 Fulham Palace Road,
Hammersmith, London W6 8JB

This Fontana edition first issued 1991

9   8   7   6   5   4   3   2   1

Copyright © Brian Callison 1990

The Author asserts the moral right to be
identified as the author of this work

Printed and bound in Great Britain by
HarperCollins Book Manufacturing, Glasgow

Prologue

It offered all the elements of a textbook evolution.

'Attacking! Tubes one and two prepare for underwater firing. Flood tubes – open bow-caps – steer zero-six-five . . . ! Sound?'

'Sir?'

'Hydrophone search again. All sectors, Stemmler. Time check, Navigator?'

'Sixteen twenty-seven, sir.'

'Which makes it nearly tea-time,' the Captain said: enforcedly casual to ease the tension, poised ready to bury his brow into the foam rubber eyepiece again. 'Stand by to check target bearing, Tower . . . Slow ahead both, please.'

Electric motors whined softly, a scatter of quietly repeated orders punctuating their battery-powered dirge. The U-boat began to rock in gentle suspension as the gleaming shaft of the attack periscope rose hissing, feather docile at Rietz's bidding to cautiously break surface again.

. . . whereupon, concealed now from his control room crew, the strictly private regret came back to the Captain's eyes.

For that doggedly steaming silhouette framed in his streaming Zeiss lens wasn't merely an abstract image – not to Rietz. Not just a soulless, Atlantic-blurred amalgamation of steel, brass and iron; wood, oakum and hemp. It was a unique creation.

Being, quite simply, a ship.

That appreciation alone established, in the Captain's view, the uncertainly approaching convoy straggler as being every bit as vital a living creature as any Tommy seaman dictating her rusted progress.

And it was a reasonable assumption that, even if a U-boat commander of Rietz's quality couldn't kill such a vulnerable target's complement, either in whole or in part, he would almost certainly destroy their vessel. Bluff-bowed and stick-funnelled she had to be over thirty years old, and thus already a veteran of a much earlier Battle of the Atlantic; panting even to maintain a bare seven knots against the creaming westerly seas while zigzagging only half-heartedly as though her master had resigned himself to accepting that, should his weary command ever aspire to reach safe haven, then a virtual straight line was the only practical course to steer.

Such abstract deliberation wasn't exceptional for Rietz. A disquiet for what he was about to do still tended to embrace the Captain during this preliminary phase of every attack; intruded, as now, upon his most precious moments of privacy. The need to destroy such proudly fashioned creatures was the one element he still found difficulty in reconciling with his duty to the Fatherland.

But all he actually said was: 'Target identification: five and a half thousand tonner. Tommy tramp. Three island scow with a bloody criminal top weight of deck cargo. Looks like timber – Christ, it's pissing down up there.'

'With a bit of luck the bastards'll drown anyway. Academic whether it's salt or fresh that kills 'em,' Chief Engineer Sindermann grinned fiercely, bearded and skull-faced with strain from his station at the trimming panel. 'Boat balanced, Herr Oberleutnant. Depth: twelve metres thirty!'

'Thank you.' Rietz rotated the periscope fractionally. He didn't comment further. Sindermann's telegram had arrived three hours before they'd sailed from St-Nazaire. It regretted to inform the Chief that his wife and two baby daughters had been killed in an RAF raid on Cologne. Sindermann had doggedly insisted on abandoning his right to compassionate leave. Sindermann wanted only to kill Tommies as a pragmatic expression of mourning.

Chief Engineer Sindermann had mourned to great effect

6

during the course of this last patrol, Rietz reflected bleakly. His new VII-C boat, hunting Sector Bruno Dora in company with other members of *Gruppe Sturmer*, had savaged one Newfound-land/UK-bound slow convoy so brutally that, during the darkest, wildest period of one bloody night, their respective hydrophone operators experienced considerable difficulty in isolating the subsea rumblings of Allied hulls crushing simultaneously under the pressure of water.

Sindermann might never, ever be totally happy again. But by *God*, on that horrific night of slaughter he'd rediscovered how to smile!

'Whereaway now, Stemmler?'

'Propeller noise still moving left, bearing zero-one-five de-grees, sir: loud and increasing. All other sectors silent.'

'Maintain hydrophone search.'

Rietz upped the scope and snatched a six-second glance.

'Come five to port – steer two-nine-eight! Switch on tubes one and two. Enemy speed, seven knots – range, nineteen hundred! Set torpedo speeds to three zero: depth three metres. Bow left – angle forty – follow changing angle!'

He downed the periscope and leaned back against the running convex steel of the boat listening to the litany of repetition; forcing himself to appear casual. The atmosphere stank of submarine and submariners – diesel and sweat and urine and cabbage. Condensation was beginning to whisp streamers of vapour around the naked deckhead lights.

'Nearly there,' Rietz announced. 'Unless she alters again we'll have her beam on in two minutes.'

'Propeller noise closing steadily: still passing right to left, sir.'

'Thank you, Sound.'

'Do please come into my web,' said Herr Spider to the Fly, Rietz thought expressionlessly: patiently. But then, the Captain had suffered far wider-ranging qualms of conscience once. A very long time ago now, it all seemed.

For, while Rietz had listened avidly like every other patriotic German to Chancellor Hitler's great speeches, and had grimly appreciated that the Fatherland had no option but to stand fast for the second time that century in the face of British provocation – a nation forced to war despite the Führer's most earnest attempts at compromise – mobilization had still heralded a period of uneasy psychological readjustment for the abruptly militarized Rietz.

For the Captain had been a peacetime merchant seaman when the clouds of war finally exploded over the Polish–German Corridor in the heady blitzkrieg days of September '39.

By the end of that month – already, at thirty-two years of age, a senior bridge officer of promise in the superb passenger ships of the Hamburg–Amerika Line and so most likely to excel at surface warfare – Rietz had nevertheless found himself appointed to Kiel submarine school while his previous ship underwent hasty conversion for her new task of raiding enemy trade lanes in the South Atlantic.

An area which he'd known intimately, and from whence he'd just returned.

So, because the Kriegsmarine wasn't any more astute than any other navy at utilizing its greatest resources, not only did that mean that Paul Rietz had to master the third – to a conventional seafarer, particularly traumatic – dimension of operating under-water, it also afforded the bitter irony that his primary task as a U-boat man would be to hunt and destroy the very merchant vessels he'd grown to respect, indeed to love, as fellow voyagers during his formative years at sea.

And thus it was that the – by then – ex-Chief Officer Rietz had found himself a considerably older, perhaps rather more thoughtful would-be fighting man than the majority of his fellow candidates earmarked for accelerated promotion within Admiral Doenitz's urgently expanding U-boat arm.

Looking back with a trace of cynicism, he'd also found himself to be quite unique.

It seemed he'd been the only fledgeling U-boat officer in the Third Reich's shiny new war machine *not* consumed by a feverish desire to win his Cross of Iron on the basis of total tonnage sunk!

. . . Those early scruples, the Captain pondered ruefully, had been given every cause to still themselves since his subsequent advancement to the harsh realities of battle command.

8

Only it seemed they hadn't been entirely suppressed: not even now. In the awareness that he was probably about to kill some of that so-vulnerably approaching ship's crew – perhaps all forty-odd of them should the gods of war feel disinclined to clemency during the space of the coming minutes – the Captain still couldn't dismiss a further nagging suspicion that he, U-Boot-waffe Oberleutnant Paul Rietz, might arguably be about to commit murder.

... Yet again! he reflected, and not without a touch of justifiable resentment. The first, and emphatically the last, time Rietz had naïvely surfaced to warn such an apparently defenceless British steamer's crew of their vessel's impending sinking, an opening round from the Tommy's concealed stern gun had blown his boat's target marker lens away in company with a good 95 per cent of his moral conscience.

That nearly fatal compassion, the low light of his maiden patrol as commander of an old Sixth Flotilla VII-B boat, had taken place over a year previously. Rietz had learned a lot since then. The simple proof of his continued diligence as a military student was evinced by the number of Allied seamen who had subsequently perished without warning as Oberleutnant Rietz's volcanic eels crashed into their hulls whereas he, Rietz, had – so far, at least – succeeded in keeping both his crew and himself alive.

The Captain shrugged wearily as time had taught him to do. Basically it all boiled down to expediency: to whether it was more profitable to justify one's view of war from above or from below the surface. The arch-criminal propagandist Churchill skilfully exploited the bloody consequence of such effectively learned German tactics as 'Unrestricted submarine warfare'. Onkel Karl's nephews – the officers and men of Doenitz's élite U-boat force – sardonically called them 'Survival'.

So the fate of the approaching merchantman's crew – the British – now caused the Captain, as with most men conditioned by two years of actual combat, only the briefest moment of soul searching. One had merely to remember that in the matter of Poland the Tommies had opted to protect the Jewish interest: had elected to become the Third Reich's enemies and thus,

9

by definition, Oberleutnant Rietz's. Moreover, that the British themselves had also helped prescribe the rules of the new sea war – or rather the lack of them – having graphically demonstrated to Rietz that one had little option but to smite one's enemies before they bloody well smote you.

Whereas his other concern: the image nudging his target marker, that deeper cause for the Captain's introspection – now she *did* still cause him more than a twinge of regret!

That lonely ship, lame and ugly as she was, had never done a damn thing voluntarily to harm him, while Rietz was coldly aware that a hit by either one of his boat's remaining two Mk G7E torpedoes of the patrol – each four hundred kilos' weight of high explosive, ready-loaded and awaiting expulsion, barracuda fast, towards the target encased within forty thousand Reichsmarks'-worth of Krupps' technology – would snap such a venerable old lady's spine clean as a rotted spar.

Participating in THAT sort of barbaric conduct, the Captain considered morosely: now that *could* quite justifiably be regarded as murder by any jury of true seafarers.

And it was that privately concealed inner conflict which really made Oberleutnant Paul Rietz – who loved ships infinitely more than beautiful women, having had intimate experience of both and thus having proved to his own satisfaction that only the ships could be said to be entirely trustworthy – so sad.

Not that Rietz had always believed that human beings were of lesser account than ships. Rietz had, once upon a time, even assumed it possible to divide his allegiance between both. Some six years previously, before the war changed everything for everybody for ever anyway, he had embarked upon a voyage into matrimony as blithely as had most of his contemporaries: in the then Merchant Third Officer Rietz's case with a Hamburg banker's daughter called Karen who'd possessed long golden hair, an exquisite body, a sexual appetite equal to his own and no greater perception than he of the reality of separation.

It had proved an unhappy passage almost from the start. Founded on such immature passion, the marriage had inevitably disintegrated into a recriminatory union of two unsuited people: she unable to come to terms with the necessarily sporadic demands a seagoing husband made on her; he increasingly resentful at being made to feel an interloper in her otherwise separate life. They had never produced a child, and now they never would. She had left Rietz twelve months before he was called to the U-Bootwaffe but, quite frankly, by then Rietz had given up caring about anybody, man or woman, outside the compass of his own crew anyway.

. . . but that ship out there had never caused him hurt.

He felt nothing but compassion for the ship.

From the tower the click of Rohde's attack calculator echoed distantly as the First Watch Officer fed constantly changing lead data to the gyroscopic brains of the torpedoes. Young Rohde was a Nazi. Very political: one of the Führer's strength-through-joy kids before they patted him on his arrogant blond head and gave him his Kriegsmarine uniform. Rietz didn't have a lot of time for Leutnant Rohde but conceded the Leutnant was good at his trade. Murdering helpless ships.

Now Grutner, on the other hand, wasn't. Grutner got nervous as the killing time approached. Sweat dripped unheeded from Navigator Grutner's nose even as Rietz watched, splashing briefly twinkling stains across his tightly grasped clipboard and stop-watch.

'We'll try a double shot,' Rietz said to no one in particular, conscious that only he, through the medium of his extendable Cyclopean lens, was privy to what lay on the surface. His eyes substituted for the eyes of all of them. It helped maintain morale to keep them informed of his intentions. 'Both eels; three-second interval.'

'No dispersal angle, sir?'

'Negative!'

'Fucking lovely. Fish in a barrel,' the Chief muttered evilly.

Rietz shoved his white cap flat aback: the Kriegsmarine symbol of command almost as coveted by Leutnant Rohde as the Iron Cross Rietz had been personally awarded by the Führer following their previous patrol – for, the Captain reflected ironically, merchant tonnage sunk! Then he half squatted, reaching for the scope handles in anticipation while feeling, as always, ridiculously elephantine in his ancient leather flying jacket and yellowed submarine jersey.

'Two minutes, sir!' the Navigator called tightly.

Rietz upped the scope, compressed into the eyepiece quickly, searching for the ship. She was there, precisely where he'd anticipated.

'Tubes one and two – prepare to fire. Range: fifteen hundred. Motors half ahead!'

He could make out the blurred outlines of boats and Carley floats; the misplacedly defiant stream of the British merchant fleet's Red Duster at her counter; but Rietz, by then, had divorced himself from such personality. Instinctively the Captain, too, had become a computer; a robot every bit as calculating as Rohde's attack-programmed fruit machine. He felt no sadness now, no moral dilemma: only the pound of adrenalin, the U-Bootwaffe hunter-killer syndrome coursing through his tautly braced frame.

A cold and somewhat unexpected facility for murderous professional detachment considering his previous misgivings, which explained why ex-merchant seaman and failed husband Paul Rietz afforded promise of becoming every bit as efficient a ship destroyer as Gunther Prien of U.47 who'd torpedoed the battleship *Royal Oak* after penetrating the Tommies' most secure fortress of Scapa Flow; as Otto Kretchmer and Joachim Shepke: eighty-four sinkings between them – even as efficient as the great Fritz-Julius Lemp who, within ten hours of Britain's suicidal declaration of war and while still a mere Oberleutnant commanding the old U.30, had torpedoed and sunk the Donaldson liner *Athenia* before aspiring to fifteen further successes including the awesome destruction of the Royal Navy's Battleship *Barham*.

Or perhaps that was to underestimate Rietz. Perhaps Rietz was in process of proving himself an ever better man. For hadn't those early heroes – the Fatherland's first U-boat aces of this Second World War – all been sunk or captured over a year previously?

Whereas on the twenty-fourth day of March 1942, Oberleutnant Paul Rietz was still alive.

And killing.

*

'Tube one . . .'

Someone choked nervously; convulsively: exploded into a paroxysm of nervous coughing down aft. Rietz only dimly heard the savage response from Maschinenobergefreiter Schauroth.

'You're on a fuckin' CHARGE, Zeissler . . . !'

'. . . *Fire!*'

The boat jolted fractionally; barely began to lift her abruptly lightened bow surfacewards before Chief Sindermann expertly compensated for the loss of trim.

'Tube two . . .'

Rietz watched tightly, dispassionately, as the doomed ship's Zeiss-magnified Plimsoll line and rusted boot topping slid further into the crystal trap of his periscope target marker.

'FIRE!'

A second jolt and an audible exhalation from those around him, the *click* of Grutner's stopwatch sharply punctuating the tension. Now they must wait again, and hide again, and wonder.

Rietz straightened; downed the scope and involuntarily stared upwards, a blind man in company with blind men, towards the streaming, pipe-intestined deckhead and the surface of the North Atlantic.

'Both torpedoes running, sir!' Harshly, from Sound.

'Thank you, Stemmler.' Studiously laconic, from their Captain.

The remains of a Westphalian smoked ham hung from a compressed air line directly above Rietz's head, swinging gently with the subsea rocking generated by the expulsion of their last torpedo. Rietz concentrated on the ham. It belonged collectively to the wardroom. Every Sunday at sea they'd lovingly cut a thick slice for each officer. No special privilege was accorded to rank when it came to sharing the ham which had, by now, turned black-shiny from over-curing in the foetid air of the boat. Only the most recently dissected plane of pig remained faintly pink and white.

How long did a G7E torpedo *take* to cover a few hundred metres of sea, f'r Christ's sake . . . ?

They'd synchronized the expenditure of both the ham and

their primary armament well. Fourteen eels had left the tubes since sailing on war patrol six weeks ago, during which period the pink and white ham plane had slowly diminished to a small circle. Only one moderate portion left for each now, surrounding a fastidiously scraped shank of bone.

Take courage. Your time has come too, Ham, Rietz thought determinedly. We're a stingray without a sting now. Good reason to eat you all up and go home ...!

A giant padded hammer boomed faint against the outer hull. Rietz found his glance drawn involuntarily past the tense, expressionless faces of the two planesmen towards Chief Engineer Sindermann. Sindermann's features were deadpan too, except that the bereaved man's careful restraint didn't quite encompass his eyes. There was a glittering satisfaction there, signalled faintly from dark and sunken voids: an exquisite misery of joy.

The Captain felt glad in that moment that he'd never spawned babies before Karen left him.

'Sweet music, eh, Obermaat? Requiem for another hearseload of Tommies.' Rietz overheard Rohde's typically tasteless and sardonic aside to his conning tower PO.

A second muffled drumbeat transmitting through the cold envelope of sea enclosing them, followed by a spontaneous cheer from forward; just as spontaneously discouraged by the senior rates.

Pity senior rates aren't permitted the privilege of silencing arrogant little shits like Rohde as well, Rietz thought grimly, making a mental note for later – Captains were!

'Two explosions bearing three-five-zero, sir,' Stemmler reported with studied formality.

The Captain saw the haggard, bearded faces watching hopefully. They'd all done well; he owed it to them. Especially to Sindermann.

'Bridge watchkeepers and gun's crew to the tower. Stand by to surface in three minutes ...' Rietz smiled bleakly. They expected it of him. 'We'll take a look at victory, before we go home!'

*

Victory was half an ancient ship still protruding from the Atlantic. Victory was a spreading carpet of cheap coal-dust from ruptured bunkers bearing hideous, ingeniously vivisected things from her fo'c'sle accommodation. Victory was having reduced the enemy to one splintered lifeboat, and that only part filled with shock-eyed survivors.

Victory, to fanatics like Rohde and tortured widow-men like Sindermann, was the legless, headless corpse, still stoutly displaying British Merchant Navy chief officer's rings around brassbound jacket sleeves, which Grutner discovered jammed behind their quadruple 20mm AA gun mounting abaft the bridge immediately after surfacing.

Victory for U-Bootwaffe Leutnant Grutner, it seemed, was being violently sick.

Victory, to Oberleutnant Rietz, demanded a further cold assessment in the rain. His stalker's adrenalin had subsided: by then he felt deflated and sour; any satisfaction derived from carrying out his professional duty was dissipated by anger with himself for making her suffer further, for not having achieved a clean kill.

Despite the two hits forward and amidships it was apparent that the victim's after bulkheads were still holding. Rietz knew that even such a mortally stricken part ship could remain afloat for days. The British deep-sea salvage service had been known to pluck similar casualties home before now, if only to retrieve their needed cargoes. The Captain had no contempt for the resourcefulness of the Royal Navy: Rietz had studied Nelson and Beattie; read *Hornblower* as keenly as any other U-boat commander.

'Put some bloody holes in her. Let the air out.'

'Fire at will . . . Commence firing!'

SLAM . . . ! *Whoosh* as the forward cannon's shell tore away to target: a brief incandescent sparkle against the distant hull. SLAM! – this time the trajectory sounding like ripping sailcloth . . . Water vapour began to spurt geyser-like from the penetrations and the old voyager shuddered grotesquely; rusted wire stays parting like flailing snakes; mizzen mast collapsing across the after end of her angled centrecastle.

Slam . . .! SLAM . . .! That bloody Tommy Red Ensign still defiant as hell . . .

SLAM!

A conqueror strangely reluctant to savour Victory in detail, the Captain still raised his Zeiss glasses – *shit*! He licked caked salt from the lenses, screwed them below his brow again, noted something fuzzy protruding from the sinking ship's side moving, it seemed, convulsively, frantically. Rietz caressed the knurled focusing wheel . . . an eight-times-magnified man slammed into close-up, irretrievably wedged within a rusted after porthole just too small to permit full egress. The enemy seaman's mouth was open: crying. The Quintessence of Victory . . .

Deliberately Rietz swung the binoculars to her counter. British Naval Security insisted the merchantmen obliterated their names while in port: British bloody-mindedness meant their crews invariably replaced them on sailing.

'Indentify for the war log,' he called harshly. 'Name: *Oberon* – Port of Registry: Liverpool.'

SLAM again from the foredeck and the acrid whiff of propellent flung back across the sprayshield by the bitter wind. The now twice-stricken victim, still embracing the trapped man, started to sag forward and down as an eerie rumble of collapsing bulkheads reached the slowly cruising U-boat across that restless bier of sundered dead. Black gushing steam and coal dust began to shriek from her spindlestick funnel.

'She's going,' one of the younger bridge look-outs muttered in awed fascination.

'Don't ogle! Keep your eyes on your bloody SECTOR or I'll 'ave you, laddie!' Landgraf snarled. Bootsmaat Landgraf had good reason to be sensitive on the surface. The Bosun's previous boat had returned to Lorient with a depth charge lodged in her forward casing dropped by a low-flying aircraft no one had even seen coming.

SLAM!

Inexorably the racked ship began to diminish into the heart of a rearing, gouting cauliflower of sea, the remaining air trapped within her finally compressing beyond tolerance to explode wooden hatch covers and vents with machine gun reports. Timber baulks began to tear loose from submerging deck cargo, spearing surfacewards to leap twenty, thirty metres into the storm-ripped sky. Faster and faster she slid, gathering a great and terrible momentum. Rietz felt inordinately relieved when the mouthing accusations from her fellow porthole voyager were finally dragged forever below the hysterical sea, but that only added to his secret anger. Compassion for the enemy's vessels was one thing: sympathy for the enemy himself was a weakness no front-line combat officer could afford.

SLAM!

Rietz leaned out over the spray deflector and stared coldly down along the slender wood-planked foredeck to where the three-man gun's crew struggled against surging icy water, often to their waists.

'I said, "hole her" – not bloody well cut her up for scrap! Cease firing: secure the gun for diving!'

They grinned up at him from under dripping sou'westers: all too briefly scruffy children playing fairground games. His men loved the dry reprimands by which their Captain disguised his affection for them and, while Rietz was careless of personal popularity, that common esteem had nevertheless proved a vital factor in their joint survival.

Rietz knew that the already superb discipline of the U-Boot-waffe became even finer honed by such mutual respect, and that only rigid order would prevent the catastrophic errors that lesser submariners had been known to make . . . once! Moreover, grim experience had proved to the Captain that only discipline of the highest resolution afforded half a hundred sweating men compressed into a noxious steel tube the courage to resist that invariably fatal paralysis engendered by the U-boat sailor's worst nightmare – depth charge attack. A seemingly never-ending dementia of two hundred-and-fifty-pound Tommy subsea bombs erupting metres from his fragile shell.

Yet such vital strength of purpose Rietz, and many of his fellow operational commanders, grimly conceded was becoming an ever more elusive thing.

For, notwithstanding the initial promise offered by the concept of *Die Rudeltaktik* – the so-called Wolf Pack strategy devised by

Admiral Doenitz himself, by which the flotillas hunted and struck in concert – and unqualified successes such as *Gruppe Sturmer*'s wholesale massacre of that last convoy, the 'Happy Time' for the U-boat crews had nevertheless betrayed signs of faltering in recent months. Too many once-familiar faces had been missing from shore base messes in between patrols; too many sister boats were ominously failing to keep appointed sea rendezvous. The word was circulating within the Service that Allied anti-submarine forces were showing a disconcerting adaptability to new tactics.

In the circumstances, while Rietz would have been less than human if he hadn't felt pride in knowing that, despite fewer and fewer volunteers stepping forward to embrace the claustrophobic terrors of an Atlantic class Frontboot, the majority of his own crewmen, even given the unlikely option, would still elect to stay under his command rather than return to the surface fleet, such endorsement of his leadership was hardly adequate consolation.

'We've seen enough,' he snapped harshly, his oath to the Führer fulfilled and suddenly weary of death. 'Hands to diving stations. Look-outs clear the bridge!'

He was still thinking about the eviscerated ship while sliding down the conning tower ladder into a controlled hubbub.

'. . . stop and clutch out main engines: switch in E-motors . . . Close outboard exhausts and induction valves . . . Engine-room and fore-ends – report readiness to dive!'

Bells, klaxons: orders and repeated orders . . .

Rietz wondered how long it would take for the few Tommies who'd made it to that single splintered lifeboat to die from their wounds or exposure unless rescue came quickly. No one had overtly referred to them while on the bridge, not even Leutnant Rohde. In the U-Bootwaffe it was considered bad form – invoking ill fortune, almost – to comment specifically on Allied survivors after the kill. The orders from Submarine High Command had been quite supportive in that context: 'No survivors are to be taken on board. We have to be hard in this war!'

The British seaman probably still protruding through drowning *Oberon*'s porthole would have subscribed to Oberleutnant Rietz's diligence in being exactly that!

'Diving readiness confirmed, sir!'

'Very good. Check main vents, Chief.'

'Check main vents,' Sindermann bellowed. The responses came like cannon shot. U-boat discipline – Rietz's discipline!

'Five clear!'

'Three port and starb'd clear, sir!'

'One and two clear . . .'

'All main vents clear, Captain,' Sindermann reported easily.

'Watch Officer clear the bridge!' Rietz snapped. There came a *clang* and he checked above his head to see a still puce-faced Navigator Grutner on the vertical ladder, spinning the handwheel clamping the conning tower hatch.

'Dive, Dive, DIVE! Open all main vents. Take her to fifteen metres.'

'Foreplanes hard-a-dive! Afterplanes – ten degrees of dive . . .'

Listening to the familiar roar of compressed air venting from the main ballast tanks he felt her dip, adopt a bow-down attitude: begin to slide below the waves.

The torpedoed ship had done exactly the same thing just moments before.

And the torpedoed men.

The U-boat shook gently to the crash of the very last wave against her fast-submerging superstructure before all became peace for victor and victims alike.

'Smoked ham for tea,' Oberleutnant Rietz decided. Quite looking forward to it.

Chapter One

They could tell something was wrong by the colour of the sky.

Even while making the recognition signal of the day on surfacing off the Loire; unusually requiring repetition at the curt request of the Naval Signal Station before permission was granted to proceed up-river – particularly so in the case of a victorious Sixth Flotilla boat returning from war patrol – the bridge crew had noted smoke from the direction of St-Nazaire.

'Not exactly a welcome on the mat. Someone up top's jumpy,' Rietz commented cynically. 'Signal to Flotilla: request situation report and current alert state. Close up anti-aircraft armament otherwise implement formal routine for entering harbour.'

By the time the hands had fallen in along the forward casing – bearded, sun-starved, red-eyed, awkwardly self-conscious in their damp-moulded grey leather dress uniforms after nearly two months of virtual incarceration below – and Rietz had conned the U-boat's slender bow slowly to starboard to begin her final homeward leg between the mud flats enclosing Charpentiers Channel, word had spread to every compartment that the base had, indeed, been hit.

Some of the younger hands looked a bit unhappy, but in general no one minded too much: particularly the senior rates. In fact, most were quite captivated by the thought that it was only right and proper: total war dropping in on the brassbound shoreside bastards every so often – cause for sardonic comment, nothing more. Another sporadic Tommy raid was hardly likely to change the course of history already predetermined by Adolf Hitler.

And they weren't far wrong, Rietz reflected. The massive hangar-like structures now rearing ahead of them above the St-Nazaire U-boat Basin had clearly been under construction for months yet had almost incredibly been spared, during the period of their greatest vulnerability, from too-close attention by the RAF. Exploiting that vital reprieve the Todt Labour Organization and thousands of forced French workers had completed nine of the fourteen proposed ten-metre-thick, steel-reinforced concrete pens under which refitting submarines and Kriegsmarine base support staffs alike could shelter while the operational crews fought the real blood, guts and terror battle out in the North Atlantic.

Even Leutnant Rohde, usually fanatical in parroting the Führer's oft-proclaimed invulnerability of the Third Reich, appeared to appreciate the irony; leaning over the spray-shield beside Rietz and scanning the still-distant dock complex through glasses.

'A grim affair, sir. Base Admin Office must've taken heavy casualties. Quite a few mahogany desks may never fight again.'

It was the first time since Rohde's appointment that the Captain had felt any affinity with his First Watch Officer. Probably the last, too. Chances were, the ex-Hitler Youth would be given his own command this time in – on Rietz's personal recommendation. If Rohde managed to keep his crew alive for longer than it took to learn to throw straight-arm salutes and scream '*Heil* Hitler!' he'd run a formidable Frontboot until the law of averages caught up with him as it eventually must with all of them. While Rietz's own devotion to duty had always been coloured by professional distaste, the Nazi-programmed Leutnant Rohde would slaughter beautiful ships or enemy seamen with equal and unimaginative zeal.

Raising his binoculars towards St-Nazaire again, Rietz frowned. There appeared to be rather more waterborne activity than usual, especially in the area of the Avant-Port and East Jetty leading up-river towards the Old Mole. While still too far away to make out detail, what looked to be the smoking wrecks

22

of several small naval craft also lay strewn along the fairway. Quite a few fires still burned in the vicinity of the warehouse area and the Old Town . . . all implying that the shoresiders had suffered not only a rude, but also an ominously recent awakening.

'Get Stemmler to chivvy Flotilla again. Demand a reply. Ask them what the fuck *did* happen last night!' Rietz snapped, suddenly irritated. The curt unwelcome from the Signal Station and this current lack of information either typified rear echelon self-preoccupation or suggested the Base had been seriously disrupted by rather more than a routine bombing raid.

'Hope to Christ they never hit Fifi Chambrelle's place down the Old Town,' Bootsmaat Landgraf muttered anxiously from below the periscope standard.

Rietz smiled drily under the binoculars. Everyone had their personal priorities. In the Bootsmaat's case it was hardly a secret that he'd long cherished a deep admiration for one Madame Fifi Chambrelle: a lady who, in the view of the boat's undisputed connoisseur of carnality, captained the tightest and most innovative freelance brothel in Occupied France; far superior to any sexual gymnasium in the U-boat crews' officially designated recreation pasture of nearby La Baule.

'Take courage, Bosun: a more positive attitude. Maybe the Tommies overshot Fifi's girls: wiped out the detention cells in which you habitually spend almost as long – and as often!'

'With respect, sir; if they did get blowed to hell, then I hope the Base Regulating Staff was inside 'em at the time.'

'Be specific, Landgraf,' Rohde grinned, good humoured as anybody at the prospect of not having to share a single cramped toilet with fifty other men for the next few blissful weeks. 'Inside the cells – or Chambrelle's young ladies?'

'Inside the CELLS, Herr Leutnant!' the Bosun barked woodenly, snapping briefly to attention. Revealing nothing, yet implying everything.

It's curious, Rietz noted absently while searching again to assess the extent of damage inflicted on their home port, how, even when one of the few truly dedicated Nazi Party crew members in this boat *does* make a joke – nobody laughs!

The Captain spread his elbows on the spray deflector to

counter the tremor transmitted by Sindermann's joyously turning diesels. Landmarks were slowly coming into view further up-river now; up past the Old Town Mole and East Jetty to where, still four miles ahead and overshadowing the Loire entrance to the St-Nazaire U-boat Basin, Rietz could just make out the southern caisson of the *Forme Ecluse* Joubert, otherwise known as the Normandie Dock: the massive dry dock originally constructed to house the building of France's greatest maritime venture, the trans-Atlantic liner *Normandie*.

. . . a grandiose pre-war gesture by the Frog-Eaters which had subsequently rebounded on their Allies for, following St-Nazaire's occupation, the complex now looming ahead of Rietz's boat also happened to represent the only dry dock on the European Atlantic Coast capable of accommodating the Third Reich's biggest ships: awesome war machines like *Scheer* and *Lutzow*, *Scharnhorst* and *Gneisenau*.

Even more significantly – *Tirpitz*!

For every strategist – British and German alike – knew that the fate of the sea war hinged on her. That eventually the mightiest German battleship of all would be forced to run the Royal Navy's blockade through the North Sea from her present base in Norway to reach the St-Nazaire facility for desperately needed underwater maintenance before again breaking out towards the Atlantic shipping lanes, once there a virtually undetectable pin in such a vast and trackless ocean, to put the final seal to Adolf Hitler's vaunted 'Plan Z': the total annihilation of the Allied merchant fleets.

There was, of course, another side of the tactical coin, Rietz reflected wryly. One which even those bar-top debaters in the U-Bootwaffe messes conceded: that if the British ever *did* manage to deny the Führer's stiff-collared big ship fleet the use of the Normandie Dock, then the outcome of the Second Battle of the Atlantic – even ultimate victory for the Fatherland itself – could well be placed in jeopardy.

Not, the pundits assured each other, that there was the remotest possibility of that happening. Not now the Tommies had foolishly permitted St-Nazaire, despite her bomb-proof submarine pens and her militarily vital dry dock, time to become, in the considered view of Naval Commander-in-Chief Grossadmiral Raeder, a quite impregnable sea fortress.

Oddly, Rietz himself had never felt totally comforted by such confidence. The same senior officers had shown a markedly similar trust in the invincibility of *Tirpitz*'s sister behemoth until eleven months ago. Until the Royal Navy achieved the impossible: intercepted *Bismarck* as she ran their northern Churchillian gauntlet; brought Adolf Hitler's Pride to battle.

And sank her!

The Captain stiffened abruptly, eyes narrowing within the Zeiss rubber cups. By God but there *was* some disturbance to the profile of the Normandie Dock, now clearly discernible even from this distance. A small grey ship appeared to have driven headlong into the massive outer caisson to lie, crumpled and forlorn, with concertinaed bows protruding slightly above the ten-metre-thick steel sliding gate barring entry to the waters of the Loire.

More reassuringly, the superstructures of two dry-docked German merchant tankers under repair still loomed above the protection of the caisson; both seemingly undisturbed in their temporary balancing act below sea level and so suggesting that the watertight integrity of the Normandie Dock itself had been unaffected by the as yet inexplicable collision.

Rietz thumbed his lenses irritably: damn the bloody Atlantic's ability to encrust everything with salt. 'Can you make out what the hell's happened, Rohde?'

His First Watch Officer, cap flat aback, scanned critically ahead, then shrugged. Rather too nonchalantly, the Captain thought.

'Looks like a torpedo boat destroyer, sir. Seems she's steamed arse over tit into the gate and bounced off. Presumably some flashy tin-can driver panicked during the raid: put his helm the wrong way . . .' Rohde smiled thinly: vindictively. 'The Gorossadmiral ought to hang the stupid bastard on a piano wire.'

'. . . and probably will, Rohde!' Rietz snapped bleakly. 'At least, in the pre-war Kriegsmarine, they only had courts martial to fear!'

'Object in the water ahead, sir!'

From Look-out Schadt. Tensely.

'What the hell NOW?' Rietz growled, fed up with bloody stress on this, what should have been their triumphal lap of honour.

'WhereAWAY ahead?' Bootsmaat Landgraf bawled. 'The trip's not over yet. Report proper, laddie, or you won't be gettin' no chance at Fifi ass this time in!'

'Green one-FIVE, sir!'

Leutnant Rohde, swinging his glasses in parallel with the Captain, still presented a study in contrived elegance: the gentleman hunter home from the sea.

'Looks rather like a body, sir.'

Rietz caressed his own focus wheel. Just as he'd done two days ago to reveal the portholed man, only this time there was no suggestion of life. The corpse drifted aimlessly on the outgoing tide, face down and buoyed by a not instantly familiar military blouse ballooned with air trapped above a webbing belt showing two brass equipment buckl . . . ?

Rietz hit the General Alarm klaxon.

'Surface ACTION STATIONS . . . This is NOT a drill!'

The grey, combat-weary line of men, shocked from their desperate need to relax in supposedly friendly waters, whirled in concert: broke in disciplined confusion as the raucous horn shrieked danger.

'. . . main deck armament – CLOSE UP!' Rietz snarled bitterly, knowing the shallow waters of the River Loire afforded no natural hiding place for a submarine while, at the same time, cursing the bastards in Flotilla who'd let them come into this without even a bloody sitrep. But the Captain didn't intend to expose his complement now: allow his boat – their boat – to become more vulnerable than absolutely necessary. Not at the trivial expense of possibly looking foolish.

'But it's *dead*, sir,' Rohde protested, incautious in his arrogance. 'Unusual as it may be, a corpse hardly presents much of a threat, surely?'

The Captain swung savagely. 'No threat you say, Rohde? Not even when the body in question – the one that you are about to recover and *personally* examine, Herr Leutnant! – is sighted adrift within one of the most heavily defended port areas in German Occupied Territory. Wearing BRITISH ARMY uniform?'

The duty harbour launch came out to intercept them ten minutes later. During the ML's approach, and despite the red, black and white stream of her Kriegsmarine Ensign astern, both Oberleutnant Rietz's binoculars and Oberleutnant Rietz's guns remained immutably locked on target.

Obviously the Base had been the recipient of a British Combined Operations raid within the past few hours. The bullet-riddled cadaver Rohde's deck party had roughly hauled aboard was that of a British soldier with corporal's stripes on his sleeves and Commando flashes at his shoulders. Bloody proof to all aboard that St-Nazaire, whether impregnable or not, had come to the end of its reprieve.

. . . suggesting that from this day onwards none of us, not even we folk heroes of the U-Bootwaffe on our sweet returns from somewhat tasteless victory, Rietz brooded sombrely as they waited, alert, can ever sleep soundly again without wondering if Churchill's roughest thugs are *en route* to square the account even as we hide ashore.

But he didn't impart any such view to those on the bridge. Instead, and only when he'd confirmed the unmistakably jaunty rake of Kapitänleutnant Leo Fischer's cap in the sternsheets of the closing vessel, did the Captain finally cock a slightly better humoured eye towards Bootsmaat Landgraf.

'It seems our Staff Officer Operations is coming out to greet us in person. What attitude would you commend me to adopt, Bosun?'

'Insist on 'im making the recognition signal of the day, sir. Same as they done to us,' Landgraf growled. 'Otherwise – though with the utmost respect, mind you – blow the balls off the bastard!'

Rietz grinned fleetingly: leaned over the shield.

'Secure from action stations: resume routine for entering harbour. Better drum up a bloody side party, Grutner, to receive Kapitänleutnant Fischer aboard.'

Navigator Grutner looked startled. 'Me, sir? But shouldn't Leutnant Rohde . . .?'

'The First Watch Officer is already privileged to be performing his duty to the Führer.' Rietz coldly indicated the foredeck where his second-in-command knelt, gingerly probing the battledress pockets of the British corpse and not at all languid any more, at the end of a furtively grinning straggle of re-forming submariners.

'Throughout our patrol Leutnant Rohde has persistently displayed a keen personal interest in the human flotsam created by our war task,' Rietz smiled thinly. 'Chance, Grutner, has at last afforded him an opportunity to engage the enemy at rather closer quarters than the range of a G7E torpedo!'

The Captain swivelled, meeting as he did so Bootsmaat Landgraf's ever so studiously expressionless gaze.

And winked.

Kapitänleutnant Fischer returned Rietz's salute with steel-edged precision as he reached the bridge.

'Some senior officers would consider it an impertinence to say the least, Oberleutnant, to find themselves intimidated by the guns of one of their own Frontboote!'

'In view of the lack of response from Flotilla to our signals, sir, I felt it prudent to err on the side of caution.'

'Is that somewhat thinly veiled criticism meant to imply,' Fischer said drily, 'that I should be damn grateful your prudence didn't err on the side of recklessness?'

'No, sir,' Rietz gestured up-river towards the grey warship smashed so ineffectually against its proportionately immovable object. 'Merely that I was briefly concerned, having recovered evidence of British military activity while deprived of hard intelligence from Command, that the enemy *had* achieved their objective!'

Fischer stared searchingly at his subordinate then jerked an iron-grey head towards the Bosun standing in wooden innocence behind them. 'And him – our notoriously irreverent Bootsmaat Landgraf? I suppose *he* suggested you should just go ahead and blow my balls off anyway, eh?'

Landgraf, sensing the eye of the storm had passed, braced himself even more punctiliously: a broad grin at such recognition cracking his cured-leather features. His Captain merely looked grave.

'In Landgraf's defence . . . only with the *utmost* respect, sir.'

Leo Fischer suddenly chuckled and grasped Rietz's hand with a warmth which, at the same time, invited no further liberties. 'By God but I'm glad to see you and your boys back, Paul. Sorry about your reception: they're still arse over tit in the Main Signals Office after last night.'

'As I said: we gathered we've not been the only ones to scent powder and shot recently.'

The veteran submariner, shrewdly aware of anxious messdeck ears by then hanging on his every word, directed a carefully composed eye towards Rietz's bridge crew.

'Impressive pyrotechnics to celebrate your return, eh boys?' Fischer dismissed the smoke-hazed port area ahead with a perhaps rather too laconic wave. 'As you see, the ranting British bulldog Winston, cowering in his war kennel beneath London, has finally mustered the courage to test his so-called terror commandos against our Biscay coast defences. While disappointed at the poor quality of opposition, our gunners were still grateful for the break in routine – Tommy afforded some bloody entertaining target practice.'

You don't really believe Churchill lacks courage any more than I do, Leo. Or that the British can't fight, Rietz thought perceptively. That's Staff Officer, U-Bootwaffe Morale talk. The official Doenitz line.

'They made sure all the burned-out old brigand achieved was a criminal sacrifice of lives.' Leo Fischer's eyes strayed to the foredeck where Rohde was concluding his interrogation of the mutilated British corpse, whereupon, just for a brief instant, Rietz saw an unexpected shadow pass across the older officer's face. Then the shadow gave way to a smile.

'Still, it did take us old hands back a bit. Shades of the last war, y'know?'

'Zeebrugge, sir? Keyes's infamous 1918 raid?' Rietz complied for the men's benefit. 'Hardly the stuff of Nelson this time then, one would have thought – their emulating, rather than making, history?'

'And reassuring, Oberleutnant. Suggests the British High Command haven't advanced their tactical thinking much: imagining they could get away with a tin-pot little operation like that in this day and age.'

The Staff Officer Operations considered a moment, then grinned openly. 'Mind you, they panicked the absolute shit out of our coastal defence boys last night. Before the shore battery commanders got their bloody brains in gear.'

He swung and slapped Rietz's back. 'Come *on* then, man, don't keep me in suspense! What's your final patrol tally? I trust you made every eel count, eh?'

'Four confirmed sinkings, sir: fifteen thousand-odd merchant tons,' Rietz was forced to respond to the man's infectious enthusiasm. Leo Fischer had won his spurs and the Flotilla's respect at the high-risk end of a target marker too; a whole world war ago now. 'Plus an escort corvette – Canadian, I think. Chopped her stern off during our *Nachtjagd* in Bruno Dora.'

. . . and, in so doing, murdered beautiful innocent ships; vilified the labours of those craftsmen who built them; created yet a further host of tearful widows, parents, children . . . gazed into the eyes of a seaman so much like myself yet, nevertheless, one whom the Führer's orders – *my* corrupted maritime skills – conspired to cast into the deep with a five-thousand-ton millstone around his neck! Oberleutnant Paul Rietz, dutiful centurion of the Third Reich, reflected silently.

'Bloody good sport. Wish to God I'd been with you, but they say I'm too old to go hunting this time around. Trouble is, they're right, Paul. I feel it – old and burdened as Methuselah, sometimes . . .'

The grey-haired senior officer inhaled the stench of U-boat venting through the tower like some nostalgia of fine wine before rubbing his hands briskly, returning to matters of moment.

'Right then: your boys will be savouring the prospect of baths, decent food, sleep – the welcoming arms of a good woman, eh, Landgraf? Or should I expand that to *women* in your case, you unconscionable old reprobate?'

'*Jawohl*, Herr Kaleunt!' Landgraf snapped to attention again, beaming. 'But – beggin' your pardon o' course, sir – I'd be grateful if you didn't insist on 'em being all *that* good either. Sir!'

Rietz smiled too. 'Permission requested to proceed to our berth? I was particularly taken by your mention of sleep.'

'Granted with pleasure. Incidentally, I'd like to accompany you if I may?' Leo Fischer sniffed dolefully. 'Pity me, Paul – a three-mile joyride aboard someone else's Frontboot and I'm actually excited at the prospect. Still, it's the nearest our respected Admiral allows me to get to a normal bloody life again.'

'Half ahead both,' the Captain ordered down the voice pipe. 'Starboard five: come to zero-four-zero!'

The diesels gushed a rumble-throated plume of exhaust while a shiver of excitement ran through the deck as Rietz's rusted black U-boat began to glide the final few miles to her reinforced concrete lair.

Fischer subsided enjoyably over the sprayshield with the casual stance of years. 'Put her to bed in Number Three shelter. Don't expect your usual conquering heroes reception, by the way. The counter-propaganda boys have more pressing events on their minds this morning.'

'You mean no band?' the Captain growled. 'No carbolic-scrubbed base staff Fräuleins waiting to embarrass my disgustingly unkempt crew with armfuls of flowers thoughtfully provided by Herr Doktor Goebbels' cameramen, sir?'

Fischer grinned. 'For an ex-passenger ship lounge lizard you're becoming a very hard-nosed U-Bootwaffe cynic, Oberleutnant. I actually meant you'll have to enter the submarine basin through the Avant-Port this time in. The Harbourmaster regrets to inform you that the grand entrance in way of his precious South Caisson has become, ah, temporarily un-navigable?'

Rietz allowed his own mouth to crease fractionally. 'We'd noticed that the Normandie Dock seems to have suffered the attentions of . . . a gatecrasher?'

'Good. I like that, Paul – a gatecrasher, eh?'

'Can't help feeling a sneaking admiration for the poor bloody

CO who blotted his copybook with such style – well on his way to becoming a Kriegsmarine legend.' Rietz frowned, intrigued. 'Who was he anyway? Damned if we could positively identify which ship she is.'

'Hardly surprising. Considering she's British.'

Rietz blinked. 'BRITISH . . .?'

'As – roast beef, don't they say?'

'*Christ*!' Rietz muttered, genuinely appalled.

Fischer looked little-boy pleased at finally disturbing his subordinate commander's aplomb. 'One of their obsolete Yankee-loaned destroyers: HMS *Campbeltown*, according to the Intelligence boys. Damn clever concept, I have to grant the Tommies that. Altered her profile completely – chopped off her heavier guns and superstructure, removed two of her original four funnels, angled the remaining brace German style . . . looked uncannily like one of our own North Sea Squadron TBDs in the dark.'

Rietz scanned the nearing hulk of the enemy ram with new eyes. Respectful eyes, but still carefully concealed within the lenses of the Zeiss, as always when privately mourning for any once graceful ship. She didn't look graceful now, he thought bleakly: just tormented in her wasted gallantry.

'Then the cheeky buggers topped her up with hard-nut commando troops and sent her in at half-past bloody one this morning, escorted by several Fairmile gunboats and a few MTBs . . . precious few managed to withdraw again.' Fischer encompassed the other burned-out wrecks scattering the fairway almost angrily. 'What the hell kind of stupidity IS that, Paul? Tommy guns and light mortars . . . wooden skitterbugs with *petrol* engines, f'r Christ's sake – sacrificed pointlessly against the firepower of Dieckmann's 280 Naval Artillery battalion!'

Rietz stirred from sombre reflection. 'It achieved something. They did land their force, sir, right where they could hit us hardest: at the heart of the Base . . . by flashing a confusion of recognition signals to the shore stations when challenged, I presume – then steaming like bats out of hell for the South Caisson while our crowd were still trying to make up their minds to shoot?'

The SOO appraised Rietz whimsically. 'A succinct evaluation. You're a quick thinker, Paul. As befits one of my best Frontboot commanders.'

'Then maybe Onkel Karl should transfer a few of *us* to port defence,' Rietz growled sardonically, read the look in Fischer's eye and added drily, 'An attempt at humour, sir!'

'I'd caution you, Oberleutnant, the Admiral isn't laughing.' Fischer lowered his voice. 'Not for the ears of your officers or the men, but we've had a bloody narrow escape. Between our own and Seven Flotilla's, Doenitz had nine VII-C boats under refit in the pens last night. If the British had done their homework properly, deployed a stronger force, they could have destroyed half the damn squadron before we woke up.'

'With respect to the C-in-C, sir, it strikes me that we still got off relatively lightly.'

'Meaning?'

Rietz shrugged. 'Surely their primary target had to be the Normandie Dock itself. Either way, the fact remains that they penetrated our defences far enough to ram the gate. Say they'd invested a little more in success – deployed a larger displacement ship rather than some light-build destroyer which folded on impact?'

'Obviously ramming it at speed would've breached it. Flooded the whole bloody complex.'

'And delivered their merchant fleet from the threat of *Tirpitz* breaking into the South Atlantic for months to come – a vast prize for the British if they'd achieved it.'

'Then thank God they underestimated the South Caisson's strength, eh?'

'That's what worries me,' Rietz frowned. 'The fact that they apparently did.'

'Don't look gift horses in the mouth, young Rietz,' Fischer growled with asperity. 'And don't underestimate their achievement, either. Ill-supported or not, last night's raid still blitzed the harbour installations badly enough to guarantee Herr Todt's Frenchie labour squads a hell of a backache in the coming weeks, apart from shaking our defence teams to the core. Forget my official line to the sailors – take it from me, man: those khaki stormtroops were bloody tigers. By *God* but they fought . . .'

A distant explosion and frenetic crackle of small-arms fire rolled down-river from St-Nazaire while Leo Fischer pounded the rail in almost comical frustration. 'Hear THAT, dammit? Two or three hundred men cut off in the midst of a Wehrmacht garrison and they're still bloody holding out – an entire night on our own home ground, yet the whole of 333 Infantry Division are STILL trying to mop up their survivors!'

The Kapitänleutnant grumbled to an abrupt halt and raised a resigned eyebrow. 'All right, let's have it! What's surfacing in your somewhat oblique mind?'

Rietz chewed his lip pensively. Something *was* wrong about the British approach. Their planning for what must have been, for them, a vital strike against the *Tirpitz*'s one critical route point to the Atlantic seemed uncharacteristically flawed . . .

'The whole tactical concept, I suppose. Their having committed a seemingly inadequate force of lightly armed troops supported by nothing more than one old warship and a few flimsy launches. Personally I find it hard to credit the enemy could ever have hoped to achieve anything more than a token landing. Nor that they weren't keenly aware of the subsequent disadvantage they would invite.'

'Disadvantage?'

'The British aren't complete fools. They must have realized that even a minor raid at this stage was bound to sharpen our vigilance: alert us to the possibility of future attacks on this coast – so why *did* Churchill sanction it? Why sacrifice a destroyer uselessly when a bigger ship would have smashed her way clear through the caisson without costing him any more in terms of casualties?'

Fischer waved vaguely. 'His back's against the wall? He felt pressured to make some theatrical gesture before his troops abandon all will to fight . . . ? The British know they're losing this time round, Rietz. Their leader with the fat cigar must be uncomfortably aware that, if he allows them to stagnate in a purely defensive posture much longer, defeatism will become their norm.'

'Churchill's also an opportunist. He would have urged his

Chiefs of Staff to make damn sure that whatever they did resulted in military as well as psychological gain – certainly rather more than they appear to have attempted.'

'Do I get the impression that you admire the criminal Winston Churchill, Herr Oberleutnant?' Fischer snapped sharply: dangerously.

'I . . . respect him, sir,' Rietz answered levelly. 'As a master of the unorthodox.'

Leo Fischer grinned fleetingly. 'Just wondered, that's all. Because the aggressive old bastard scares the *shit* out of me!' He shrugged. 'Take a tip: save yourself the speculation. Command wouldn't listen, even if you did come up with the correct answer. You and I, we're U-boat men, Rietz: the darlings of the media, the Third Reich's death and glory supermen – who, by definition in the view of our masters, can't possess a grain of imagination because anyone who did wouldn't sail in these claustrophobic tubes of shit in the first place!'

'They're probably right at that,' Rietz muttered, leaning forward to the voice pipe. 'Starboard five – engines half speed!'

Approaching the point of departure from the Loire main channel into the Avant-Port, they were close enough to distinguish the larger calibre shell holes and bloody carnage wrought by Kapitänleutnant Dieckmann's Loire batteries upon the so-fragile form of the enemy warship. Half of *Campbeltown*'s crew, a stupefying proportion of the commando troops embarked within her, must have fallen at their action stations long before she'd even reached what all aboard *must* have known was intended to be her final and quite irrevocable destination.

Lowering his gaze, the Captain's eyes fell to the dead corporal on the foredeck. Rohde was walking expressionlessly aft, having left the soldier lying honourably to attention; boots upturned to the smoke-raddled sky and a blanket covering his warrior face. Rietz was glad of that. Glad that even Führer-child Rohde had gained some respect for death.

What kind of men ARE you, our so-dedicated enemies, that you could voluntarily have endured such a firestorm; made such gallant sacrifice for *nothing*? the Captain wondered bleakly. But then, U-Bootwaffe Oberleutnant Rietz had reflected upon that same riddle many times before. Every time he tracked a defence-less Allied ship in his target periscope.

Why DID you throw yourselves upon our German bayonets with such little hope of victory . . . ?

Paul Rietz gained his answer less than one hour later.

At twenty-nine minutes past ten, to be precise: on that same morning of Saturday, March the twenty-seventh, 1942.

When five tons of time-fused explosive concealed within the crumpled fore-ends of HMS *Campbeltown* finally detonated as she still lay, contemptuously dismissed as a further threat by those in command of the St-Nazaire defences, hard against the almost impregnable South Caisson of the *Forme Ecluse* Joubert.

Chapter Two

———◆◆◆———

The full perfidy of the British Combined Operations planners became apparent to Rietz in the split second when Navigator Grutner, always an officer of nervous disposition, finally did lose his head.

They had just reached the stage of the patrol dreamed of by each and every Sixth Flotilla man from the moment he sailed for the Atlantic battle – his boat again gliding silently through the Avant-Port lockway, but inward-bound this time – when *Campbeltown* exploded some six hundred metres from them.

Rietz himself wasn't aware of any audible detonation, such were the vagaries of explosive substances. He was conscious only of a massive flash which, for a split second, seemed to freeze every face; still every hand around him in an incandescent blink.

Then had come the blast; skipping and rumbling across the red pantiled roofs of the Old Town lying, in part, between them and the Normandie Dock; expanding and pulsing on a front of lethal debris with the hot wind clutching at the slowly moving U-boat's bridge and deck crew; causing her to shy to port, her long bow to sheer momentarily for the west wall of the lock.

'Stop both – half astern starboard! St'b'd thirty the RUD-DER!' Rietz snarled, grabbing for the voice pipe, reacting automatically as Kapitänleutnant Fischer cannoned involuntarily into him.

'Sorry, dear boy!' Fischer apologized uncertainly, elegantly, then looked up at the sky above the *Forme Ecluse* Joubert and muttered, 'Jesus *Chris* . . . !'

The detritus created by several tons of high explosive expanding instantly within a steel capsule began to return to earth and water over a wide area of St-Nazaire. Sucked first into a huge ascending column of rolling black and grey smoke, the lethal spew began. Glowing steel shards from the forepart of what had been, until half a heartbeat before, an apparently neutered warship – glass; river spray; masonry . . . parts of military vehicles and 20 mm coastal defence battery guns and baulks of splintered timber.

And parts of human beings. A ghastly rain of human intestines and limbs and heads and torsos and rather less readily identifiable Things . . .

Rietz was to learn later that, such had been the complacency of the German custodians of the Normandie Dock, that by ten o'clock that morning the frail ramship *Campbeltown* had already become an object of considerable interest to anyone with enough rank to command access through the ring of guards surrounding her. That indeed, even while some enemy commandos were still defying capture in certain parts of the town and other bloody-minded Tommy prisoners, uncooperative to the point of unreasonableness, were being futilely interrogated as to why they *had* attempted such a pointless gesture, several hundred officers and officers' wives and officers' girlfriends had gathered to see and be seen, and to view the curiosity, and chat about the great event in the night, and take snapshots and maybe pick up the odd souvenir.

Bits and pieces of that theatre-going élite began to splash in the water around the U-boat as prudent crewmen threw themselves flat along the casing, some more agilely than others. First Watch Officer Rhode, either excessively brave, shocked or stupid, merely bawled furiously for them to stand fast: appalled at such self-serving dissolution of firm Hitlerian discipline in what should have been their moment of triumph. Particularly at this one supreme moment of his own operational career when promotion was on the horizon and a senior Party man might conceivably be around to view his gladiator's return.

Something hard and white struck Rietz a painful blow on the leg. He looked down. It was a hand – a woman's hand.

Unquestionably a woman's hand, Rietz decided numbly. Still with red-painted fingernails on still slowly contracting claws: still proudly displaying on one bloodless talon a large diamond and emerald ring . . .

His vessel still sheering hard for the WALL!

'Half astern port!' he roared. 'Grutner! Get down and take charge of the after casing – get a fucking LINE ASHORE!'

But Navigator Grutner only stared back at him with an even more bovine look than usual though, to give him his due, Grutner didn't show the nervousness he normally evinced on receiving even the simplest order. Grutner, in fact, was managing to maintain a remarkable composure considering the war he'd shown such aversion to had just exploded around him.

'Bastards!' someone began screaming from the foredeck, 'Oh the bloody Tommy BASTARDS . . . !'

'Sick Berth Attendant to the forr'ad *casing*! Where IS that idle bastard SBA?' another hoarse voice bellowed.

Small stuff was still splashing into the lockway around them. Ambulance and fire bells clanged in the distance while the previously sporadic firing from the town suddenly regenerated to a hysterical crescendo. Rietz suspected the unseasoned Wehrmacht garrison troops were panicking, shooting at anything which moved, British or French: not knowing where the next attack was coming from.

'Get a fucking TOURNIQUET on 'is leg!' again from forr'ad. 'Come ON, man – *below* the fuckin' knee, Streicher! It's his fuckin' foot's blown off; not 'is fuckin' HEAD, *Dummkopf*!'

. . . Grutner still transfixed his Captain with that placid, unblinking stare. It was then that Rietz noticed that only the upperworks of Navigator Grutner were actually observing him: balanced neatly on the shattered gunmetal bowl of the port-bearing compass.

The rest of Grutner's best-uniformed corpse was jammed bizarrely between the twin periscope standards high above their heads, transported there by the jagged steel plate, compliments of the Royal Navy, which had assisted Grutner to achieve such sterling composure.

The U-boat jolted, bumped hard against the lockway wall and

came to rest. Grutner, clumsy even in death, fell off the compass bowl and young Lookout Schadt fainted.

'Stop BOTH bloody engines!' Rietz growled, mortified.

Leo Fischer shrugged out of his heavy greatcoat and laid it gently over as much of Grutner as a greatcoat would conceal.

'If that's your usual standard of shiphandling, Oberleutnant,' he pronounced solemnly, 'I'm damned if I'm going to hitch another passage in *your* boat.'

Have we become so hardened to death and destruction in this war, Rietz brooded sombrely, that a young man can be torn to pieces before our eyes, yet all we do is make black jokes in the pretence that such an appalling sight has no effect on us?

But Rietz didn't consider the Kapitänleutnant insensitive. They were all shocked to the core by the horror of what had happened; each man reacting according to his capacity for self-discipline. Fischer's having survived one previous war as a U-boat man was already proof enough that the veteran Staff Officer could summon considerable fortitude under fire.

As could – apparently – Bootsmaat Landgraf.

'Put it back, Landgraf,' Rietz said carefully, trying not to vomit: especially not in front of Grutner. 'On second thoughts – give it to me to keep until someone comes for it.'

'Sir?'

Rietz raised an interrogative eyebrow, patiently challenging the almost convincing bewilderment on the Bosun's leathery face. He couldn't help feeling a little pleased at being able to display such presence of mind himself, for that matter.

No one else had noticed, following the brief diversion caused by Navigator Grutner's major upset, that the diamond and emerald ring had miraculously disappeared from the bleached hand on the deck.

Nor that the fastidiously manicured appendage had since moved, either of its own volition or, rather more credibly, with surreptitious assistance, to the after end of the bridge. That it now lay significantly – and thus still quite capable, it seemed, of pointing an accusing finger – hard alongside the enterprising Landgraf's starboard boot.

*

It proved all the more galling then that, six days later, despite having voluntarily stayed on the base to oversee his boat through her operational refit, and notwithstanding having proved to Kapitänleutnant Fischer that he was a submarine officer both of steel and of probity, Oberleutnant Paul Rietz was nevertheless relieved of his command.

Rietz glowered along the forward casing, now stripped of gratings, from which electrical and hydraulic cables sprouted in a nightmare dockyard monkey puzzle. Lit by the harsh overhead arc lamps of the bombproof refitting shelter, the blue staccato flash of welding torches; the stink of burning paint; the almost frenetic clatter of tools on steel further conspired to create a troglodyte pandemonium.

'Why? Because I hit the dock coming in?' he flared, taken aback.

'Don't be *bloody* silly, Oberleutnant,' Leo Fischer retorted with matching vigour. 'And don't shoot the messenger, either. I'm just the postman around here: others make the decisions.'

Rietz opened his mouth.

'. . . and *don't* ask me what your next appointment is,' his grey-haired mentor pre-empted. 'I really haven't the first idea. Let's just say something's up. Command's had the shits ever since the Tommies left their calling card. Even officers who had absolutely no responsibility for coastal defence are being moved around – the clearing of yardarms and the click of Staff umbrellas can be heard from as far away as Berlin. It's called panic!'

'Then may I ask who takes over my boat?' Rietz asked tightly.

'Rohde. He's been recalled from leave,' Fischer said. Then shrugged. 'Not my choice. But there again: I didn't agree with Hindenburg's appointment of Hitler as Reichschancellor back in Thirty-three, either.'

'There aren't many who'd admit to that,' Rietz felt slightly diappointed. He'd always assumed Fischer to be an intelligent and far-seeing German.

'Sir,' Fischer reminded him absently.

'. . . sir.'

The Staff Officer Operations grinned.

*

'All right, Paul: feel free to speak your mind. Which, of course, you will anyway.'

'With or without the "sir". Sir?'

'Keep the "sir" in, just to make up for the ones you missed out. Otherwise – off the record.'

'Then, Kapitänleutnant Fischer, sir: as an ex-Merchant Mariner I wish to place on record that I am fed up to the *teeth*,' Rietz grated savagely, 'with being fucked about by the *fucking* NAVY!'

'Be ready in an hour and you'll have the chance to complain to those who can do something about it,' Fischer said, quite unruffled. 'Personally I have a feeling, young Rietz, that, as far as you're concerned, the Navy's only just started.'

The blacked-out dockside office, dark and dingy at the best of times, was yellow-lit by a single desk lamp as the still disenchanted Rietz, followed more circumspectly by Leo Fischer, barged through the door without knocking.

Then halted. Abruptly.

Three men were waiting; two standing, one sitting easily behind a battered desk. All were Kriegsmarine officers: all wore long greatcoats and peaked service caps rimmed with the gold oak leaves denoting high rank.

The observation from the sitting man was sharp, yet not without a trace of humour.

'I trust, Herr Kapitänleutnant, your approach when entering unfamiliar enemy waters is rather less confrontatorial than your present mode suggests?'

Rietz slammed to the salute: elbow bent, flat-palmed naval style. From the two most senior officers the gravely returned compliments followed the same pattern. U-Bootwaffe men together seldom used the more formal Nazi greeting: not even their Commander-in-Chief, Karl Doenitz, despite his undoubted devotion to the Führer and the Movement.

The third, an angular man, carried the four rings of a Fregattenkapitän. His arm extended stiffly to the accompaniment of clicking heels. Rietz didn't recognize the Captain, who wasn't wearing Submarine Service insignia, but instinctively decided he wasn't going to like him.

'*Heil* Hitler!'

But Rietz was more concerned with the faces known to every German submariner.

'I apologize, Herr Admiral. I was not expec . . .' He focused his eyes correctly, unseeingly, ahead in best Bootsmaat Landgraf style. 'With respect, sir: Oberleutnant Paul Rietz, Sixth Flotilla *Befehlshaber der Unterseeboote*, reporting!'

'With equal respect, young man, I am not in the habit of confusing the ranks of my officers,' Doenitz corrected. 'If I address you as Kapitänleutnant – then a Lieutenant-Commander you must surely be, eh?'

'Congratulations, Rietz,' the taller staff officer smiled fleetingly, 'on a well merited promotion.'

'Thank you, Herr Konteradmiral,' Rietz echoed uncertainly. There were many tales of the Service's 'Godfather', Eberhard Godt; Doenitz's closest adviser and Deputy Commander of the U-Bootwaffe since the pre-war days when U-boat Headquarters had been located in a wooden shed in Wilhelmshaven Dockyard before moving to Paris and the Boulevard Suchet.

Surely the wheel hasn't turned full circle? Rietz thought uncertainly, allowing his eyes briefly to encompass the gloomy interior. His involuntary lapse wasn't overlooked.

'Be reassured, Kapitänleutnant. This is a discreet meeting for reasons which will shortly become obvious.' Godt looked around drily. 'We are not yet considered so insignificant by comparison to Reichsmarshall Goering's Luftwaffe that the Führer has re-consigned us to wooden sheds again.'

Eberhard Godt, like Onkel Karl himself, commanded the unswerving willingness of the Frontboote combat crews to drive themselves to the limits of endurance: as much as anything by his determination that everything possible would be done to ease the misery of their existence at sea. It had been Vice-Admiral Godt who'd conceived of the proxy 'damage control marriages' by which already over-stressed U-boat men on patrol and separated by several thousand miles from their – usually under such pressing circumstances, pregnant – girlfriends could, in simultaneously conducted ceremonies both at home and afloat, ensure the respectability of the forthcoming offspring.

'Be at ease, Rietz. And you too, Fischer.' Doenitz, a smallish man seldom given to expression, rose from the chair before indicating the fifth attendant at that unorthodox rendezvous.

'Allow me to introduce you both to Fregattenkapitän von Strelow of B-Dienst.'

'Sir!'

'B-Dienst . . .?' Rietz shot an alarmed glance towards Fischer, now only his unexpected equal in rank. The Sixth Flotilla's SOO merely returned an imperceptible shrug: obviously Leo had not been made aware of the purpose of this clandestine rendezvous either.

But: *Beobachtungs-Dienst?* The German Naval Observation Service; the intelligent Intelligence boys – the code-breakers? Rietz speculated anxiously. Found more commonly in the high-security radio monitoring section of Kriegsmarine Headquarters on Berlin's Tirpitz-Ufer than in Occupied France . . . Surely to Christ they weren't intending to promote him into a *desk* job?

Doenitz's expression hardened. The conventions had been observed.

'Stand advised that this meeting will be regarded as top secret. You will also bear in mind, should you feel inclined towards comment, Kapitänleutnants Fischer and Rietz, that von Strelow bears details of an operations . . .' The C-in-C paused, his warning clear. '. . . ordered by the Führer personally!'

Being an unmistakable signal to us to think carefully before voicing our slightest reservations, Rietz interpreted, conscious of suddenly conflicting emotions.

On the credit side, the operational reference at least suggested the prospect of his continuing in an active service role. One somewhat more challenging than ambushing some poor bloody merchantman! he reflected hopefully.

Yet Doenitz and Godt, on the other hand, must already have been aware of what was to come – and didn't like it. The very fact that their own Admiral's disquiet had been so thinly veiled afforded an ominous significance. Karl Doenitz counted among Hitler's staunchest advocates: only his gruff affection for the men of his beloved U-boat Service might strain that loyalty near

44

the point of open dissension – meaning, almost certainly, the threat of unacceptably high casualty figures to his already over-stretched fighting Arm.

Of which – Rietz could hardly fail to note – he, a newly promoted and currently unemployed Kapitänleutnant, just happened to be the only front-line member present . . .'

The C-in-C gestured to von Strelow. 'You will proceed with your briefing.'

The Intelligence Officer bowed. Too complacently, Rietz thought. Exuding all the arrogance of Hitler's authority.

You're making a mistake, Berliner, he predicted, mildly diverted. Von Strelow would have been better advised to display at least token discomfort at becoming the focus of Onkel Karl's disapproval. The formidable little Admiral, tipped by many senior officers to become Grossadmiral Raeder's eventual successor, still commanded Hitler's ear if not the Führer's full appreciation of what his U-boat crews had so far achieved in dictating the tide of battle.

'Gentlemen,' von Strelow began. 'On being informed of the criminal British attack here against St-Nazaire, the Führer . . .'

'Spare them the Headquarters propaganda, Captain,' Doenitz interrupted brusquely. 'My officers are acutely aware that the *Campbeltown* operation was a legitimate assault by highly motivated troops.'

The courier from Berlin frowned, betraying a touch of asperity. 'Very well, sir. Then I confine myself to stating that, in view of the damage inflicted upon the Normandie Dock with its consequential delay to the deployment of *Tirpitz* in the South Atlantic, the Führer has declared himself to be . . . ah . . .'

Von Strelow faltered, searching his diplomatic vocabulary.

'Berserk with fury, Captain?' Godt, who knew exactly how far he dared go before Doenitz, supplemented drily. Rietz saw Fischer suppress a grin: their Leader's propensity for ungovernable rage had hardly remained a State secret.

'I would prefer to describe the Führer's reaction as "vigorously displeased", sir,' von Strelow retorted sharply. 'Suffice to say, the senior Wehrmacht officers responsible for the defence of this area have already been disciplined.'

'In other words, it can get bloody cold on the Moscow Express,' Godt observed acidly.

'For those who failed to search *Campbeltown* before she exploded, the opportunity of enjoying such minor discomfort may well prove elusive.' It became von Strelow's turn to draw only the thinnest of veils. 'Do I really have to stress, Herr Konteradmiral, the whole extent of our Führer's anger at the military embarrassment this British adventure has caused to the Third Reich?'

'No, you do NOT!' Godt bristled; finally exploded.

'That didn't take long,' Fischer whispered cheerfully.

'We have already been subjected to a more-than-adequate reminder of the penalties for those negligent in their duty to Germany – a reminder, von Strelow, both impertinent and totally unnecessary to we of the U-Bootwaffe!'

'Sir?' von Strelow looked quite taken aback. Rather as Lieutenant Rohde invariably managed to appear whenever anyone dared imply the enemy were also human – that Allied survivors left adrift in a freezing sea might merit at least token compassion.

A Staff man to his keelplates, Rietz reflected contemptuously. Worse – a Party zealot. He can't recognize his own imprudence: his offensiveness to proper seamen blinded as he is by the final sanction in the signature he carries.

'From now on you will bear in mind when addressing my U-boat men, Fregattenkapitän,' Doenitz reinforced nevertheless, cold as diamond ice, 'that motivation is not required. That it is enough merely to state the Führer's wish!'

A stirring belligerence, Rietz applauded silently, somewhat wryly. Unless, of course, one just happens to be the heroically unprotesting U-boat man in question.

Von Strelow came to uncertain attention.

'I was merely anxious, Herr Admiral, to convey the Führer's strength of determination that Operation Juggernaut *will* procee –'

'Then bloody well get ON WITH IT, MAN!' Doenitz roared.

Ahhh, Rietz thought, suddenly rather more preoccupied with his own yardarm than von Strelow's discomfiture. Now I suspect we're getting to the crux of it. Of why I, the combat officer, find myself privileged by such distinguished company . . . *Operation Juggernaut*, eh?'

'One does have to concede it has a fine Teutonic ring to it?' Leo Fischer whispered boot-faced beside him. 'A true Wagnerian flavour. The kind of clarion-call any good German should be proud to give his life for?'

'As you instruct, sir!' Von Strelow was tight-lipped: barely concealing his resentment. 'Then, first I propose to outline the general operational scenario . . . Immediately following the *Campbeltown* incident, the Führer ordered we of B-Dienst to identify an appropriate target for retaliatory action. He particularly stipulated it should call for the . . . ah, penetration of some coastal fortress area so far considered by the enemy as impregnable – in essence, a target worthy of a seaborne German counter-strike not only audacious in concept but which will, by its destruction, so devastate British morale that they must flinch from further provocative attacks against our own coastal bases.'

'The first rule of war – apart from brevity!' Fischer muttered *sotto voce*: ' "Know thine enemy . . ." So where the fuck was Adolf when the history books were handed round *his* class?'

'The Führer has since approved our outline proposal for just such an operation. One which he has personally code-named "Juggernaut".'

'You chose the phrase "outline proposal",' Fischer, the operations man, picked up instantly. 'Then presumably our presence here means the U-boat Arm has been allotted the task of detailed planning?'

'. . . and execution?' Rietz, the combat commander, supplemented keenly.

Von Strelow looked petulant. 'Because of the necessary involvement of your Atlantic submarine groups during the lead-up phase – yes! The Führer has decreed that Operation Juggernaut will henceforward become the executive responsibility of the U-Bootwaffe . . . B-Dienst will, of course, advise on matters within the Intelligence spectrum.'

'You are appointed Staff Officer Plans and Operations to the Juggernaut project as of this moment, Kapitänleutnant Fischer,' Doenitz said. 'Delegate the Sixth Flotilla's routine Staff duties to your Deputy SOO without further explanation. For security reasons, avoid Base Supply channels: submit your logistic requirements directly to Konteradmiral Godt.'

'Aye, aye, sir,' Fischer nodded coolly – remarkably so, Rietz thought, considering Leo hasn't yet been given the first idea of what it is he has to plan.

'The time scale, sir?' he asked.

'The reporting phase of certain enemy dispositions is to commence immediately. Appropriate orders will be radioed to your Atlantic U-boat Groups *Sturmer* and *Dranger* at midnight tonight.'

'And the date of the actual attack?'

'Its precise timing will be contingent on those reports. But the Juggernaut Force itself must – I repeat, gentlemen: *must* – be formed and operational by the first week of May. Five weeks from now.'

'Not long,' Rietz judged critically. 'Certainly not long enough to set up any kind of major assault. It's got to suggest some form of hit and run operation. In and, hopefully, out – from wherever it is when he gets around to telling us.'

'At the risk of compromising such laudable brevity, von Strelow,' Godt interrupted with dry perception, 'perhaps you should identify for Fischer and Rietz which particular impregnable British fortress the Führer has in mind. Regrettably we still have a wide choice until such time as our Luftwaffe keep their boast of two years ago – to annihilate the Tommies' coastal defences.'

'Southampton Water, Konteradmiral.'

Rietz blinked, momentarily disconcerted – so the Brits really had exposed a raw nerve within the High Command when they ventured here to St-Nazaire? Now, it seemed, the Führer's response was to thrust a stick straight back into the hornets' nest. The enemy maintained a necessarily massive anti-submarine presence in that region because of its proximity to the Occupied Channel ports. With that prospect in mind, a challenge promised to be the very least offered by Operation Juggernaut.

'With respect, sir, getting a U-boat in there undetected would make even Gunther Prien's foray into Scapa Flow pale by comparison.'

The Admiral allowed the corners of his mouth to twitch. 'Agreed, Rietz. But then, I don't believe I heard von Strelow actually specify that a U-boat *was* to carry out the mission.'

Rietz swallowed, somewhat at a loss.

'Sir?'

Von Strelow looked patronizing. 'You give the Führer little credit for military realism, Kapitänleutnant. He conceded our view that to commit a submarine to those waters would almost certainly invite its immediate destruction, and that alternative means of deploying your task element should be devised.'

Is he now trying to tell us, in his pedantic Party jargon, that we're about to embark upon a U-boat operation – but without a bloody U-BOAT . . . ? Rietz conjectured wearily, anxious only to get to the point.

'We looked, therefore, to our predictions of enemy shipping movements . . .'

'Meaning, no doubt, the observations which Admiral Canaris' Abwehr spies and Fifth Columnists send from Allied ports?' Godt displayed a touch of disapproval that modern war must necessarily be conducted by such underhand ploys.

'Supported by data provided from my own department's interception and analysis of enemy naval radio traffic – yes, Konteradmiral. You would, I trust, concede that it is only by such means that we have been able to propose a quite imaginative strategy to penetrate the ring of British steel protecting Southampton?'

'Imaginative?' Rietz queried, instantly supsicious.

'In essence, our raiding force will infiltrate the Royal Navy's guardships in the guise of . . . can I say, a Trojan horse?' The Captain looked rather pleased with himself. 'Yes indeed: a Trojan horse could be a most apt description!'

'A Trojan what?' Leo Fischer grunted.

'*Horse!*'

Rietz and Fischer stared at each other.

'An allegoric reference,' von Strelow snapped, plainly disappointed by such negative response, 'upon which I do not propose to elaborate before concluding the overall scenario.'

Shit, I should've guessed! Rietz thought savagely. The bastard throws in the most intriguing comment so far – then intends to keep us in suspense until the last moment.

'Then would it be too much to ask if your overall scenario allows for our being informed of the bloody TARGET?' Fischer retorted hotly.

Von Strelow did smile at that, to give him his due. Like a patronizing skull, and for the very first time.

'Naturally. The target the Führer has selected . . .' He paused then: deliberately milking his moment at centre stage to the full. '. . . will be Southampton's King George the Fifth Dry Dock, Kapitänleutnant. At the very heart of the port complex itself.'

Fischer scowled at that. Well, it did seem an inappropriate moment for humour considering the Captain's previous demeanour, but the tit-for-tat similarity with *Campbeltown* – the 'you blew up ours so we'll blow up yours!' element – simply had to be too ludicrous to treat seriously.

'The gates of which our valiant Trojan horsemen will then, no doubt, be expected to ram, eh?' Leo rejoined, black sarcastic despite Doenitz's sharp glance. 'At full speed, of course: and laden with high explosive?'

'But of course,' von Strelow said.

Quite matter-of-factly.

Obviously surprised even by the NEED for such a question!

There followed a thoughtful silence: not even Doenitz seeming anxious to meet the blank stares of his subordinates.

Until . . .

'Jesus CHRIST, I don't believe it!' Fischer muttered, utterly dumbfounded.

Rietz, however, found himself as much intrigued as disconcerted. He didn't understand yet: particularly von Strelow's maliciously vague reference to a Trojan horse. Almost as though the bloody man was implying the British guardships would welcome, rather than repel, the Kriegsmarine dagger aimed at their heart?

But the overall thrust was clear.

So it IS to be a German *Campbeltown*, by God! he thought, not entirely displeased at how detached he'd become now the speculation was over. Perhaps Doenitz had been right after all:

that all one *did* have to do was to outline the task to a U-boat man . . .? Or had Leo been rather closer to the truth during their passage up the Loire – that only those unimaginative enough not to dwell upon the eventual manner of their death were suited to becoming U-boat men in the first place?

For Paul Rietz, despite his outward cynicism, had always maintained faith in the Führer's enterprise. There *had* to be more to the Leader's thinking than an apparently childish act of revenge? Rietz simply couldn't bring himself to believe that Adolf Hitler would order such an overly theatrical gesture irrespective of the German blood it would surely demand; its cost in sacrificed lives.

Of course he wouldn't!

. . . *would* he?

Yet the Tommies had many dry docks: Southampton's King George V represented only one of several available to their larger ships within the Allied territories, affording nothing like the strategic hammer blow to their maritime plans that the loss of the *Tirpitz* facility had inflicted on Germany. Even its permanent destruction, however audacious, would hardly fulfil the Führer's stated intention of making the British flinch. More than likely it would merely serve to harden their bloody-minded national resolve!

On the other hand the eyes of Germany had, for months, been focused trustingly on the Kriegsmarine: anticipating a victory at sea to compare with Rommel's North African campaign; the Luftwaffe's lightning decimation of Poland. Yet Grossadmiral Raeder's Navy had so far seemed incapable of justifying such public confidence. The war for the surface fleet had never really begun: a temporary setback, Rietz appreciated – there was no uncertainty in his mind that they would eventually gather way to smash the Allies in every ocean. But nevertheless, even the U-boat offensive was drifting into temporary stalemate; *Bismarck* had unbelievably been pounded into a tomb for two thousand officers and men within nine months of her proud commissioning. Now her massive sister had been brought to impasse, trapped – as they in that jaded workmens' hut in St-Nazaire were only too bitterly aware – in her Norwegian fjord with nowhere left to run to . . .

So maybe Leo Fischer had indeed stumbled on the right motive in his river passage musings – but had simply attributed it to the wrong national leader? Rietz felt a surge of revigoration at that prospect – that it was, in fact, their own Führer rather than Winston Churchill who was omniscient enough to realize that, unless his sea forces presented the Third Reich's people with a victory of flair and style to counter the *Campbeltown*'s success, then a cancerous acceptance that Britannia did indeed rule the waves might well become Germany's norm.

'To restore the honour of the Kriegsmarine, gentlemen,' Godt confirmed, trying, at least, to convey the impression he considered the mission's aim even remotely attainable. 'The most coveted prize for any German Naval officer.'

Abruptly Doenitz rose from his chair. Just for that one un-guarded moment Rietz felt a surge of unease; could have sworn he detected a flicker of – almost of *sadness*, could it have been, in the Admiral's scrutiny . . . ? An instantly controlled regret for the futility; the wastefulness of it all? Mirroring the selfsame emotion which Rietz himself experienced each time he, too, gazed duty-bound upon those his orders were about to commit to destruction?

But then the moment had passed.

'The task must be for volunteers. Single men,' the Commander-in-Chief said bleakly. 'Nevertheless, because you have qualities I believe are vital to the task, I offer you combat command of Juggernaut, Kapitänleutnant Rietz.'

Rietz felt all eyes upon him: but he didn't dare betray his true reaction before those military men: not trapped as he was – as they all were, even von Strelow – in the sterile webs of platitude demanded by their duty to the Fatherland.

'I consider it an honour to serve my Führer in whatever manner he sees fit, sir,' he heard himself recite.

Even though conscious only of the most exquisite, the most painful irony of all – that he, the counterfeit man of war: the ex-merchant mariner who loved ships with such passion – had been chosen to enact every seaman's greatest nightmare.

To drive one such ship, along with her crew – along, no doubt, with himself – to almost certain suicide.

Chapter Three

'The owl?' Rietz said uncertainly. 'What the hell have owls and *ants* to do with anything?'

Fischer didn't answer for a moment: just sat on the edge of the desk and lit a cigarette, looking thoughtful.

The immediate pressure was eased. Doenitz and Godt had left for nearby Kerneval and, following the British raid, the guard-reinforced chateau from where they ran the real deep-sea U-boat campaign. Of lesser consequence, Fregattenkapitän von Strelow had gone too – in his case, presumably back to Berlin and his meticulous, eavesdropping war of cyphers and whispers from the ether, and stiff-armed obsequiousness to Service and Party superiors alike.

Doenitz's parting salute had been punctilious to Fischer and Rietz, perfunctory to von Strelow: the C-in-C's resentment for those who had persuaded the Führer to commit precious U-Bootwaffe resources to Juggernaut clear in his final remark.

'It is regrettable, gentlemen, that while B-Dienst have seen fit to recommend to the Führer an admittedly imaginative attack concept, they have proved singularly unhelpful in devising the practical means by which it can be achieved. The U-boat Service has, as usual, been placed in the situation of the Owl and the Ants . . . You will submit your joint operational proposal to me by 1800 hours tomorrow!'

'Once there was a rainstorm in the forest.' Fischer blew an elegant smoke ring and pierced it with his cigarette. 'It created a flood which separated two ants from their nest. Eventually they

53

went to seek advice about their predicament from The Wise Old Owl – in our case, the Führer. Requiring only a moment's thought, the Owl retorted, "It's simple, Ants. You merely have to fly across the water and your objective is achieved." '

'With respect, Kapitänleutnant,' Rietz growled heavily, still unsure of quite how to treat his new peer, 'but aren't you being just a tiny bit bloody ridiculous?'

'Exactly what the Ants thought,' Fischer grinned. 'Only they, like you and I, didn't dare voice their opinion either, in case the Owl ate them. So: "But how precisely, Wise Owl," the Ants contained themselves to asking meekly, "do you suggest we go about flying across the water?" The Owl looked down upon them from his lofty perch, and shrugged. "*I* concern myself only with strategy," he said haughtily. "I leave it to insignificant creatures like yourselves to work out the tactics!" '

'Go screw yourself, Leo,' Rietz said, finally deciding.

But his initial disconcertedness had begun to subside. Now the adrenaline of prospective action was taking charge – Rietz's all-too-familiar periscope syndrome. Powering him through the peacetime seaman's distaste at what his war duty compelled him to do, to a detached analysis of how best to go about the pedantics of killing.

And however dismissive Fischer appeared on the surface, Juggernaut *was* an imaginative concept; even Doenitz himself had conceded that much. Truly a German *Odyssey* in the making.

Even better than its mythical precedent, he thought hopefully. For when Ulysses commanded Epios to construct a great wooden horse, then left it at the gates of Troy while pretending to withdraw his besieging army, he'd had to rely entirely on the artlessness of the defenders to drag both it and its concealed Grecian Kommando inside their previously invulnerable walls . . .

'You look introspective. Can't say I blame you.' Leo lit yet another cigarette and eyed Rietz quizzically. 'You're going to get the shit kicked out've you and your boys before Juggernaut's over. You do know that, don't you?'

Rietz sidestepped the challenge. There wasn't *that* much adrenaline in his system yet.

'Just thinking. How much smarter von Strelow's crowd could prove to be than Ulysses. Homeric god or not, Leo, he was still utterly dependent on the enemy's cupidity to enable his raiding force to gain entry to the heart of the city – whereas, if we *can* pull off the first stage successfully, then when I and my contemporary warriors do finally sail for England bearing our high explosive gifts, we can hope to arrive not only as expected, but as welcome guests.'

'Your extra half stripe still wet and already you're hinting I was wrong,' Leo Fischer lifted a gently mocking eyebrow. 'That our somewhat unattractive Fregattenkapitän *has* apparently grasped one useful principle of waging war after all?'

'Am I?'

'That if one does feel obliged to attack Britain out of pique, dear boy – have, if nothing else, the prudence to attack it with a British ship!'

'While von Strelow demonstrates either a cold-blooded disregard or a naivety bordering on cretinism for the military practicalities of the mission, his argument in support of it must have been hard for even Hitler to refute,' Leo mused drily. 'It's based on a logical premise for a start. Which, compared with the normally convoluted tactical thinking of our other Kriegsmarine Wise Owls, must have come as a breath of fresh air to the Führer. Even I concede it might work – until you break for the dock, of course, and they rumble you!'

When any Allied merchantman embarked upon a war voyage, the Naval Control authority at her port of departure signalled her coded details and ETA – her expected time of arrival – to the defence forces at her destination. It did seem to follow, therefore, that to invite unopposed entry to Southampton Water, one merely had to present oneself on schedule, and in a form which offered the Tommy guardships precisely what they'd been pre-warned to anticipate – yet one more unremarkable Allied merchantman completing a home run after having survived the U-boat gauntlet.

'But she would have to be genuine, as von Strelow so blithely insisted,' Leo cautioned. 'A real enemy ship arriving from a legitimate voyage. A counterfeit with forged credentials can't hope to fool the British, dear boy: particularly following so closely on their own *Campbeltown* deception – dammit, they invented the ploy themselves, and "you can't kid a kidder", as the Americans would say.'

'Which only leaves you and I – Onkel Karl's Ants in what rapidly appears to be turning into a war of allegory and allusion,' Rietz muttered ruefully, glancing at his watch, 'with one minor sticking point to surmount within the next seventeen hours.'

By six o'clock that evening they had to devise, for the eagle scrutiny of both Doenitz and Godt, a way to steal a British freighter.

Without the British knowing about it.

'. . . one thing I've learned about von Strelow,' Fischer grunted morosely, two hours and fourteen half-smoked cigarettes later. 'He may have studied *Mein Kampf* assiduously, but the bastard's never once read Mrs Beeton.'

'Mrs Who?' Rietz queried vaguely, rubbing his temple savagely to counter the weariness of frustration. So far the key element for the furtherance of Operation Juggernaut obstinately remained an ingenious twinkle in the eye of its proponent – and a practical impossibility in the view of its delegated executors.

'Mrs Beeton. An Englishwoman of their Victorian era. She wrote a book; still considered the definitive text by the British on housekeeping and cookery. In it she included a recipe for rabbit pie.'

'You have an astonishing capacity for the irrelevant.' Rietz hurriedly forced a smile to cover his irritation, not yet being all that sure of his ex-Flotilla superior.

'Irrelevant, but not entirely divorced from our current preoccupation,' Leo shrugged. 'That particular recipe began: "First, catch your rabbit . . ." Unfortunately our particular rabbit will weigh in at around eight thousand tons gross, be running at eighteen knots, will be instantly suspicious of any attempt to stop her . . .'

'. . . and can scream "enemy attack" at the top of her electronic voice given the slightest perceived threat?'

'I should've stuck to horses. Theoretical rabbits provide far too complex a challenge,' Leo growled, crushing his weed and lighting another. 'Let's summarize the problem again. Your most likely passport through the Tommy defences – and as such, your potential ramship – appears to be a fast Allied cargo liner: the *Java Star*.'

'Currently discharging in New York, according to Abwehr's spy on the spot.'

'So by roughly the end of June, again according to Abwehr, she'll complete loading her war cargo, including ammunition, in Norfolk, Virginia: final destination – Port of Southampton,' Fischer mused. 'She's then almost certain, because of her speed, to receive orders to return independently and without escort . . . It's on that return voyage that *you* have to hit her. Quite how, von Strelow hasn't yet managed to work out.'

Rietz frowned. Fischer had highlighted the one aspect of the Fregattenkapitän's briefing which had niggled at the back of his mind ever since Karl Doenitz made his acid reference to Owls and Ants.

'Don't you think there's something odd about that? Something a bit Trojan horse-before-the-cart? All the effort von Strelow appears to have put into identifying one particular ship – yet the bloody man obviously hadn't given a moment's thought to the feasibility of capturing her! Almost as if . . .'

'As if what?'

'I don't know. He just seems remarkably conversant with the details and whereabouts of that one particular ship, I suppose.'

'He *is* an Intelligence Officer. As well as a complete shit,' Fischer pointed out reasonably. 'With full access to the fruits of Canaris' espionage network including the predicted movements of Allied merchantmen. He's *supposed* to anticipate, dear boy. That's his job.'

'It doesn't make him a fortune teller. Remember, he stated he'd prepared the Juggernaut scenario for the Führer only as a reprisal for the *Campbeltown* raid – but that only took place six days ago. AND caught our whole High Command, including B-Dienst, with their pants down.'

'So?'

'So, von Strelow's first action appears to have been to prepare an astonishingly detailed appraisal of one Allied vessel among dozens of possible candidates for ramship ... hardly a first priority when Hitler's screaming for an overall strategy?'

Fischer began to fidget irritably. 'All right – what are you getting at?'

'I really don't know,' Rietz muttered. 'I can't put my finger on it, Leo. It just makes me wonder why he chose the *Java Star*, that's all.'

'Because, laying aside for a moment your paranoia which suggests you've spent far too long underwater already, dear boy, she's unarguably ideal for the task,' Leo rejoined. 'What *does* worry me more is that, while Onkel Karl chose you because you're ex-Merchant Service, moderately intelligent, remarkably cool in action, and show a loyalty to the Fatherland which I personally consider excessive to the point of imbecility . . .'

'Thank you for your moral support,' Rietz growled.

'. . . your command of the English language is at most, despite your having served in the Atlantic passenger trade, moderate – and with a positively execrable Germanic accent! Should you ever perchance be forced to bluff it out eyeball to eyeball with the Royal Navy, they're hardly going to believe you were born in Tilbury or Leith.'

'Then I'll just have to chance playing the part of a block-headed Dutchman: there are a lot of them in Tommy ships. Haven't accepted the inevitable.'

'It's a weak link.'

'The whole bloody plan's a weak link between concept and completion.'

'At least she's fast, this *Java Star*,' Fischer grunted. 'Built just pre-war, suggesting she'll be strong. Heavy scantlings.'

It was Rietz's turn to smile drily. 'Which she'll need to be – when they rumble me and I'm left with limited time to ram the dock before they shoot the shit out of her.'

'I couldn't have phrased it more succinctly myself, dear boy.'

'You already did!' Rietz sniffed.

'Remember, too, that according to Abwehr's intercepted copy of her provisional manifest – which speaks volumes for Uncle

Sam's security and virtually guarantees our winning the war because they, the Allies, appear to be even more careless than we are with military secrets . . .'

'I know,' Rietz broke in hurriedly. Fischer's good-humoured support had already proved itself precious beyond measure, but sometimes it did tend to wander a little off course. 'The *Java Star* is scheduled to load in the order of eight hundred tons of assorted munitions as part of her cargo. Right?'

'Obliging of them really. Considering what we have in mind for her. Saves your coping with the physical problem of carting around several tons of IG Farben explosives as your demolition package. It'll be like a holiday cruise for your boys. Once you've captured her, all they'll have to do is take aboard detonators and fusings – even those ready-rigged by B-Dienst's whizz-bang technicians.'

'I wondered about that as well. It seemed an odd caveat: yet another emphasis on trivial detail,' Rietz frowned. 'For whatever reason, von Strelow leaves us to tackle the major operational planning, yet nominates some unspecified team of shoreside armourers to supply a simple timing device which any experienced U-Bootwaffe torpedoeman could prepare blindfolded.'

'Better it's not too simple in this case. Something nasty, full of anti-tamper pitfalls should the enemy's disposal people get to it in a hurry. The Brits won't be as complacent as we were over *Campbeltown*: they'll twig immediately that you've driven a floating bomb into their dock. Your team can't be allowed more than twenty minutes at maximum to clear the area before she's got to blow.' Fischer grinned; irritatingly candid again. 'More constructive for you to pray it's foolproof against the shock of impact, eh? Now, where were we?'

'Where we were two hours ago, Leo. Still trying to work out how I can throw a bridle over my Trojan bloody horse!'

'Norfolk to Southampton is roughly, what . . . three thousand three hundred miles?' Rietz muttered, brows meeting in weary calculation. 'Which means at eighteen knots – say sixteen as her actual speed of advance allowing for anti-submarine zigzagging – and assuming her to follow one of the standard Allied ocean

59

routes, her homeward passage will take roughly eight and a half days.'

'During which time she'll be shadowed and reported by Patrol Groups *Sturmer* and *Dranger*. We'll know her precise position, course and speed during every moment of her voyage.'

'Theoretically, doesn't that advantage already put us one step ahead of your industrious Mrs Beeton?' Rietz couldn't resist the temptation to digress this time, and with a certain sarcastic relish. 'Presumably *she* had to hunt her rabbit before she could attempt to catch it.'

'She was also at liberty to shoot the damn thing if it ran away: a course of action which you are constrained by simple common sense from taking,' Leo defended stoutly. 'The *Java Star*'s officers will already be jumpy as hell at sailing *sans* escort. One whiff of *force majeur*, my embryonic young Ulysses, and she'll break radio silence: Juggernaut's going to be compromised before your boys can pull a trigger. Complacency in the British Merchant Fleet went down with the *Athenia*, remember? They've all seen too many of their sister ships sunk; hauled too many boatloads of survivors aboard. None of them are likely to drop their guard . . .'

Rietz blinked. 'Say that again.'

'What – ALL of it?'

'You said: survivors!'

'Did I?'

'I think, Leo,' Rietz said, not really believing he was reckless enough even to propose it, but daring to all the same, 'you've just suggested how at least a Trojan *rabbit* might be persuaded to crawl, quite voluntarily, under our piecrust.'

Chapter Four

—◦●◦—

The ship was very old – nearly fifty years old, Rietz had discovered from her Log – but she would do to perform the short-term task he'd conceived for her in what, it seemed later, had been that moment of reckless aberration.

Come to that, nobody had shown enthusiasm for it: the device by which Rietz proposed to overwhelm and capture his necessarily British-as-roast-beef Trojan horse in mid-passage without the British being aware that such an impossible coup HAD taken place – but then again nobody, Owl or Ant, had been able to come up with a better subterfuge: nor felt the suicidal impulse to tell the Führer, who had decreed the destruction of a dry dock irrespective of the cost, that it couldn't be done.

It hadn't stopped them giving their professional views, of course. Not in private.

'You're crazy!' Leo Fischer had erupted when Rietz first speculated aloud on how a British master *might* just be persuaded to drop his guard enough to take aboard armed German sailors in the middle of the Atlantic, in the middle of a war. With Germany.

'. . . absolutely and utterly CRAZY, young Rietz!'

Then Leo had halted. And looked fiercely thoughtful. Until, slowly, a wistful smile had twinkled and spread from the weather-beaten corners of his seaman's eyes. 'But by *God*, with such an experience in prospect – especially for anyone who's been a U-boat commander – I wish, more than ever, I was going with you, laddie!'

Seventeen hours later, Konteradmiral Godt had taken one look at their Juggernaut operational plan: noted exactly what Rietz demanded in the matter of logistic support from the Fleet, to say nothing of how Rietz proposed placing himself and his attack group at such risk even before they entered into the most perilous phase of all, and exploded.

'This suggestion – it's bloody ludicrous! It forces me to seriously question, Kapitänleutnant Rietz, whether you aren't absolutely and utterly . . . utterly . . .'

'Crazy, Herr Konteradmiral?' Rietz had obliged a little wearily. But he'd already seen how Godt could play the wooden-faced military game of camouflaged resentment every bit as skilfully as that arch-master of implied criticism, Bootsmaat Landgraf, and would understand. And if he didn't; if the Godfather proved to be a smaller man then Rietz had judged him to be . . . ? Well, Rietz didn't intend for one moment to pursue a career in the Kriegsmarine after they'd won the war even if he did live to see that day, which seemed increasingly improbable. And anyway, he was fed up to the bloody teeth by then with people wanting to take him out of U-boats – which he was just getting used to – and pressuring him instead to sacrifice himself for the Fatherland in ever more propaganda-efficient ways.

Karl Doenitz, on the other hand, had studied Rietz's plan intently before frowning coldly from his desk.

'This proposal of yours – this double bluff to gain control of your ramship? Damn it, Kapitänleutnant: your request is tantamount to my endorsing an operation within an operation.'

'Nevertheless, give me your unqualified support, Herr Admiral,' Rietz snapped, eyes fixed unblinkingly ahead, 'and you afford me at least the optimum prospect of carrying out the Führer's order.'

The C-in-C's eyebrows lifted briefly, fractionally, towards Godt.

'Deny it, and be held directly responsible should you fail, eh? You're being reckless, Rietz. You must be aware that the waters of this office can hold as much danger for the imprudent as any protected by the Royal Navy?'

'I assure you, sir, that were the circumstances less pressing, I would steer a course well clear of either option.'

Doenitz leafed through, frowning a moment longer. 'This is incomplete, man. Where is your escape plan? You've made no recommendations, no request for support facilities to withdraw your force after final impact?'

'Britain is an island, sir. The King George Dock is one of their most heavily defended potential targets ...'

Rietz hesitated then. It had been the hardest fact of all to come to terms with – the acceptance that, from the moment he felt that massive caisson collapse beneath his Trojan horse's weight, for he and his men the war would be over. At best, a Tommy POW camp would be their lot until the Third Reich did finally march against England. And at worst? If they couldn't – if the British fire proved too intense to permit them to withdraw from the *Java Star* within twenty all-too-fragile minutes ...?

'With respect: not having had the benefit of Fregattenkapitän von Strelow's planning expertise, I have confined myself only to making what I consider are practical proposals.'

For that one long moment Doenitz had sat back and scrutinized him intently.

'I see that, apart from your first and most outrageous demand, you have also requested me to assign one of my U-boats to your tactical command to support you in the capture of your ramship?'

'Yes, sir.'

'But you propose that, once having accomplished that specific task, it should then be released to take up general patrol duties?'

'I considered it a logical submission. Yes, sir.'

'Then you have made your second error, Kapitänleutnant. By assuming I would send any of my men into combat without offering them at least some prospect of withdrawal, however remote.'

The C-in-C rose then, to stare expressionlessly at the portrait of Adolf Hitler which dominated his office.

'It is incumbent on we of the Führer's U-Bootwaffe, Rietz, to take every justifiable risk in order to offer our comrades hope as a fair exchange for their gallantry ... You are formally reprimanded, Kapitänleutnant, for omitting to propose that same

U-boat should surface off an appointed rendezvous as near to Southampton as feasible on, say, three consecutive nights following Juggernaut? To repatriate any of your survivors who can make their way there.'

He turned and shook his head.

'You realize, of course, that you are quite mad, young man?'

'So I understand, sir.' Rietz stiffened even more to attention.

'As a Bavarian Hare!' Godt, who'd remained quiet until that moment, reinforced severely. 'In my candid opinion, sir, this officer is not only impertinent, but also every bit as irresponsible as the British pirates who singed our beards at Nazaire.'

'Then we're both agreed,' Doenitz growled. 'So find Rietz a suitable ship. Also, assign one VII-C boat from Sixth Flotilla to his overall command as he requests . . . Oh, and one more thing, Godt?'

'Admiral?'

'Call for rating and non-commissioned volunteers for extra-hazardous duty. I suspect you'll be confronted by our roughest, most aggressive U-Bootwaffe reprobates: particularly those from his previous boat.'

Admiral Karl Doenitz smiled then. Rietz didn't know anyone who'd actually seen the Admiral smile.

'We'd better give Rietz the number of supplementary mad-men he requires, eh, Eberhard? Before he blackmails us even further?'

Ten days later Rietz was given his ship. They'd found her abandoned in a backwater of the Gironde Estuary. Within forty-eight hours, on Godt's orders, they had effected the minimal repairs necessary for her to make her way to a high security berth in Bordeaux where she'd been handed over to Rietz.

Her name was the *Stralsund*.

Typically, Rietz felt apologetic towards her, which was quite illogical considering she *was* only a ship, without any heart other than a reciprocating compound one powered by steam. But he still felt strongly that she might have been excused for believing she'd earned the right to die peacefully, without further disturb-ance, in the warm French mud where she'd lain for the past twelve months having already served her Führer diligently in war.

For the *Stralsund* had already created the stuff of legend in her day as one of the greatest of the early blockade runners. Many German merchantmen had been surprised in foreign waters by the suddeness of hostilities. To avoid capture by the British, most of them had concurred with their sealed orders and sailed to neutral ports where they were interned along with their crews – but not the ageing *Stralsund*.

Caught in the Java Sea, her master had immediately swung north, running the gauntlet of Dutch warships patrolling the Molucca Passage before, with remorselessly emptying bunkers and a top speed of seven knots, the indomitable *Stralsund* had then steamed two thousand miles to the friendly Axis port of Myazaki, Japan. She'd made their triumphant landfall with her crew ripping up the last of the old lady's wooden hatch boards to keep her fireboxes red.

And there she'd waited for instructions from Berlin; ready-loaded with raw material desperately wanted back home. Teak, wolfram, quinine, rubber . . . eventually her orders had arrived through the German Naval attache in Tokyo – *Sail for any German or Occupied French port*, the Führer had commanded. As simple as that. Half a world to cover, along routes still dominated by Allied seapower: one already exhausted ship; thirty-four Hamburg seamen. And German courage.

'Yet you did it, by God,' Rietz thought in wonder as he gazed over her still desolate decks. 'Ran the Tommy blockade at a snail's pace, disguised as a variety of Allied flag vessels; sailing under false colours with false names painted at your rusted counter.'

And now he was forcing her to war again. But a much shorter distance this time: just far enough to achieve his first objective – the beguiling of his real Trojan horse, the *Java Star*. So she didn't have to live much longer, decay much further, before being called upon to give herself finally for the glory of the Third Reich.

'Perhaps you and I both, old lady,' Rietz reflected sombrely, fingers absently caressing the scarred teak rail of her starboard bridge wing. 'And Chief Sindermann and Bootsmaat Landgraf and those twenty other German boys who've volunteered to sail in the wake of Ulysses with me . . . for in the next few days violent death must come as a certainty for you, and an uncomfortably distinct possibility for the rest of us.'

He shivered despite the early morning warmth, and felt embarrassed for himself because of it. Not ashamed, though. Rietz didn't feel ashamed of his fear of dying: only of being seen to possess such a fear. There must have been a great many, he consoled himself by thinking, among the British sailors and soldiers embarked within *Campbeltown* during her last voyage towards explosive self-sacrifice, who suffered much the same chill trepidation.

It was ironic, really. How, while every fighting man tended to turn, albeit for cold comfort, to the knowledge that others had gone before him, he, Rietz, consistently drew his greatest strength from the actions of those sworn to destroy his own country.

'What kind of men ARE you, our so-dedicated enemies?' he still remembered questioning only a few short weeks before off St-Nazaire while gazing down at the Tommy Commando corpse lying on his old U-boat's foredeck. 'That you could voluntarily have endured such a firestorm; made such gallant sacrifice?'

He knew now. They were ordinary men who had been called upon to become extraordinary men for one infinitesimal moment in the history of war. And had responded because courage was to be found in as many guises as the fear which, by definition, spawned it.

A man without fear does not require to be brave, and thus cannot be considered heroic. It follows, therefore, that only a frightened man – one as apprehensive as I myself about what is to come – can claim to be truly courageous, Rietz decided, recognizing his pomposity but, despite that, feeling the better for it. Surely being the front-line commander, the overt man of steel, the attack leader, didn't preclude him from a little private self eulogy just like anyone else, did it . . . ? Then immediately felt contempt for even that brief weakness as, glancing over the tattered canvas dodger, he saw Chief Engineer Sindermann leading broken-nosed Maschinenobergefreiter Schauroth on a morose survey of the dilapidated winches and wires and ringbolts littering their very temporary warship's foredeck.

For Sindermann was, perhaps, the most heroic among his Trojan horsemen, yet Sindermann had never been called upon to conquer fear as most men knew it. Sindermann's courage had long been proved: had demanded constant renewal from the moment a British bomb fell on a small house in Cologne, by his continuing to fight for something despite already having lost everything.

Rietz braced, forced himself from such dangerous philosophy; shoved his white cap flat aback and leaned over the bridge front. It was time to assume the actor's mask: the counterfeit *élan*.

'Tell me, gentlemen. Is this lumbering box of rust and shit going to get us further than the Fairway Buoy?' Rietz the grim-jawed insensitive; the calculating ship-killer already with the Cross of Iron at his throat called sardonically, seeing Schauroth's grin bolstered, as Rietz intended it should be, by his mission leader's obvious self-confidence.

'Sweeten the target with a Union Jack, Herr Kaleunt,' Sindermann's hollow-bearded intensity burned back without any calculated theatre at all, 'and we'll drive you and your guns through the lower holds of hell to hit the bastards!'

'ROHDE! In my old boat?' Rietz snapped disbelievingly. 'He's barely ready for command of his first routine patrol, never mind as the linchpin of an operation calling for flexibility and intuition – neither of which Rohde possesses! Apart from being a politically programmed arsehole, the boy's got a by-the-book mentality . . . I don't intend to place the lives of my men in Rohde's hands, Leo, and that's flat.'

'OK!' Fischer said, turning for the chartroom door. 'I'll tell Godt. He may mention it to Doenitz in the passing, or then again, he may just have you shot on the wharf down there without wasting Onkel's time.'

He was waiting patiently on the sun-washed wing when prudence finally overcame Rietz's anger.

'Look. Keep it to yourself, Paul, but we've lost three Frontboot already this month. U74 with Friedrich; 573 . . .'

'Heinsohn?'

'And Rathke. In U352!'

'Jesus,' Rietz muttered.

'It could get worse. Preuss hasn't reported in yet: he's overdue by seventy-two hours. There simply aren't enough blooded commanders to fill the gaps, and Doenitz insists the Atlantic battle groups take priority. Apart from which . . .' Fischer hesitated then, looking uneasy: not at all Leo's usual style.

'Apart from which – what?' Rietz growled.

'Doenitz wasn't given a choice. Von Strelow – and you know as well as I do, that means Hitler himself – particularly specified Rohde's appointment as your close escort.'

Rietz swung at the roar of Mercedes engines to frown down at the heavily guarded wharf where two camouflaged Naval trucks had pulled up. Men, still in U-Bootwaffe grey, were vaulting from them to stare silently, disconcertedly, up at the rusted *Stralsund*: the deck complement of his Juggernaut Force picked in the main, as Doenitz had shrewdly predicted, from his previous crew.

A crew who had elected to follow me, their tried and trusted Commander, blindly rather than serve under Rohde, he reflected, helpless as ever to do more than rail against this further, seemingly capricious, irony of war. Yet that same immature young officer will now be the very man upon whose skills the success of Phase One – our all-critical ploy to capture the *Java Star* – is to depend.

But then Rietz hesitated: frowned even more fiercely as yet again that still amorphous warning bell rang at the back of his mind.

For WAS it pure chance . . . ? *Was* Rohde's appointment to Juggernaut quite such an arbitrary choice by Berlin?

Because they, the von Strelows: the Party Men who strutted the bombproof corridors of the *Tirpitz Ufer* and took decisions over crystal glasses of Schnapps regarding how other men should die – they would certainly have done their homework even if only to protect themselves in the event of failure. They must have considered Rohde's fitness report: appreciated full well Rietz's bluntly expressed concern that his ex-Number One's

68

arrogance, his propaganda-fed contempt for British resolution combined with his lack of tactical command experience could well lead to Rohde's proving an over-confident U-boat leader. The most dangerous kind of consort on a very delicate operation.

Therefore – and even more incomprehensibly – they, the Führer-advisers, must, like Rietz, have realized only too clearly that, should the Oberleutnant make one mistake; take one overly impetuous action, he would almost certainly destroy Juggernaut's chances of success before Southampton Water ever opened ahead of the Trojan horse's bows.

And anyway – why specify *anybody* to support Rietz? Why not let the U-Bootwaffe pick its own personnel: take ALL the responsibility for failure should that be the case?

'Why Rohde?' he snarled. 'And don't give me that crap about the shortage of battle-seasoned captains, Leo! At our present rate of losses, half the white-caps we're committing to the Atlantic Theatre have come straight from Command School, green as grass. I made it clear in his fitness report that if – but only *if* – he learns fast, then Rohde might just survive for long enough to become a formidable huntsman before he meets his *Götterdämmerung*. But he needs the discipline of Pack direction: he's not ready to be let loose on his own . . . So why DOES von Strelow want him in particular out there with me?'

'I don't *know*, dammit!' Fischer took a deep breath and faced Rietz squarely. 'Oh, the hell with it – you're going to find out anyway next time you call at the Base. Your Oberleutnant Rohde was flown up to Berlin for a secret briefing two days ago. Top Luftwaffe priority. Couldn't resist letting everyone in the wardroom know that much, smug little bastard. But that's all he's given away.'

Rietz turned to gaze down from the wing again: the alarm bells clamouring loudly now.

Landgraf was chivvying his small flock into two ranks along the wharf. 'Get fell IN, Leinweber! Oh, *do* try an' stop bein' a dozey little bugger this trip out, Schadt . . . You there – Feiler, is it? Get your forage cap rigged fore an' aft proper: you're with the cream o' the U-Bootwaffe now, even if you ain't never seen no submarine like the one in front o' you!'

The British NCOs must have sounded exactly the same, preparing their squads to board *Campbeltown*. Again Rietz wondered if the enemy troops had been told, as his volunteers had, that the chances of their returning home before the war was over were extremely remote indeed.

Even more so now, he feared. Since they'd been placed in the hands of Oberleutnant Rohde.

'Suddenly I don't trust anybody, Leo,' Rietz said on an impulse.

'Von Strelow?'

'All the Owls.'

'A well founded reservation, I fear,' Fischer grunted, looking more serious than Rietz had ever seen him look before. 'There's something more devious afoot than a simple pin-prick against our enemy, my boy. Something not quite sporting . . . Watch your back!'

Chapter Five

There was no band when the *Stralsund* sailed on her very last voyage to war. No flag-waving; no carbolic-smelling girls; no last-minute morale boosts from senior officers . . . not even a bloody moon.

'Let go aft,' Rietz called quietly into the darkness. 'Hold on to your forespring – engine, dead slow ahead.'

He leaned out over the port wing, eyes probing astern as – bluff bow still restrained from moving ahead by their one last tenuous manilla link with the shore – the *Stralsund*'s battered counter began to swing off the berth.

A jet of dirty smoke shot from the old ship's funnel; soot hung acrid about the bridge, while the deck of a steamship began to vibrate beneath his feet for the first time in nearly three years. It smelled, felt and sounded good: benign somehow. The easy sigh of power harnessed for trade, as opposed to the throated roar of a U-boat's diesels created only to maim and destroy.

'Stop engine.'

'Stop engine . . . Engine stopped, sir!'

There was no Leo Fischer to wish them bon voyage either, and that hurt Rietz more than he cared to admit. For weeks they had worked and planned closely together: Rietz had learned to value his veteran collaborator's sometimes dry support, particularly when his sense of duty to the Führer gave way, in the face of what that loyalty demanded from him in return, to black foreboding.

But now even that camaraderie had, it seemed, been a mere

operational expediency: an illusion. The last time he'd seen Fischer had been two hours ago when, during the tense pre-sailing waiting after every contingency had been anticipated and only imagination remained to fill the mental void, Leo had announced his intention to take a final scout around the ship . . . and never even bothered returning to the bridge to bid Rietz farewell.

The ship was still pivoting on the spring rope, lying angled to the wharf now, near-vertical stem gently nudging the scarred timbers. Rietz could just make out the silhouettes of those who had guarded her from prying French eyes standing silently on the quayside, watching impassively as their mystery charge left on her secret business of war. Only one rifle-slung sentinel even risked going so far as to lift an arm in mute farewell. Their orders were to be incurious, but – Rietz found himself smiling then, albeit wryly, into the gloom – but by *God* how they must have speculated on what part such a wheezing hulk proposed to play in the Führer's grand design!

A part which, nevertheless, it was time to assume.

'Let go spring. Engine slow astern.'

'Slow astern, Herr Kaleunt!' The evocative jangle of the bridge telegraph echoed by Sindermann's engineroom repeater from far below: the hiss of worn slide valves and the abruptly reversing clatter of connecting rods carrying faintly through the blacked-out engineroom skylight abaft the funnel.

'Engine running slow astern, sir.' Landgraf, from the wheel-house managing to inject an almost comical note of surprise in the confirmation that his old shipmate, Sindermann, could have achieved such a miracle as propulsion from machinery more fitted for the breaker's yard.

'All gone forr'ad, sir.' Clearly, matter-of-factly from Becker on the fo'c'slehead. Seems a good boy, Becker, Rietz mused absently, watching the quayside slowly regress into black anonymity as the ship began to gather sternway. Pity that what we're about to do will barely afford time to test more than the calibre of his courage. Still, temporary though our relationship promises to be, it's at least refreshing to have a second-in-command not totally blinded by the lustre of the single gold stripe he's been accorded . . . especially when compared with Leutnant – sorry:

Ober-bloody-Leutnant! – Rohde, as they've now seen fit to make the little turd.

Junior Lieutenant Rudi Becker had joined two weeks before: the only other commissioned officer allocated to the *Stralsund* – an economy which illustrated, Rietz could hardly fail to note, the real measure of Doenitz's optimism regarding the prospects for their return. The youngster had appeared aboard one early morning as diffidently as Rohde would have demanded recognition.

Rietz had chanced upon him standing hesitantly at the brow: a twenty-year-old carrying his entire personal kit in a brown paper bag. A very *small* brown paper bag! Such frugality on Becker's part suggested not only that whoever had briefed him had been brutally candid about his future career prospects in the Kriegsmarine following Juggernaut, but also that Leutnant Becker himself possessed a commendable degree of realism.

Even more so in that he'd turned up wearing a loud checked shirt above, of all things, moleskin trousers.

'And who the *hell* are you?' Rietz had growled in astonishment.

'Becker. I . . . er, think I'm the First Lieutenant,' the boy had retorted dubiously, eyes still betraying the glaze of first introduction to his new sea appointment. Then he'd taken a grip and retorted stoutly, 'Come to that – who the hell are *you?*'

'I'M JUST THE BLOOD – !' Rietz had halted abruptly in mid-roar, conscious of the young man's gaze pointedly hoisting in the anonymity of his own informal rig: Rietz's stained canvas trousers encompassed by the thick leather belt with its seaman's sheath knife and marlin spike; his multi-coloured Swedish wool jersey; the wood-soled Belgian seaboots. But the *Stralsund* was about to embark upon a voyage of lies. Uniforms and marks of rank, like the ratings' U-Bootwaffe base haircuts, the saluting and otherwise sacrosanct Navy bullshit . . . all those had been left ashore with the personal letter each man had been permitted to write home, and which would be retained in Godt's safe until the final casualty toll was confirmed.

'I'm Rietz, Mister Becker. Kapitänleutnant! And at least I *know* I'm the Captain,' Rietz had said, willing himself to look fierce. 'So the quicker you let the hands know you're my Number One, the bloody better!'

Becker had done just that. Quietly and efficiently: never having found the need to lift his voice once. Rietz found himself hoping keenly that Becker would survive –

'Stop engine.'

'Stop engine, sir!' *Jangle, jangle* . . . 'Engine stopped, Herr Kaleunt.'

Lifting his binoculars Rietz thumbed the lenses through habit, then remembered he wasn't aboard a fast moving U-boat with a tower height only metres above the surface any more, and snatched a last glimpse forward: searching for the quayside and, more specifically if the truth were known, for any last-minute appearance of Kapitänleutnant Fischer. But there was nothing to be seen now. No Leo. No shore. No indication other than a pooling swirl of black water that the *Stralsund* had ever lain there.

Which was just as it should be.

He turned and faced aft. They were nearly clear of the creek now: still making sternway into the mainstream of the Gironde. A topsy-turvy relic, he thought, suddenly feeling very lonely. Steaming backwards to extinction.

'Starboard thirty. Engine slow ahead,' Rietz the fearless, the Iron Leader, called. 'Oh, and – Landgraf?'

'SIR?'

'DON'T sound so bloody over-awed *every* time we turn a screw!'

Nearly three in the morning. The wind had freshened by the time *Pointe de Grave* came abeam and the motor gunboat which had escorted them down-river pulled away on a surge of rising water to leave the enigmatic *Stralsund* alone . . . so far as the coxswain and crew of the MGB were aware, anyway.

Meticulously Rietz scanned the arc of sea ahead through the Zeiss without any great anticipation. The rest of the German Navy – particularly the element he was searching for – ran strictly on orders and to time. Rietz, on the other hand, had opted to sail earlier than prescribed: prudence suggesting he allow for Chief Sindermann's being forced to effect last-minute adjust-ments or even – if the gods did choose to set against them – major repairs. The long-untried state of the *Stralsund*'s fifty-year-old main engine was one of many imponderables which would plague the Captain until he achieved his crucially timed interception of the *Java Star*.

Not that Rietz lacked confidence in Sindermann; only in how long Sindermann might require to perform a routine miracle of ingenuity should such a demand be made. The Chief would get her running again somehow despite the pathetic stock of spares available to him. He'd fabricate them himself if need be, from tin lids or steel scrap or brass salvaged from less vital fittings, because Sindermann had spent the bulk of his seagoing engineering life in the employment of owners even more impecunious than Hitler's Kriegsmarine, and had thus learned to keep a ship under way with curses, sweat and little else.

For Sindermann, in common with Bootsmaat Landgraf and the rest of his Trojan horsemen, had been slected not merely for his proven steadiness in action, but because he was ex-Merchant Service. Rietz had prescribed that singular qualification right from the start – even First Lieutenant Becker had spent his fledgeling months as a deck cadet with Deutsch-Afrikanische of Hamburg before German merchant officers became largely redundant for reasons not too divorced from why the old *Stralsund* herself had been forced to become a blockade runner ... but Operation Juggernaut would only succeed as an act of theatre, albeit a very violent one, in which every player could find himself under close scrutiny by his enemy peers, whereas the merchant seaman's way of doing things was often at odds with the professional Navyman's. One unwitting slip at that point could kill them all.

... like my bland assumption that we're all alone and therefore safe right now, simply because I can't see anything, Rietz thought grimly. Allied submarines operated in Biscay just as freely as their own U-boats, and Rietz himself had proved more destructively than most that a cautiously deployed periscope presented little evidence of menace.

Don't do what I do – do what I say! he chided himself ruefully. *It seems I'm better at giving orders than at bloody well setting an example.*

Not that he had to in this instance. The hands had all seen

and heard enemy ships dying: learned the hard way what a moment's inattention to duty could invite. The watch lookouts wouldn't require any graphically detailed threats from Bootsmaat Landgraf to know that every flickering whitecap against a black night sea might well herald a consequence; every imagined break in the dark horizon, the enemy. The difference now was that, for the very first time, Rietz and his ex-huntsmen had to condition themselves to war as experienced by the hunted.

Even so, as the shoreline of Occupied France faded astern and the veteran *Stralsund* began to lift her squat bow to the first real deepwater seas, Rietz couldn't help but succumb to a dangerous nostalgia: leaning over the bridge front with the wind riffling his hair and pretending unashamedly, little boy-like for those few precious moments, that there wasn't any hate in the world, and that vessels like the one he'd previously commanded didn't seek to kill other vessels like the one he now commanded. Just savouring the movement of a trading ship again, and simply watching with never-diminished fascination as luminescent skips of seaspray flung high above rails already deformed by a legion of storms to carry, spattering and hissing with excitement, across the fo'c'slehead.

A movement in the darkness dragged him guiltily from his reverie – Funkgefreiter Stemmler, yet another refugee from his previous crew. Rietz had been flattered in a masochistic sort of way when his former hydrophone operator had volunteered. He'd been perfectly aware that Stemmler, almost as subtle a communicator of lower deck criticism as the Grand Master Landgraf, had regularly conveyed by the merest lift of an eyebrow or the suck of a tooth his view of Party Member Rohde's competence as a U-boat officer.

But then, Stemmler didn't like any officers. Stemmler showed rather too open resentment sometimes. Got a bit *too* familiar.

. . . nevertheless the man's current willingness to follow Rietz into unspecified hazard rather than remain with Rohde and risk perishing in what promised to be an all-too-specific manner proved Funkgefreiter Stemmler at least to be a man who spoke with his feet as well as his teeth.

Rietz grinned despite his irritation with himself. There would indeed be a great tooth-sucking and lifting of knowing eyebrows between Stemmler and Landgraf when the Oberleutnant's ego did finally cause him to make his first and last mistake as a Frontboot commander.

Rietz stopped grinning suddenly and, instead, began hoping to Christ that wouldn't occur on *this* trip!

'Coded signal just come in from C-in-C, sir,' Stemmler said. 'I haven't acknowledged.'

'Give it to Leutnant Becker in the chartroom. Tell him I'll be there in a minute.'

'Aye, aye, sir.'

'Nice cruise line number for you, this, Funkgefreiter,' Rietz called after him. 'No more hydrophones. A Sparks' berth aboard a ship where radio silence is mandatory?'

'The transmitter's buggered anyroad, Herr Kaleunt. Like the rest've this old shit bucket they've . . .' Stemmler prudently went full astern then. And sucked a tooth.

'Let's reach an understanding here and now, Stemmler,' Rietz suggested ever so pleasantly. 'You learn to cope with your dental problems, and I won't have you court-martialled for dumb insolence when we get back to Sixth Flotilla, eh?'

Stemmler's grin flashed in the gloom, but the real art lay in knowing when it was permissible to exploit a liberty.

'Yessir. Sorry, sir. Mistook you for someone else f'r a minute . . . Is that, er, a guarantee, by the way, sir? That we'll definitely *get* back to base when this is over?'

'And don't fish either!' Rietz countered severely.

For, equally, the art of being a captain lay in knowing when the liberties had to stop.

Leutnant Becker was still the only other man aboard aware, so far, of the purpose of their mission. The others would learn what adventures lay in store in a few more hours when Rietz intended to brief them. The Captain very much doubted if Stemmler would manage to honour their pact on that occasion. Not without a great deal of orthodontic self discipline.

Becker had almost completed decoding the signal when Rietz handed over temporary charge of the watch to Landgraf and joined his executive officer in the cramped, red-lit chartroom.

Passed through Doenitz's operations plot, it relayed the first target contact report originated by a U-boat – U736 in this instance: at that precise moment some three thousand miles away and patrolling the West Atlantic seaboard with *Gruppe Sturmer*. Hopefully it would also be the last to come from the C-in-C. From then on, to limit the risk of British interception and possible compromise, no further signals would be transmitted from shore with reference to the mission, other than in some unforeseen emergency. The shadowing U-boats would simply rattle off a cryptic – and, to Tommy ears – apparently meaningless update of the *Java Star*'s daily progress.

'Confirmation that our potential ramship sailed last night, Kapitän. She's already on her way across.'

'Nicely anticipated. Hats off to Abwehr and B-Dienst,' Rietz murmured softly.

'The *Java Star* came under *Sturmer* surveillance as soon as she cleared the US coast at twenty-three hundred local zone time. She's assumed to be heading for Allied Ocean Route *Oboe*.'

'Then so shall we. Anything else?'

'Yessir. Tracking responsibility has now been passed formally from Abwehr to the U-Bootwaffe . . .'

Meticulously Becker finished transcribing Stemmler's neat columns of cypher then drummed his pencil softly, a little nervously on the chart table: the only outward indication that he appreciated its full import.

'. . . and C-in-C's given us final clearance to intercept. Juggernaut transmissions will now cease!'

Rietz eyed his deputy curiously. For a German young enough to have spent his formative years on a school diet of National Socialism and *Mein Kampf*, Becker showed commendable restraint.

'No histrionics at this point, Leutnant? Not even some brief but stirring reference to Duty and Fatherland?'

'No, sir,' Becker said. Then smiled tentatively. 'Too scared, sir. Worse than that – I can never remember all the words of *Deutschland Über Alles*.'

'Thank God!' the Captain growled.

He didn't consider it too grave a flaw in Becker's military

aptitude, though Oberleutnant Rohde undoubtedly would have. But then, Rohde would probably have insisted they all sang it going into Southampton bloody Water!

An event which had suddenly taken one significant step closer to realization. The waspish Fregattenkapitän von Strelow had at least been proved right about the value of Admiral Canaris' spies working their United States net. His B-Dienst Intelligence cell had been channelling their reports to Rietz almost daily, updating the American coastal progress of his pre-selected Trojan horse.

. . . or of Mrs Beeton's rabbit, as Leo chooses to call her. Rietz couldn't avoid succumbing to a touch of waspishness himself. Damn the bloody man for not doing the decent thing by the crew, never mind me. Not even turning up to cheer *them* on.

It was then that a sudden unsettling thought struck him.

'Who drafted and encoded that signal? Presumably it *was* Kapitänleutnant Fischer?'

'Er . . . No, sir. A Kapitänleutnant Karl-Heinz Richter.'

'Godt's personal aide,' Rietz frowned. It didn't make sense. While Richter obviously held the Konteradmiral's confidence, he was still a Base Staff administrator. There shouldn't have been any necessity for him to draft signals; play an operational role – so what the *hell* had happened to Fischer . . . ?

The anomalies since Rietz's introduction to Juggernaut were beginning to assume a significance which, in retrospect, surely transcended coincidence? Von Strelow's so vague and yet so precise initial briefing – the paradox of the man's totally inadequate military preparation measured against his intimate knowledge of one particular enemy vessel out of many . . . Intelligence detailed enough even at that early stage to mark her precise whereabouts . . . even the likelihood, since confirmed by Abwehr, of her carrying *munitions* in her return cargo . . .

Then had followed the Fregattenkapitän's seemingly illogical insistence that a novice Frontboot commander – worse, that the hidebound and psychologically immature Rohde – should be appointed Rietz's tactical consort and thus, thanks to Doenitz's unexpected sanction, the one slender hope that at least some of his Trojan horsemen might achieve a withdrawal had vanished.

And finally had come the most unsettling twist of all.

The revelation that the same Oberleutnant Rohde, an officer ostensibly under Rietz's direct operational control, had nevertheless attended a secret Berlin briefing . . .

Rietz stood for a moment, thoughts racing: only vaguely registering the gentle tremor of the slowly turning engine; the familiar creak of timbers; the pendulum sway of hanging oilskins to the movement of his already condemned *Stralsund*.

Sustained throughout his previous role as an unwilling ship-killer by fierce loyalty to Adolf Hitler, Rietz had never really thought to question an order before. Since his promotion he'd been preoccupied only with the mechanics of a different kind of war, and of keeping his volunteers alive for long enough to ensure at least their profitable sacrifice for the Fatherland.

Until now! Because suddenly, with the Juggernaut die irretrievably cast, a new and quite alien disquiet had begun to crystallize in the mind of Kapitänleutnant Paul Rietz . . .

'It's nearly time, sir. Zero four hundred,' Becker reminded him circumspectly.

Rietz nodded, and turned for the black-out curtain swinging stiffly across the chartroom door. Before he brushed it aside, he hesitated.

'The Ants and the rainstorm, Leutnant? I wonder if it ever occurred to them that their Wise Old Owl may have had an ulterior motive in encouraging them to cross the flood?'

'Sir?'

'It doesn't matter,' the Captain said. 'It's a damned unlikely story anyway.'

She rose out of the sea to starboard with a deceptive gentleness. First her search and attack periscopes so often privy to Rietz's own very private regrets – now simply distant, slender needles feathering the Biscay surface into little cuts of foam.

Then came the tower, glistening menace somewhat muted to a black, featureless silhouette dimly seen against the marginal light of the coming dawn: smashing carelessly through the seas while spilling a by-then hysterical cargo of displaced water in cataracts through the after rails of the quadruple AA mounting which U-boat men cynically called their rose garden.

But which, on one occasion, bore more fruit than roses, the Captain remembered grimly, thinking back to the day of the mutilated British Chief Officer, when Navigator Grutner became sick at the sight of victory.

Finally her foredeck casing, bow trimmed slightly up, breaching like the back of some great killer whale and carrying upon it her cannon: barrel secured fore and aft and passive now; not elevated and trained predatorily outboard as it had appeared when Rietz deployed it to rip the already dying SS *Oberon* even further apart.

An act of savagery which, by my albeit unwitting order, denied yet another fellow seaman any last opportunity to disengage from the four thousand ton millstone which I had hung about him, Rietz thought harshly . . . and one after which I, the executioner, embarked upon a smoked ham tea with great relish because such monstrous inhumanity is considered perfectly excusable in this war – quite laudable in fact: Iron Cross With Oak Leaves stuff – as long as one remembers, later, to shield it from one's conscience under the veil marked: Duty.

'She looks good after 'er refit, sir,' Landgraf the more practical grunted beside him. 'Not so good as when you had 'er, but still smart, all the same.'

'Then now's your chance to request a transfer back aboard, Bosun,' the Captain retorted, grateful to be drawn from his black reflection.

'Begging your pardon, Herr Kaleunt, but is it zero eight hundred you said you was proposing to brief us on what little game we're playing under your command, sir?'

Rietz frowned: sometimes Landgraf's thought processes *were* inclined to follow a somewhat obtuse course.

'While I've got you all in a receptive mood after breakfast – affirmative!'

'Then c'n I give you an answer at – say . . . five *past* eight, sir?'

'Go to hell, Landgraf,' Rietz said amiably, lifting his glasses. There was a slight bloom of salt on the lenses from being at sea again, but he didn't wipe it away. It was a welcome myopia.

Even magnified eight times the bridge crew's heads above her angled spray deflectors were unidentifiable – or all but one. Rietz smiled humourlessly below the Zeiss. Oberleutnant Rohde hadn't learned yet that his coveted white commander's cap presented the perfect aiming mark on all but the darkest night. Particularly for a Tommy bomber attacking from zero altitude.

A red-shaded signal lamp stuttered briefly towards *Stralsund*.

'Recognition signal, sir,' Stemmler called quietly.

'Reply!'

Stemmler's shutter clattered.

'Add – Proceed according to Phase One Opord. Maintain station five cables astern of me. Essential, repeat essential, you observe submerged routine during daylight hours.'

A wraith of funnel smoke curled around the *Stralsund's* bridge, eerily reflecting the stroboscopic flashes of Stemmler's lamp.

Is it yet a further irony, or a compliment, the Captain mused, idly scanning the group on the distant U-boat as he waited, that while I have been accorded the somewhat dubious privilege of commanding this lumbering, defenceless scow, Rohde the Party Child, unarguably my inferior both in rank and in expertise, sails to his war task in a vessel which can run faster below the surface than mine can above it?

It was then that Rietz stiffened abruptly: fumbled with the focus wheel of his Zeiss . . . there was one figure, taller than the others on that dimly seen bridge and standing apart. Much further aft, braced against the attack scope standard as if unused to the motion of the sea . . .

But Stemmler had finished and there came one blood-red flicker of acknowledgement from their lean consort before the harsh echo of her diving klaxon carried faintly across the intervening sea, while the U-boat's tower began to clear in a rush of activity.

Whereupon Paul Rietz could only gaze in frustration as the first exhausting flurries of compressed air roared from her venting ballast tanks and her long, predatory bow began to submerge . . . and feel a cold prickle at the nape of his neck the like of which he'd never experienced before: more acutely aware than ever of a growing unease for the morrow.

Because if he HAD been correct in his interpretation of that fleeting glimpse . . . then what in God's name was Fregattenkapitän von *Strelow* – a Headquarters desk man – doing?

Sailing to war aboard a Front Line U-BOAT?

Chapter Six

Rietz was to experience a further, if rather different, prickle of apprehension at finding himself abruptly confronted by the unfathomable during that first night of their voyage in search of violence.

Less than half an hour after Rohde's boat had withdrawn into the secrecy of Biscay, in fact.

It was still grey-dark enough for an already galvanized imagination to run rife, with the salt wind continuing to increase from the west and the seas having gained enough strength by then to lift their effervescent tops clear above the weather deck bulwarks and gurgle cheekily at whosoever walked upon the ship.

. . . when the Captain chanced upon a ghost. The Phantom of the *Stralsund*.

Unsettled by what he'd seen – or thought he'd seen – and desperately needing to think, Rietz decided to take a turn about the decks. Landgraf was perfectly capable of overseeing the bridge watch while Becker laid off their first provisional course to intercept the *Java Star*: a simple navigational exercise which, in practice, was fraught with chance.

Their target ramship, homeward bound at last but still some three thousand miles away on the other side of the Atlantic, represented, in scale terms, merely a minute aberration on the surface of an ocean. She was advancing broadly towards him at an overall rate of some sixteen knots. His worn-out *Stralsund* might, by a concensus between God and Chief Engineer Sindermann, hope to maintain seven in a reciprocal westerly direction. At their combined closing speed, therefore, they would reasonably expect to occupy the same few hundred square miles of sea in just under five days' time . . . and at that juncture, God – who, without any help at all from Sindermann, created rain and fog and spindrift – would take exclusive command.

In conditions of poor visibility ships could still pass within a rifleshot of each other without either being aware of the other's presence.

So Rietz was, in effect, embarking upon a giant cat and mouse game, but there the analogy stood on its head. In this case the mouse, his raddled, diminutive *Stralsund*, was hunting the sleek cat, and with one unique advantage – his mouse would be assisted by the eyes of wolves!

Despite his mystification over von Strelow's unlikely reincarnation as a man of military daring, Rietz found himself smiling ruefully as he descended the final rusted ladder to the after welldeck.

'Indeed, Herr Wave,' he remarked to a nearby sea which lifted and sighed a liquid sigh as if calling for privileged attention, 'this voyage really *is* developing into a voyage worthy of Noah himself. Horses first . . . then owls and ants and rabbits? Now, cats – mice . . . even WOLVES?'

The wave said nothing. Just gurgled in embarrassment at being singled out for such unexpected intimacy before sinking back to jostle for anonymity among its countless fluid fellows.

But the Captain could at least feel hopeful that the odds in favour of a successful convergence lay with him. Already U736 had reported the *Java Star*'s master to be heading for Allied Ocean Route *Oboe*, one of the known sea gauntlets enemy merchantmen bearing Uncle Sam's charity were forced to run in order to keep Britain's foundering island fortress afloat. Should she deviate from that apparent intention, then Rietz would be informed and the *Stralsund*'s course altered accordingly.

The irony of the quarry's situation was not lost on Rietz, by then beginning seriously to question whether or not he *himself* might be a fellow victim of war's duplicity. While running Doenitz's blockade the *Java Star*'s crew would be nervous irrespective of their undoubted courage: her officers constantly alert to the slightest sign of attack . . . yet the truth was that for the next five days – and purely because every operational U-boat in the Atlantic theatre WAS looking out for her – such apprehension was quite uncalled for.

The British Motor Vessel *Java Star* had suddenly become the most jealously protected, indeed quite the safest ship, in the worl . . . !

It was then that the Captain became diverted from such philosophical rumination.

. . . for that was the moment when he first heard The Noise.

Rietz sensed immediately that the sound carrying above the sigh of the waves came not as a natural consequence of the *Stralsund*'s movement. A ship rolls or pitches, even performs both at the same time in a confused seaway, but with a certain rhythmic predictability in all but the most hellish weather. It is that predictability which gives an experienced mariner his sea legs: his ability to anticipate the next gyration. On the other hand any unsecured objects aboard, not having the sixth sense of a seaman, are simply compelled by the laws of physics: swaying or jolting or sliding to bring up hard against the nearest restraint – but always in harmony with the motion.

The sound which caught the Captain's attention, halted him abruptly in his tracks, hadn't followed that pattern. It was much more a metallic, non-conforming sort of noise – the sort made, say, by a chain being dragged wearily across a steel deck?

. . . and then came the first disembodied moan!

Rietz glanced uncertainly around, confident that no member of his assault team would be reckless enough to play such puerile tricks, and most certainly not on their Captain. Tension enough was present in every turn of the screw: no one needlessly aggravated it by indulging in stupid horseplay.

Horseplay . . . ? *Trojan* horseplay, naturally. Bringing me full circle to Noah's bloody Ark again, Rietz thought wryly, deciding he'd been mistaken and that it really was time he turned in. U-boat service had taught him it was his duty, as commander, to sleep whenever he had the opportunity: to store as assiduously as ammunition, food and fuel what could, at any moment, become an all-too-evasive necessity.

Mentally shrugging, the Captain continued aft until he came abreast of number five hatch ... whereupon he heard that same chilling, somehow distant cadence accompanied – quite unmistakably this time – by a rattle and clank of chain not in any way influenced by the motion of the ship ...

Childish though he knew his reaction was, Rietz still felt a finger-nail of unease trace delicately to the base of his spine. And not without a certain justification. A deserted deck at night can be an eerie place to all but the most insensitive. Moon-cold shadows inch remorselessly across plate and planking as the ship leans to the sea: expand and contract in a myriad of unease-provoking images – silhouetted ventilators curve long necks surmounted by what could well represent the bulbous heads of devouring sea monsters. Blocks and hooks and rails become fashioned by the mind into nightmare crustaceans: into slimy Awful Things rising from shipwrecked centuries of dead men who sleep forever in black ooze a thousand fathoms deep ... Into ghastly giant mol-luscs squirming aboard to reach for, and almost touch, before drawing back when the deck slants again and the shadows regain their familiarity just in time to save you.

And then there are the sounds of a ship passaging alone in the middle of an ocean in the middle of a night. Or rather the paradoxes they imply. For it is deathly quiet – and yet it isn't quiet at all; certainly not to someone who believed, as Rietz did, that each and every ship communicates in all sorts of ingenious ways: not merely by its constant articulation of wood against steel, but also by exploiting the elements. That it is the ship herself, and not the sea she casts aside, which hisses and rumbles in contempt. That when the sensuous breath of the wind caresses a ship it is she, through the vocal chords of her rigging and not the wind, which moans – sometimes even shrieks aloud with ecstasy – at such erogenous interplay.

But no ship, so far as Rietz was aware – not even his already complaining *Stralsund*, by then wheezing and exhausting and voicing a quite understandable resentment at being forced to this final metronomic passage – no ship actually *clanked* . . . ?

For one illogical moment he found himself regretting not having thought to carry a sidearm. Then realized just how ludicrous such a precaution would have been in any event. The threat had to come from not-at-all-illusory British torpedoes and naval shells against which a Luger pistol, even a Schmeisser sub-machine-gun – the only weaponry aboard anyway – afforded derisory protection. While, quite frankly, should the day ever dawn when a perfectly well-adjusted German officer had to consider arming himself for combat with the supernatural . . . ?

Rietz grinned toughly, just a little self-consciously, and continued.

The resonant clatter, the undulating wail, the eerie subterranean drag of metallic fetters rose again . . . !

This time Rietz really did stop dead in his determined tracks. He couldn't dismiss it any longer. There *was* something hiding among the dank, angular hiding places of the well deck. Something haunting in its persistent claim for his attention.

And if that *was* what it was attempting to do, then it was making a pretty damn good job of it!

This, Rietz thought, beginning to feel faintly hysterical, is bloody *ridiculous*! While I'm fully aware that Fregattenkapitän von Strelow has undoubtedly proved himself a duplicitous bastard for some as yet inexplicable reason, am I seriously to entertain the quite bizarre thesis that he – having conspired, presumably, with Admirals Doenitz and Godt; with Ober-bloody-Leutnant Rohde AND, for that matter, with Adolf Hitler himself – has actually tricked *me*, Kapitanleutnant Paul Rietz on detached special duty from Sixth Flotilla *Befehlshaber der Unterseeboote* into not so much conducting heroic deeds of derring-do against the enemy as playing unwitting host to some lunatic maritime *Walpurgisnacht* . . . ?

The eldrich clamour sounded yet again. Even more distinctly, and from almost below his feet.

The answer appeared to be 'yes'!

'Oh, *shit*!' Rietz the cynic: the centurion with the Cross of Iron at his suddenly very dry throat, swallowed. 'Now it's in the HOLD!'

*

87

It was then that Rietz began to get angry.

By GOD but hadn't he proved more than adept so far at bringing himself to confront much more dreadful images than this ludicrous troglodyte: this . . . this noisy *nonsense?* Didn't, every night, his closing eyelids reflect a savagery of doomed part-ships and drowning, burning, eviscerated sailormen as intimately as if gazing upon them for the very first time through his attack lens? Nightmare *visions?* He, Paul Rietz, ate, lived and slept hand in hand with nightmare bloody VISIONS! He, Rietz, had *created* horror – MADE fellow creatures into ghosts: ate smoked ham for tea while other men were still slowly sinking to the bottom of the sea where HE – U-boat warrior Rietz, the most terrible monster of all – had consigned them!

Savagely Rietz kicked at the wedges retaining the neatly tucked-in corner of number five hatch canvas: secured after sailing against whatever assault the weather might mount against them. At least until they met with the *Java Star* anyway, and such seaman-like precautions became irrelevant.

Below Rietz's feet the Beast began to bellow: flail with metallic fetters in echoing response.

'You want noise, Creature?' Rietz shouted back, yanking next at the hatch bar. 'I'll give you bloody NOISE . . . !'

The *crash* of the steel bar clattering on the iron deck reverberated through the after end of the empty ship like a giant drum. The Captain became dimly aware of shouts from forr'ad; running feet as the Watch alerted: but Rietz was furious now. Rietz didn't give a damn for the Beast below.

With superhuman strength he began to haul at the heavy hatch-boards, upending and sending them tumbling to the deck: opening enough of the square for a man's shoulders to enter while, all the time, the Creature howled a blood-curdling welcome.

The old ship rolled sullenly, resentfully at such cavalier treatment, allowing the first light of dawn to peer briefly into the rusted, dripping cavern below – and Rietz finally SAW it. The Beast. The Phantom of the *Stralsund*! Blood-matted hair: red-rimmed eyes glittering from its upturned head: squatting in simmering menace . . .

'Oh, JESUS!' Rietz blurted, recoiling in shock.

Slowly, stiffly, the Creature drew itself to its full height.

'What the FUCK,' Kapitänleutnant Leo Fischer grumbled in weary frustration, 'took you so long to GET here?'

Chapter Seven

'Your flailing the deckplates with a chain stopper to attract our attention – that I *do* understand,' Rietz complained peevishly after escorting the bloodied Fischer to his cabin below the bridge and, more practically, out of earshot of the crew. 'But why all the . . . the caterwauling? You scared the absolute hell out've me, Leo. I hope you realize that.'

Already reassured by Fischer's spirited response to rescue that the Kapitänleutnant's wound was more messy than serious, he watched irritably as the *Stralsund*'s unscheduled supernumerary tentatively explored his injured scalp.

'Caterwauling? I was *singing*, dammit! Morale, y'know: keeping the spirits up?' Leo winced. 'It just so happens, dear boy, that it makes for an extremely long night – battened below in an empty hold all on your own.'

'If that was your idea of harmony,' Rietz decreed emphatically, 'then both you *and* Becker are disqualified from the chorus of *Deutschland Über Alles*.'

'Eh?'

'Forget it,' Rietz growled. 'You're still not going to Southampton, Leo.'

'Haven't the faintest idea of what you mean,' the tone-deaf phantom frowned innocently.

'I seem to recollect your once remarking you'd give anything to be going with us.'

'Implying I stowed away down there?'

'Well, didn't you?'

'Be careful, Paul,' Fischer warned, his expression suddenly bleak. 'Your extra half-stripe hardly gives you *carte blanche* in what you choose to say. There's still the matter of seniority between us.'

'And I'm still tactical commander of Juggernaut as well as captain of this ship. You'll transfer to Rohde's boat after dark tonight.'

Leo eyed him thoughtfully. 'Bullying your own Staff Operations Officer? It's a fine course you're steering, and a risky one.'

'I'd have thought that observation applied rather more to your own current escapade. Anyway, Doenitz said much the same thing. I still won the argument.'

'Of *course* you did,' Fischer agreed. 'You blackmailed him into letting you blow yourself up productively instead of frittering your aggressive talents before a firing squad.'

There came a knock on the door and Stemmler entered carrying two steaming mugs.

'There's a drop of Schnapps in 'em, sirs. First aid, compliments of Bootsmaat Landgraf.' The Operator squinted sideways at Fischer, hoping to learn something.

'Real coffee, Funkgefreiter?' Leo asked blandly, not at all susceptible to bribery.

'*Ersatz*, Herr Kaleunt. The Base Supply Chief said he didn't plan to waste good French stuff seeing we weren't likely to get the chance to use it all up – whatever *that* meant?'

'Eight bells, Stemmler. That's when you all get briefed and not before,' Rietz said. 'So just pay the money you wagered Landgraf on loosening our tongues with a taste of his contraband alcohol, and go away.'

Following Stemmler's reluctant withdrawal he gestured at Fischer's broken scalp. 'Hadn't you better let me take a look at that?'

Leo presented his head cautiously. 'I did wonder when you were going to show some sympathy.'

'I didn't mention sympathy.'

Rietz examined it: a nasty contusion but superficial. He thought Fischer would live, and was glad of that. He'd felt more dispirited than he'd cared to admit, even to himself, by Leo's failure to oversee their departure. Now he knew why . . . But was he being just a little too sanguine about his friend's prospects for longevity? The consequences of Fischer's turning up aboard the *Stralsund en route* to battle promised to be both summary and savage. Yet Leo wasn't crazy: he must have known that if he didn't come up with a damn good reason for having deserted his post as shoreside link with Juggernaut, Doenitz would be left with no choice other than to court martial – and then hang – his recalcitrant staff officer.

Because if Doenitz didn't . . . then the Führer's SS most certainly would!

Unless, of course, the Tommies got Leo first, as now seemed most likely.

'What happened anyway?' he queried, deliberately keeping his anxiety low key.

'I wondered when you were going to ask *that*, too,' Leo retorted petulantly.

'Leo, I'm trying very hard not to lose my temper. Your being so bloody evasive doesn't help. No more than my being forced to the conclusion that, whatever action I take, you're still in deep trouble.'

'Damn right I am. Particularly if Onkel Karl persists in the misconception you so obviously hold – that my being here represents some sort of irresponsible, reckless adventure on my part.'

'No, don't tell me – let me guess the rest,' Rietz countered, unable to resist a touch of malice. 'Before we sailed you went for a last check on an empty hold; just happened to slip off the ladder . . . and eventually woke up only to find yourself imprisoned aboard. Leaving you no option, naturally, but to carry on to the target as a reluctant hero?'

'I'd *deserve* to be shot for dereliction of duty if I claimed that as a defence,' Leo observed, dangerously mild.

Abruptly, a little melodramatically, he rose and moved quickly to the cabin door. Opening it sharply he looked outside. Rietz frowned blankly. There was nothing to be seen apart from the pink tinge of the new day painting the crest of a passing wave as the *Stralsund* rolled.

'No,' Fischer said, closing the door again. 'That's not what happened at all, so don't be so bloody quick to jump to conclusions, laddie.'

'Oh,' Rietz muttered, disconcerted by Fischer's abrupt change of demeanour. Suddenly he became aware that the man was under considerable strain despite his outward nonchalance. This was the professional Fischer who had long survived as a U-boat man: the veteran with the steely eye and the authoritative bearing which invited no further liberties.

'I'm sorry. My inference was unwarranted,' Rietz said stiffly, angry at himself. 'My concern for your situation led me to exceed the bounds of comradeship.'

The older officer shrugged. 'No need to go completely overboard, I'm not *that* thin-skinned. And anyway, what I really meant was: save your most immediate concern for yourself and your men, Paul.'

The unease returned full circle to Rietz's mind. All his earlier forebodings about Juggernaut: the *Java Star*; about the secret meeting between von Strelow and Rohde, to say nothing of that same Fregattenkapitän's still totally incomprehensible presence not half a mile astern of them, came flooding back.

'Meaning precisely what?'

'Damned if I know,' Fischer said grimly. 'But *someone's* trying hard to wreck this operation, and whoever he is, he stands pretty close to home, Paul: perhaps even close to Adolf Hitler himself. One thing I *am* certain of now, is that some threat a damn sight more sinister than anything the British might have devised awaits us in the not too distant offing.'

'Us, Leo?'

'Us! Unless you're prepared to transfer me to Rohde's U-boat at gunpoint I fully intend to stay here, aboard the *Stralsund*.'

'Why?'

Leo Fischer grinned then. But there wasn't any humour in it. Not any more. Somehow Rietz sensed that all the humour had been left behind in France.

'Because, despite your overly romantic assumption, I didn't embark on your little cruise through choice. I'm aboard because someone in your crew intended I should be, Paul – and by God I'm going to oblige them.'

'Someone in my *crew?*'

'Who made one mistake. When he left me in that hold he assumed I was dead.'

'*Dead* . . . ?' Rietz knew he was repeating himself: that his jaw was gaping foolishly, but he couldn't help it. 'WHO, for God's sake?'

'I don't know that either – yet!' Leo growled darkly. 'All I *do* know is that, a few minutes before you slipped out of Bordeaux, some bastard tried to smash my skull in. With a chain stopper!'

Rietz didn't keep them waiting. There was no element of self-importance in the Captain's make-up. No sooner had Landgraf reported the crew assembled on the swaying welldeck than he clattered down the bridge ladder to walk briskly aft accompanied by Fischer.

He left Becker in charge of the ship. The Leutnant knew their war task and how they were to embark upon it, and so had already been accorded an officer's privilege of enjoying an even greater time in which to anticipate his likely vivisection.

The faces looked up expectantly at his arrival: stolid, deliberately expressionless faces, each contriving to conceal from its neighbour any hint that this was more than an ordinary day, and that the face belonged to anything less than an extraordinarily hard-boiled fighting man.

And Rietz looked down upon those faces and felt pride and respect all mixed up with, and therefore unforgivably despoiled by, a terrible burning anger.

His pride, he freely conceded, was in part a selfish indulgence: arising from the knowledge that they had freely elected to follow him, Rietz, into the, as yet, unknown.

'And why shouldn't I feel flattered?' he thought unashamedly. 'What leader could be so unemotional; so self-effacing as to deny such an unqualified accolade?'

His respect arose from his knowing most of them more intimately even than the mothers who bore them – Landgraf; Sindermann; Stemmler . . . he, as their Captain, had already stood shoulder to unflinching shoulder with that stout majority, challenging death to make its bid for each and every one of them in the cold black pressurized abyss where the U-boats fought their unforgiving war.

Whereas those faces he didn't know so well? Didn't feel quite such affinity for? Rietz felt proud of them too, and respected them simply because they were there.

All but one. And that still-faceless face explained the Captain's inner rage. Because it had to be the mask of either a traitor or a spy or, worse, of a German who owed allegiance not to his trusting fellow comrades-in-arms but to some darker element of the Third Reich which even so dedicated a servant as Kapitänleutnant Paul Rietz privately conceded did exist. An enemy within who now, following the event of Leo Fischer's broken head, suggested himself as being the most likely – as well as by far the most demoralizing – source of threat.

Rietz intended to execute such a cancer personally, just as soon as his identity was revealed. Coldly, and without compunction irrespective of which uniform he'd replaced with his present counterfeit merchant seaman's rig.

But until then the Captain had a duty to the others. To send them good-humoured into battle . . .

'Eight bells,' he called sardonically. 'Close the book, Landgraf, the betting on our destination's over.'

'Kapitän?' The bewildered stamp of Bootsmaat Landgraf's heels on the rusted deck came as an entirely predictable reaction. 'I c'n hardly believe I 'eard you right, sir – ME?'

'You, Landgraf,' the Captain confirmed patiently. 'Come on, then: let the wardroom in on the odds you've been offering any man fool enough to place his money with you. Kapitänleutnant Fischer here's enjoyed the comforts of the *Stralsund*'s steerage class so far – he *needs* a bloody good laugh.'

He got one then. They all did. Their former Flotilla Staff Officer's dishevelled reappearance in the early hours had already helped to ease the strain, divert speculation in the fo'c'sle messdeck over breakfast. Only Bootsmaat Landgraf managed to maintain a look of mystified innocence on his leather-seamed face while all about him the guffaws rose at the Captain's approach to the very grave business of killing.

Or alternatively, of course, to being killed.

'Come *on*, Bosun, you're not usually so reticent – how about a Yankee target? Easy meat, but three thousand-odd steaming miles away. What odds did you offer my lads on our sailing against America?'

'Twenty to one against, I'd figured, sir,' Landgraf finally beamed, abandoning all pretence. 'Then I listened to Chief Sindermann's language through the engineroom skylight an' upped them to fifty. There hasn't been many takers even at that.'

'Russia, then?' Fischer joined in. 'What about Ivan . . . ? Now he's an ugly one, but even a polar bear might well present a soft underbelly to a foxy little warship like this, eh, Bootsmaat?'

'Still ten to one against, Herr Kaleunt. There's a few Reichsmarks on 'im, mind. Some o' the boys took a flutter that Kapitänleutnant Rietz might just be daf . . . *crafty* enough to alter northwards soon.'

'The world's our oyster, man. You must have taken money on the rest of the world, too?'

'Took most of it on really wild cards, sir. These lads is gamblers: can't resist an outside bet. Mind you they got to be – to have volunteered f'r this lot, if you sees my drift?' Landgraf shook his head sadly. 'But they're simple lads, sir. Not proper U-boat men. One half of 'em is thick as two short planks when it comes to figurin' odds, while the other half shouldn't never have been weaned off their mother's milk.'

The Bosun's amiable insults were met by equally amiable grins from the crowd. Rietz noted how the tension had eased already at such unexpected banter, and was gratified. It would return soon enough when he called a halt to the fun.

'But you're not simple, are you? I know you, you old brigand. You've offered innocent young men a ludicrous price to suck them in, hoping that when we get back to Nazaire you can buy yourself a piece of Madame Fifi's business on a permanent basis?'

'Hundred to one. Who could resist it, sir?' Landgraf leered, not at all offended. Then he eyed the Captain cleverly. 'Except on the one destination that *might* just have slipped your mind, sir?'

Rietz raised an artless eyebrow. 'Another target option, Bosun?'

The Bootsmaat looked smug. 'With respect, I think I knows you well enough too, Kapitän. You've always been a man to go f'r the balls of the organ grinder, not the monkeys.'

'Meaning Churchill, eh?'

'That's where my money says this ship's going. England, sir.'

Rietz nodded sagely across a suddenly hushed sea of faces. 'And what miserable odds are you risking if I *do* confirm the *Stralsund*'s bound for Britain?'

'How CAN you think so badly of me, sir?' Landgraf sighed, wounded beyond measure. 'I'm still prepared to give these brave lads 'ere four to one, seeing they're shipmates.'

'As much as four to one?' Rietz echoed, genuinely surprised.

'ON, sir!' the irrepressible old matelot grinned. 'Not many took me up on the offer, but a man's gotter make a living.'

'The old skinflint's done it again,' Fischer growled without a trace of surprise. 'Taken a fortune in unlikely bets by offering odds so bloody unattractive that no one thought it worthwhile to speculate on *his* guess as to field favourite.'

Whereupon Leo, who already knew both the *Stralsund*'s real destination *and* Bootsmaat Landgraf, grinned wide as the English Cheshire Cat in *Alice*.

Rietz, on the other hand, was Landgraf's Captain, and captains do not wish themselves to be seen as uncharitable in victory. Rietz, therefore, fought valiantly to constrain his euphoria at actually achieving what he'd previously considered an impossible dream – to preside over the fall of arch-schemer Landgraf.

'Then from now on, Bootsmaat,' he submitted with velvet smoothness, 'I'd advise you to make that living of yours as the undeniably competent seaman you are ... and *not* out of attempting to corrupt your seniors with contraband alcohol; your juniors by promoting illegal wagers and – *most* particularly, Landgraf – NOT out of trying to read my bloody mind!'

Rietz did permit himself the merest ghost of a smile then. But only that of a man concerned to encourage a lost sinner more easily to regain the path of righteousness.

'It would be asking too much of you, Bosun, to bear a banker's responsibility for carrying money into action. Happily, you won't have to. Instead, you will be able to relieve yourself of every pfennig you owe until your burden is eased and your pockets are empty . . . All outside bets win – the *Stralsund* ISN'T going to England!'

Landgraf's smirk crumbled into comical disconcertedness while, all around, the jeers and laughter rose to gale force.

Before ceasing. Abruptly! As the Captain's tone took on a sudden edge of steel.

'The news you've all been waiting for, gentlemen. The destination of this ship . . .'

It sounded ridiculous in retrospect, even to Rietz.

'. . . is the bottom of the Atlantic Ocean!'

'Jesus, how defeatist can you GET?' someone muttered blankly, disbelievingly, from the back.

'She will be sent there in five days' time,' Rietz continued steadily, 'by a salvo of torpedoes from Oberleutnant Rohde's U-boat.'

There came a very long silence then. No one spoke. Not even the ship.

Especially not the ship.

'Er, c'n I ask where *we'll* be when that happens, sir?' Stemmler asked eventually: dubiously. Forgetting even to suck a tooth.

'Still here, Stemmler,' the Captain made it sound as if it was the most obvious thing in the world. 'Still aboard the *Stralsund*!'

Chapter Eight

Rietz had watched too many courageous submariners gnaw absently on white-knuckled fists, particularly during the interminable seconds between the firing of a too-close depth charge and its ultimate violence, to imagine that he, alone, sailed less than eagerly to war.

He'd seen even the most resolute stare surfacewards with fear-translucent complexions under such stresses; willing dulled eyes to penetrate what could well represent the steel carapace of their very own tomb in the next shuddering intake of breath. He'd observed the most indomitable nevertheless sweat a palsied varnish enough to fill a whole boat with the stink of incipient panic ... Rietz had, in fact, spent far too much time in the company of brave men pushed to breaking point: been too close to the stark reality of combat, to take Doktor Goebbels' strident assurances regarding the unshakable aplomb of the German fighting man *too* literally.

On the other hand, and to be perfectly fair to the Reichsminister for Propaganda, Goebbels had probably never been landed in Rietz's situation either. Had never found the need to break the news to that same – quite *remarkably* intrepid, one could only assume – German fighting man, that the dim-witted bastard had just volunteered to get himself blown up.

Very possibly, twice!

Either way, Rietz never had anticipated that *his* fighting men, volunteers or not, were exactly going to fall about with enthusiasm once they learned just how close to the razor's edge this particular voyage WAS scheduled to take them.

'So give it to 'em straight, but don't expect a round of applause, dear boy,' Leo Fischer had commended with his usual dry counsel. 'The imminent likelihood of being slaughtered for one's Fatherland not only concentrates the mind wonderfully: it also tends to bring out the cynic in the most aggressive of us.'

Leo, as ever, was proved absolutely right.

The silence had held ominously firm on the *Stralsund*'s afterdeck while Rietz described the mission's aim, and how he intended to achieve it. How he planned to seize the *Java Star*: what he proposed to do with her captured enemy crew – and how they would then transform her into a gargantuan Trojan horse steaming straight into the pages of Kriegsmarine history.

And why, in particular, he'd deemed it necessary for a German U-boat to torpedo German seamen sailing aboard a German ship in order to make the rest of the adventure possible: a curtain-raiser to action promising such an awesome military fuck-up in the event of error on Oberleutnant Rohde's part that even Bootsmaat Landgraf had, it seemed, found himself deprived of appropriate comment.

Or perhaps not, knowing Landgraf, Rietz found himself speculating, not without a certain small-minded satisfaction. The Bosun's being struck dumb, and with that slightly glazed look, is more than likely caused by his still trying to cope with the infinitely greater trauma of losing money.

Nevertheless the Captain really did begin to feel he was clutching at straws. The men simply continued to stare blankly back at him, implying much the same conviction of his being quite mad as that already evinced more openly by Doenitz and Godt.

'I intend to intercept the *Java Star* in the guise of a neutral Swedish vessel bound for an American port,' the Captain declared firmly.

Still silence!

'It is unlikely,' he pressed on doggedly, willing a response, 'that her master, once having identified the Swede flag we shall by then have painted on our topsides, and noted our, ah, less-than-warlike profile – will consider it necessary to take avoiding action . . .'

Rietz eyed them almost defiantly.

'By the time we've closed to some two miles on the target's bow, you will all have mustered out of sight in the midships section of the *Stralsund*. Each man will carry a concealed side arm . . . At that point, Oberleutnant Rohde will place two G7E torpedoes into us.'

'Fucking HELL!' an anonymous voice muttered.

'But clear of the centrecastle where we'll be waiting,' Rietz supplemented hastily, not wanting to give it to them *too* straight. 'One aimed for our bows; the second into our after ends.'

Beside him, Fischer tried to help by looking bored at the prospect of such a dull event. Rietz decided to experiment with a touch of understatement. 'We will then abandon in the boats, acting in the demoralized manner one might anticipate from a brutally torpedoed neutral's crew.'

It was then that the break came.

'Beggin' your pardon, sir, but demoralized won't need no acting,' Maschinenobergefreiter Schauroth interjected darkly. 'I ain't forgot Oberleutnant Rohde shooting that mock attack on the Cuxhaven Ranges – just waiting f'r 'im to put a brace of live eels into us in the right place is gonna guarantee *me* shitting myself for real!'

That sparked the first few grins, albeit notably hollow ones. Quite a few of them had witnessed the occasion when Rohde, as Rietz's newly appointed and overly confident First Lieutenant during their old boat's working-up period, had miscalculated deflection so wildly he'd placed a salvo of practice torpedoes neatly into the Fleet towing vessel instead of the target.

'Then maybe Kapitänleutnant Rietz can have you climb the Tommies' side ladder first, eh, Schauroth?' Fischer joked astutely. 'Save us the trouble of rigging someone to smell like a panic-stricken Swede, for a start.'

'Save the trouble o' shooting the buggers, more like,' Landgraf finally growled with sepulchral disgust. 'One whiff o' Schauroth with the trots, Kaleunt, an' the Brits'll chuck their hands in. Prob'ly abandon over the OPPOSITE bloody side!'

The gust of laughter at the frustrated bookmaker's return to the lesser matter of war brought a surge of carefully concealed relief to Rietz. He knew then that he hadn't been wrong: that he had, after all, picked the right men.

All but – it seemed – for one . . . ? He blanked the unease from his thoughts, concentrating on the job in hand: giving them what they expected from their Iron Father.

'It is essential that we catch the Tommies with their pants down; particularly to prevent her radio operator from alerting the British coastal stations of her capture – to that end, each man will be allotted a key point to secure as soon as we spring our little surprise. More on that later, but . . .' he contrived his most ferocious Captain's scowl, 'to conclude – and largely for the benefit of those among you who will undoubtedly feel compelled to question the Commander-in-Chief's decision to sacrifice this splendidly appointed vessel in pursuit of realism . . .'

Rietz fixed each and every one of them with pointed gaze, especially the now grinning Landgraf.

'Kapitänleutnant Fischer and I have already, in our own inadequate way, considered less dramatic alternatives. Our just waiting conveniently in the *Java Star*'s path in rubber rafts, for instance – which Tommy merchantmen don't carry anyway – and pretending to be Allied survivors, will NOT fool her crew for a minute . . .'

The Captain smiled a smile as sour and full of implied menace as any smiled by Fregattenkapitän von Strelow.

'Therefore do *not* come up with any crap about how YOU would have planned it. Be good enough to save the messdeck from endless strategic discussion – and *me* from the inconvenience of court martialling anyone who isn't bloody well LISTENING!'

He felt gratified to note that each face now revealed only resolution for the task ahead as they slammed to attention in chorus.

'Aye, AYE, sir!'

'Any further QUESTIONS?'

'KAPITAN!'

'*Yes*, Bootsmaat Landgraf?' Rietz sighed wearily.

'With respect, sir – but what odds WOULD you consider sporting, sir . . . ? On Oberleutnant Rohde's puncturin' us in *exac'ly* the right places?'

For the next five days the *Stralsund* wheezed and rumbled eastwards, closing with asthmatic determination – and surely no one could ask for more of a ship? – the geometrically prescribed intersection of two course lines on Becker's chart intended as her own execution place. Deeper and deeper into the battleground of the Atlantic – and yet only twice were they ever given cause to believe that other ships and men shared that ocean with themselves.

On the afternoon of the third day, Lookout Schadt had sighted a masthead cutting the edge of the southern horizon. By the time they'd gone to action stations, which was a stirring if somewhat pointless thing to do, the single masthead had given birth to a whole forest of mastheads; all moving slowly and purposefully across the edge of the world towards the British Isles.

Rietz and Fischer watched bleakly: each frustrated by the awareness that, had they still been Frontboot captains, an enemy convoy promising such rich pickings would have offered itself as manna from heaven. Toothless as they found themselves aboard the *Stralsund*, they could only turn sharply and run away, disturbed that the formidable concentration of merchantmen had apparently evaded both *Sturmer* and *Dranger* undetected.

Or, even more ominously – that it hadn't! That battle *had*, perhaps, already been joined further west, but with Doenitz's wolf pack driven off leaving the Allied escorts triumphant in a new-found, if temporary, turning of the tide?

Their spirits were restored a little during the following night. When they chanced upon the fire in the sky.

At six minutes to three, the blackness to starboard was rent by a massive, white-hot flash. And then another, just high enough above the curvature of the earth to imprint a hanging incandescent spot which only gradually faded from the retina of the eye. And then followed the red glow of fire, reflecting eerily from the low cloud ceiling: flickering and expanding as though Heaven itself had suffered ignition while, gradually, their ears became aware of the rumbling and booming of distant explosions.

Chief Engineer Sindermann came on the bridge and hung pleasurably over the wing beside Rietz, wiping his shiny face with an already oil-soaked sweat rag and sniffing the wind.

'Benzine tanker,' Rietz said. And felt sad for the dying ship.

'God's Kitchen, Kapitän. You can almost hear the bastards cooking.' Sindermann's teeth flashed in awful appreciation. 'Barbecued *Schweinefleisch*. In petro-gravy!'

Rietz felt even more sad.

For Sindermann.

They never were, of course, entirely alone.

Each evening, following twilight, the lean black hunter which was their submarine escort had surfaced astern as a dimly observed shadow to breathe fresh air and recharge batteries and allow her sun-starved troglodyte crew the all-too-brief privilege of relaxing, by rote, beneath the stars.

No communication passed between them. Rietz had nothing to say to Rohde either operationally or personally. The coded reports of their quarry's progress, transmitted twice daily from U-boat Groups *Sturmer* and *Dranger* and snatched by Funkgefreiter Stemmler from the ether, merely confirmed that the *Java Star* was continuing as predicted along Route *Oboe*.

During daylight hours, Rohde's boat again reverted to a trailing periscope only sighted as an occasional feather of spray cutting the turmoil of their slowly dissolving wake. Sometimes, because there *was* little else to do except watch and wait, Rietz leaned on the after bridge rail with binoculars trained steadily astern to catch a fleeting glimpse of it. It had begun as a casual diversion: an unashamedly childish game of hide and seek with the Cyclopean optic so long privy to his own secret emotions, and through which Rietz himself had looked upon many condemned ships. Though never, he reflected wryly, on a potential victim in circumstances so bizarre as this.

But before long even that innocent amusement became the

catalyst for unsettling speculation on the Captain's part. What equally private thoughts preoccupied the man who, in turn, gazed through the periscope at him? Come to that – who's eye WAS it? Was it, for instance, conceivable that Rietz's brief sighting on their first morning at sea had indeed been correct, and that control of the shadowing periscope belonged, not to Oberleutnant Rohde but to Fregattenkapitän von *Strelow* . . . ? Ridiculous it may be, but was such a hypothesis really any less likely than that Rohde, a novice commander remarkable only for his slavish adherence to the Party line, could have received separate orders affecting Juggernaut in the first place? Orders about which he, Rietz, the Mission Commander, knew nothing . . . ? And if so – why? To what purpose? Even assuming von Strelow *had* been their instigator – even conceding that the Captain from Berlin DID sail in secret company aboard their U-boat escort – was it remotely credible, in view of the Führer's directive, that a middle-ranking Staff officer would risk any pact counter-productive to the ultimate destruction of the British dry dock?

Unless, of course, such conspiracy did originate from even further up the Nazi hierarchy, as Leo Fischer had darkly hinted – even, God forbid, from Adolf Hitler himself? Yet if THAT was the case, then where did Karl Doenitz and Godt, both long noted for being fiercely uncompromising in their loyalty to their U-boat men, fit in . . . ?

He couldn't risk transmitting, himself. But why, for instance, had neither admiral attempted to query what must surely have seemed their own Operations Officer's ominous disppearance from his duty post? The orders provided for emergency transmissions from shore: there wouldn't be that much risk attached to one – why, then, had Command not made, at the very least, a signal warning Rietz of an event so obviously material to the *Stralsund*'s sailing as to defy coincidence?

Funkgefreiter Stemmler would surely have intercepted it? Stemmler had successfully picked up every Juggernaut message transmitted by the U-boat groups themselves – ergo no alerting signal from Headquarters had ever been made.

. . . Rietz lost it there. A merchant seaman for most of his life, the Captain was finding himself ill-equipped to debate the finer nuances of High Command intrigue – apart from which, Paul Rietz, by then irrevocably committed to giving his life if necessary for the Fatherland, was coldly aware that he simply couldn't *afford* to reflect too hard on the more sinister interpretation of such an omission. Permitting himself to brood too much would have destroyed him: rendered everything he'd ever fought for, all he'd ever valued as a patriot, worthless.

Because the obvious assumption had to be that Headquarters hadn't made a signal because they already KNEW Leo was aboard. That either Karl Doenitz or Godt, or more than likely, both, bloody well *knew* Fischer had sailed to war – AND presumed him dead, for that matter! – in number five hold of the *Stralsund*.

Yet the natural extension to *that* appalling hypothesis could only lead U-Bootwaffe Kapitänleutnant Rietz inexorably to the further, utterly devastating, conclusion that the attempt to murder U-Bootwaffe Kapitänleutnant Fischer MUST have taken place either with the acquiescence of, or – worse – at the express order of . . .

U-Bootwaffe COMMAND?

He didn't mention his dark imaginings about the signal that apparently never was, to Leo Fischer. No more than did Leo, who must surely have been, at the least, disappointed that his own seeming evaporation had caused such little stir back home, broach the subject with Rietz.

Leo may have taken a different and less disturbing view: would certainly have looked for a more flattering explanation than his being irrelevant, but Rietz, as conscious of the need for a German officer to maintain face as anybody, just couldn't bring himself to embarrass Fischer further by raising the matter.

After all: how could one even *suggest* to a man who had served his Fatherland diligently in two world wars that, on his next confronting the enemy he might be better advised to look, not to his front, but to the comrades-in-arms – particularly the senior officers – at his back?

*

Notwithstanding such understandable moral cowardice in the face of his friend, Rietz still remained, for all his romantic pre-war deals, a resolute pragmatist.

The Iron Cross at his throat already illustrated that. Peacetime dreamer or not; once they'd made Paul Rietz a combat commander of the Third Reich he'd proved that, when the call of Führer-duty sounded, he was more than capable of divorcing himself from superfluous emotion and focusing only on the task in hand. That singular trait – Rietz's so-called periscope syndrome – had so far accounted not only for his being able to kill ships with a ruthless efficiency matched only by his love for them, but also for his capacity to override, if not completely still, the uneasy voice of conscience within.

And so it was to prove once again, as the *Stralsund* steamed ever closer to her first and last target as an official warship, that the Captain concentrated less and less on debating the who's and why's of his mission, and applied himself to dangers more immediate.

Which, excluding what seemed to be fast becoming the almost irrelevant ones promised by the Royal bloody Navy, he reflected with ever-growing and, despite his determination to stay cool, bitter cynicism, can only stem from someone already infiltrated aboard the *Stralsund* – which takes me back full circle to 'Who'?

Unfortunately being a pragmatist didn't make him a detective. Rietz had never even been able to complete a jigsaw puzzle unaided as a child. But it did, at least, help him come to terms with having too little time before they confronted the *Java Star* to do much about identifying their undoubted enemy within anyway.

Other than call Radio Operator Stemmler to the bridge to try and unravel just a little of the tangled web he'd deduced himself into.

'Think hard, Funkgefreiter,' he said, standing well clear of eavesdropping ears. 'Are you quite certain you couldn't have missed intercepting a signal originated by the C-in-C?'

Stemmler looked positively taken aback. Thoroughly shaken in fact, Rietz thought, secretly reproaching himself. He hadn't meant to imply that Stemmler had been remiss in his duty.

Stemmler, like all the men, had enough to preoccupy him without extra-curricular pressure being added through the undisciplined paranoia of his Captain.

At the same time he felt justified in betraying *some* small irritation at what he considered was Stemmler's quite uncharacteristic over-sensitivity.

'Oh, for Christ's sake, don't you start going prima donna on me, Stemmler,' he growled. 'I'm not questioning your assiduity so much as your equipment – *could* it be failing to pick up broadcasts on the C-in-C's pre-arranged Juggernaut frequency?'

'No, sir,' Stemmler said, still a bit truculently. 'The receiver's performing adequately. Headquarters haven't tried to contact us during any of the prescribed listening periods or I'd have heard them . . .'

Rietz detected a more familiar Stemmler then, as the Sparks regained a little of his former presumption. 'As per the Signals Appendix of the Opord – IF you recall, sir? *No traffic from Command will be initiated other than in extreme Operational necessity . . .*? Might there, ah, *be* an operational necessity for the C-in-C to call us, in your view, sir?'

'When I do require assistance with the details of the Opord, Funkgefreiter, *or* in making tactical assessments,' Rietz assured him levelly, 'then I promise to consult you. Until that time, just you concentrate on my earlier advice – about pushing your bloody LUCK?'

Stemmler's briefly regained brashness evaporated as he slammed to wooden-faced attention.

'JAWOHL, Herr Kapitän!'

Well, Stemmler's got *that* message loud and clear, at least, Rietz brooded, watching his radio man leave the bridge and not really knowing why he felt so sour.

. . . so why do I have the feeling that I haven't so much unravelled one skein of the web – as unearthed yet another?

There existed, as it happened, one further and entirely personal uncertainty in the Captain's already over-burdened mind. It concerned the less complex but, for him, equally important matter of courage.

Rietz still wasn't quite sure how stoutly *he* – never mind his crew – would face up to being torpedoed by what, until recently, had been his own Frontboot.

Inevitably, and to his unfettered relief, the point in their voyage was reached where conjecture ended, and he was about to find out.

Just before seven o'clock on the morning of the sixth day a Juggernaut report of the target's progress was received by Stemmler; encrypted as part of an apparently routine operational transmission from *Gruppe Sturmer*'s U253, then some seventy nautical miles ahead of them.

Rietz took one glance at the chart and knew they would almost certainly be in action within three hours. The weather promised to hold both for interception and, he reflected philosophically, for boating.

Not for swimming, though. It very seldom was after a torpedoing. Exploded ships bled oil and entrails which made poor companions for a man restricted by his lifejacket. He remembered the choking scum of coal dust which marked the going down of the Liverpool-registered *Oberon*. That, in turn, re-conjured a more than inopportune image of her bug-eyed rider sliding, trapped and screaming, to the bottom of the . . . !

The Captain shivered involuntarily: a macabre sensation quite divorced from temperature. More as if he'd been briefly touched upon by a dead man's malice.

'Making something of a change,' he resigned himself with wry whimsy before applying himself to the chart, 'from being haunted by spectres of mistrust, disloyalty and – dare I even think it? – possible treachery.'

'Rig our Swede Flag over the side, Becker, then ensure everyone gets a damn good breakfast,' he said cheerfully. 'As many eggs as they want. Sausage: plenty of coffee . . . Whatever the mermaids have in mind for us, I rather suspect we won't be lunching aboard today.'

She betrayed herself first as a single hair on the blue-grey pate of the horizon: fine on the port bow and exactly where Rietz had visualized raising her when he'd first conceived his madcap solution all those weeks before.

The *Stralsund* had, perhaps, forty more minutes to live. The Captain couldn't help wondering if she knew it, and if there was anything he could do to ease her coming ordeal. But there probably wasn't.

Leutnant Becker came out of the wheelhouse and stared expressionlessly ahead. Rietz could see the boy was trying hard to look cool.

'What about our code books, sir? D'you want me to get them from your cabin safe and stow them ready in the weighted bag?'

Rietz looked severe.

'Don't you think it more prudent to confirm the cut of the enemy's jib first, Mister Becker? Make damn sure she *is* the *Java Star* before ditching confidential books and generally entering into unseemly panic . . . ? Look first for a heavy-lift Mannesmann tube derrick at her foremast.'

Becker looked a bit crestfallen.

'Yes, sir. Sorry, sir.'

Rietz relented. Better to do everything possible now, while there was time.

'No, you're probably right. Nip down – but *don't* be long.'

'Aye, *aye*, sir!'

Becker turned a little too quickly for the ladder, betraying his true excitement. Not, it seemed, that the young First Lieutenant was the only one to count chickens. Most of the non-watch crew, some of them already shrugging into their cork merchant-service style lifejackets, were already drifting to the proximity of their abandon-ship stations as word of the sighting went round. Rietz wondered drily whether that implied absolute faith in his judgement as a planner, or common mistrust of a probably trigger-nervous Oberleutnant Rohde's ability to hold fire until the operationally prescribed time and distance.

In general, though, he observed approvingly, their demeanour would suggest an insensibility to high explosive enough to impress even Doktor Goebbels.

A few held mugs of steaming coffee. Some of them were still masticating the remnants of what had almost certainly been the most fulsome, if not the most relaxed breakfast they'd ever had since being inducted to the Service. Maschinenobergefreiter Schauroth continued to gnaw with unconcealed appreciation on the bitter end of a formidable *Leberwurst*.

Either belying his – frankly terrifying – prediction of rectal uncontrollability, the Captain thought, grateful to command such quiet heroes at such a time, or stoking up for it.

Leo Fischer came beside him and stood watching while Rietz's horsemen lined the rusted boat deck guards: faces turned into the wind the better to observe what could, if things went wrong, prove their own premature Nemesis. Rietz noted how they nevertheless still slouched easily with elbows akimbo, one foot raised to the mid rail: unconsciously adopting the attitudes of seamen temporarily under-employed throughout voyages immemorial.

'Don't you sometimes feel, Leo,' he found himself speaking with unaccustomed difficulty, 'that to have been born a German at this time: into the dawn of the first thousand years of the Third Reich, is a great privilege?'

Having been moved to such candour it shocked Rietz a bit, therefore. When he turned, aware of a lack of response from Fischer.

The older officer was gazing down at the men with an expression of . . . almost an expression of *misery*, could it have been?

Yet surely that was unlikely?

Excitement; fear; determination; pseudo-jollity – they were the emotions one expected of the true *Junker*: from officers of Fischer's calibre under the adrenaline anticipation of action.

'But surely not *misery*,' Rietz debated uncertainly. One tended to assume that misery was only reflected in the weak and the pressed and the uncommitted?

. . . or by those forced to harbour some unbearable knowledge?

But, as seemed to be proving the norm in that increasingly perplexing Odyssey, the pace of events was about to afford the Captain no more opportunity to dwell on the curious behaviour of his contemporary than on the identity and, for that matter, the motivation, of their enemy within.

For, even as he satisfied himself that the approaching ship *was* their target and finally, coolly, gave the order to Action Stations before raising his faithful Zeiss above the *Stralsund*'s soon-to-be-drowned bridge rail: confirmed that the officers of the steadily holding British vessel were still unsuspecting, had indeed been lulled by the neutral declaration on his own ship's sides . . .

That heralded the moment in which perplexity itself took a quantum leap.

Propelled U-Bootwaffe Kapitänleutnant Paul Rietz, in fact, into a bewilderment of previously unimagined horror.

Chapter Nine

The Captain had always anticipated that the greatest strain on morale, particularly during the closing minutes of their time of waiting to greet Rohde's eels, would arise out of enforced inaction.

But he also knew they would come under intense scrutiny by the *Java Star*'s watchkeepers, and that the sight of too many crewmen on deck during a chance meeting between vessels in the middle of the Atlantic would immediately raise suspicion.

As a consequence, though the two ships were still some distance apart, the majority of the *Stralsund*'s complement had already mustered on her starboard side boat deck, unseen and – most difficult to tolerate – unseeing: constrained to wait as blind men imprisoned in a shooting gallery, prey only to escalating apprehension.

Certainly Rietz could count on his horsemen being better conditioned than most to impotence in the face of stress: a not unfamiliar condition to any U-boat man who'd ever been pinned on the bottom. Each one who now sailed with him had long learned to endure it as the price of tilting at Hell for the Führer, but the Captain had still directed, nevertheless, that the First Lieutenant should take station on the starboard bridge wing where the men would at least see *him*, and hopefully draw on the nonchalance they expected of their officers.

Of course, being the Man of Iron that he was, he would have been caustically dismissive of anyone's suggesting his positioning young Leutnant Becker out there might have been motivated, not only by combat psychology but by the likelihood that the starboard wing would prove a much safer place to *be*, aboard a ship about to be torpedoed on her port side . . . ?

For a few – her special sea-duty morticians, Rietz could hardly fail to reflect with sombre resignation – there would be vital tasks to preoccupy them up to, and even past, the *Stralsund*'s final moments as a whole ship. They were, perhaps, the more fortunate of his crew. Undertaking the last necessary rites would help stay any inclination they felt towards panic.

He himself, as the High Priest conducting her watery interment, intended to remain on the wing nearest to both the enemy and to Rohde's incoming torpedoes. Never actually having been blown up before, he could only assume it the most logical place from where events – so far as they *would* be controllable without bow or stern – could be controlled.

Supernumerary Kapitänleutnant Fischer had elected to stay with him. Despite his rank, Leo had no prescribed function in the Juggernaut scenario other than to take automatic command should both Rietz and Becker be killed or severely wounded. That was the way of the German Navy – again the men expected it, and Rietz knew that Fischer would observe such a stricture to the letter.

Bootsmaat Landgraf had closed up to the *Stralsund*'s wheel. His was the privilege of being her very last helmsman. Rietz was confident that Landgraf, phlegmatically applying an occasional spoke to prevent her head from falling away from the final course she would ever steer, would stay there while the whole world erupted around him if necessary, and only go to his boat when his Captain ordered it so.

As would Funkgefreiter Stemmler, far out of sight by then in the *Stralsund*'s ancient rabbit hole of a radio room. A good man, Stemmler, for all his tendency to over-familiarity. And so he'd need to be, for Stemmler's duty would be a lonely one – to listen until the last moment for any transmission from their quarry which might compromise the mission. It was unlikely. Unless under attack herself, the *Java Star* would be bound to radio silence by British Admiralty orders – but Rietz had long learned not to take chances.

God only knows, he'd considered resentfully. The unlikely

seems to be proving the routine on this adventure to date, without my inviting complacency to insinuate its lethal head.

But the loneliest and by far the most dangerous duty had gone to Maschinenobergefreiter Schauroth: he of the undiminished capacity for *Leberwurst* and the awesome bowel movement.

Schauroth had volunteered for the task of stopping the *Stralsund*'s ancient main engine as soon as Rohde's torpedoes struck. Should the hit on her stern fail to snap her shaft, still the thrust of her steadily churning propeller, it would then prove imperative to take the way off the ship before any boat could be launched. Otherwise, as the lens of Rietz's periscope had all too graphically illustrated on previous haunting occasions, as soon as her lifeboats touched sea they would be swept astern before the falls could be released: hurled against the towering steel wall of her still-moving hull and smashed to pulp in the maelstrom of her passage.

Chief Sindermann had initially demanded that final and sad responsibility of throttling the stalwart heartbeat of the *Stralsund*. Tall, cadaverous – himself haunted by images more precious; more terrible than any the war had inflicted upon Rietz – the Chief had argued fiercely that he was in charge of the engine: that it was his traditional right to remain below until the very last.

But Rietz had overruled him despite his understanding. Sindermann's primary duty had to lie aboard the *Java Star*, for the success of Juggernaut could well depend on Chief Engineer Sindermann's Merchant Service expertise to restart her modern diesels and take her to Southampton: drive her hugely and suicidally into the maw of the British dry dock ... whereas there was a strong possibility that whoever remained within the *Stralsund* might not even make it to chance a second dying in the enemy camp. She was old and fragile: held together by rust and optimism. Even if Rohde's eels ran true and simply bracketed her engine space she could still break up quickly. A man might never be afforded time enough to negotiate the shiny maze of ladders to her upper decks, following the coming torpedoing.

Rietz knew it. Sindermann knew it.

And Maschinenobergefreiter Schauroth knew it.

Which was why the Captain had, for the second time in minutes, found it so damnably difficult to frame words as he'd grasped Schauroth's bear-like paw and wished him well.

'Get out quick, Schauroth,' he'd urged. 'Soon as we're hit, shut her down, man. And get the hell out of there without waiting for an order.'

. . . he regained the power of speech shortly thereafter, though.

When, with less than twenty minutes to go, Rietz glanced tensely over to the port wing – and suddenly realized that the First Lieutenant was still missing.

Had never, it seemed, returned from below deck with the confidential books!

Rietz swung angrily, as reproachful of himself for his unawareness as with Becker for such irresponsibility.

Beside him Leo Fischer raised an eyebrow; once again languid enough to grace the most hot-blooded *Junker*. Despite his irritation, Rietz was reassured to note that, for all Fischer's earlier and disconcerting reaction, his contemporary appeared to have regained his former warlike *élan*. Now Leo hefted his German Navy model 9mm Luger – issued that same morning to each man aboard – with the critical approval of a small arms connoisseur: appreciating to the full the pistol's fine-hanging balance.

'We have a problem?'

Droll. Underplayed. No one could ever have suspected Leo was anticipating becoming a casualty of the sea war within the next few minutes. Suddenly the prospect didn't seem quite so formidable to Rietz, but he still glowered ill-temperedly.

'BECKER's going to, when I find him. D'*you* know where he's got to?'

'Out on the starboard wing?'

'No, he's not.'

'Well, he was . . . what, ten minutes ago? You talked to him.'

'That was before he went down to my safe. To weight-bag the code books ready for ditching.'

Just for a moment a shadow passed across Fischer's eyes; too briefly to identify, but Rietz could understand his perplexity.

'You think he's still below decks?'

'Where else could he be?'

Fischer engaged the sear of the Luger, prudently checked that the engraved legend, *Gesichert* – Made safe – was exposed above the thumbpiece, then slid it into the shoulder holster concealed below the rough duffel jacket they'd found for him; a far cry from the immaculately tailored Kapitänleutnant's rig he'd shipped aboard in.

'I'll go down and chase the wretched child up.'

Rietz snatched an anxious glance ahead through his glasses. The British ship was still some distance off and holding course to pass down the *Stralsund*'s port side. He lowered the Zeiss to scan the heaving water separating the two ships, but detected nothing. It seemed Oberleutnant Rohde had at least gained enough from Rietz's tuition to deploy his target periscope judiciously.

'No, I'll go,' he decided. 'If the dozey little bugger needs his arse kicked I'd rather do it without an audience.'

Leo opened his mouth to protest, then saw the look in Rietz's eye and thought better of it.

'Then, if your Gestapo-like inclinations really *do* have to take precedence, don't let thuggery override prudence. You wouldn't want to miss being torpedoed, would you?'

The safe hung open in the cramped cell which had euphemistically passed as the master's cabin of the *Stralsund*. It stank of stale cabbage and mildew and the booze-laden breath of a host of German tramp steamer captains long dead through kidney failure. For all his sympathy for the ship, Rietz wasn't going to miss spending another restless session in her foetid skipper's berth.

The weighted bag lay open on the ragged settee; D-ring lock unsecured and two of the six confidential books they'd carried still lying carelessly beside it. Whatever had caused Becker to leave them unattended *must* have demanded an urgent response: Rietz couldn't bring himself to accept that his previously conscientious First Lieutenant would otherwise have shown such contempt for the sacred military cow of document security.

But an urgent response to WHAT . . . ? Apart from Becker's unquestioned sense of discipline, what *could* have proved more urgent than the need to get back on an open deck before they got their bloody TAIL blown off?

Rietz snarled 'SHIT!' kicked the berth in childish frustration then stuffed the loose books in the bag, snapped the D-ring shut, and hurried for the door. Crewmen waiting tensely by the davits swung nervously as he stepped across the coaming to the boat deck.

'Anyone seen Mr Becker?'

'No, sir!'

'The First Lieutenant went in there – into your quarters – about ten minutes ago, sir,' young Schadt, awkward, giving the vague impression of a cuboid penguin in his cork lifejacket, volunteered. 'He definitely hasn't come out since.'

Which meant that Becker could only have left the cabin by its alternative exit, an internal stairway leading down through the officers' accommodation and saloon and eventually to the engine-room . . . but for what POSSIBLE reason?

Rietz shoved the heavy leaded bag at Schadt. 'Take this to Kapitänleutnant Fischer on the bridge – he'll know what to do with it!'

Schadt looked relieved at being given something to do.

'*Jawohl*, Herr Kapitän!'

The Herr Kapitän looked wistfully up at the blue sky: thought, Dear Lord, *please* don't let Führer-child Rohde be TOO trigger-happy . . . ?

Then stepped back inside what was about to become a highly efficient millstone, to look for Rudi Becker.

'Certainly the drowning of your grease-encrusted place of epi-curean alchemy will never be mourned,' Rietz remarked to the ship in passing, as he checked her deserted galley before descending ever deeper upon his urgent quest.

'No more by the legions of sea cooks who've performed their insanitary balancing acts within its cockroach-infested confines than by the half-century of undernourished German trampship men articled to your fo'c'sle and so condemned, no doubt, to a never-varied diet of rancid salt pork and pickled nameless things, and the only real fresh meat to pass their lips being weevils in the mouldered blackbread.'

Now the very last victims of the *Stralsund*'s galley had gratefully abandoned it to the fish. Only the charred cadavers of Kriegsmarine-issue breakfast sausages that not even Maschine-nobergefreiter Schauroth had managed to consume, rolled forlornly in a metal pannikin on the cooling galley stove, while a slowly dehydrating tar of *ersatz* coffee simmered sluggishly in a companion dixie. Mugs, cracked plates, rusting metal cooking implements . . . all hung and swung and tinkled a lonely carillon orchestrated by the metronome roll of the ship: the subterranean hiss and pulse of her still steadily turning main engine . . .

The Captain halted uneasily: listening.

For WAS the *Stralsund*'s heart really beating quite so determinedly? Or could he detect, through the stethoscope of her frail deck plating, that it was beginning to lose its previous steady rhythm – slowing almost imperceptibly? As if, say, the steam pressure delivered from her corroded boiler tubes was gradually falling . . . ?

As if, with only ten – fifteen minutes at most – left labour before its weary components could rest forevermore at the bottom of the sea, its gleaming connecting rods were nevertheless connecting a little less assiduously; its crankshaft cranking less enthusiastically; its slide valves sliding more slowly, admitting a little less steam alternately above and below each piston . . . indicating that the fires of her belly were prematurely dying: starved of the coal which heated the water which made the steam which impelled the engine which turned the shaft which . . . !

Yet if *so*, then – irrespective of any riddle posed by his disappearing First Lieutenant – what the hell could now have happened to SCHAUROTH? Who had, all said and done, taken it voluntarily upon himself to ensure that the *Stralsund*'s furnaces too would be kept fed and trimmed until steam was no longer required . . .

Rietz, already forming a chilling image in his mind's eye of a G7E torpedo about to leave its tube, began to run for the internal access to the engineroom.

The heat hit the Captain a physical blow as he came to a skidding halt at the head of the engineroom ladders. Below him a complexity of slippery, near-vertical steel rungs ultimately led down, past the control platform at which Schauroth might already have been expected to be standing by, to the engine bedplates and the stokehold itself.

There was no sign of Schauroth, and no point in calling for him. The compound hiss and crank of flashing connecting rods and – as far as Rietz, a deck man, was concerned, various other eccentrically moving protuberances recognizable only to ships' engineers – dominated the meagrely lit and crypt-like space which housed the *Stralsund*'s ancient propelling machinery.

For a brief moment he stood peering uncertainly into the abyss, frankly unnerved at the prospect of descending further into that bedlam hot-oil-nauseous environment. Suddenly Rietz, the U-boat man, came to appreciate more than ever the courage of those Allied Merchant Navymen who also fought their war against his own kind from far below the level of the sea: defied mine and torpedo and the second-by-second choice such likely encounters offered of whether to die by drowning or by scalding or by . . . !

A metallic *crash* behind him, and the Captain whirled, nerve ends rapidly fraying.

'*Jesus!*'

An unsecured steel door creaked slowly, innocuously ajar again as another sea returned the ship to the roughly vertical. Above the door a brass plate, now virtually obscured by decades of carelessly applied paint from the days when they'd even bothered to paint the *Stralsund*, declared with considerable difficulty: *Engineer's Store*.

There was a light burning within: a single fly-blown bulb in a corroding bulkhead fitting. Rietz moved unthinkingly to reach for the switch, intending to extinguish the unnecessary extravagance before he hesitated, smiled wryly at his own ludicrous economy.

. . . then caught sight of the upturned FOOT!

The one he could see just inside the storeroom. The one lolling with such slack articulation on the ankle to which it presumably belonged?

The Captain couldn't make out further detail. Not from where he stood. Just that single foot. And one black shoe.

Both moving lifelessly . . . in bizarre unison with the gently swinging door.

Chapter Ten

With reactions already fine-tuned as piano wire, Rietz moved instantaneously; lunging for cover, twisting to press his shoulders flat against the mildewed bulkhead adjacent to the open door while, at the same time, desperately clawing his own Luger from its holster.

Sweat stung his eyes; formed itchy, pendulous crystals trapped in the mesh of his eyebrows, glistening with the shine of fear and shock and of being far too bloody HOT in that accursed hell hole!

Yanking the milled grips of the weapon's toggle he coldly released them; felt the reassuring *snap* of the returning breech-block as it forced the first round into the chamber. At least his gun was cocked – at least, in this latest numbing confrontation with the *Stralsund*'s seemingly inexhaustible almanac of grotesque manifestations, he did *have* a bloody gun!

Get a GRIP on yourself, man, Rietz thought savagely. God DAMMIT but this *is* 1942, not the Middle Ages – and you *are* a U-Bootwaffe officer! Remember the fool you made of yourself the last time, over Leo Fischer's ludicrous materialization? And, whatever hellish event *has* taken place – that's certainly no GHOST, d'you hear . . . ? Ghosts: even the most sophisticated; the most sartorially conscious of spectres, don't wear woollen bloody SOCKS . . . !'

Apart from which, the time scale of the Juggernaut Opord hadn't allowed provision for the needs of paranormal debate . . . Rietz sucked in a deep breath: barrel-rolled around the door frame to finish up with legs straddled squarely across the entrance, extended Luger fanning to cover every aspect of that threatening space . . .

And heard someone croak: 'Oh, my GOD!'

It was all a bit humiliating: the voice being distorted by such a terrible anguish that he only recognized it as his own when he began to retch.

Not that Paul Rietz had any reason to feel ashamed of his initial reaction to the contents of the storeroom. Even the most brutalized of warriors would surely have displayed some sign of being taken aback: *some* small discomposure?

Had they chanced as unexpectedly as Kapitänleutnant Rietz did, upon a charnel house?

The foot, as well as the black shoe and the sock and the subsequent sprawling leg and so on did belong to U-Bootwaffe Maschinenobergefreiter Schauroth.

And Schauroth *was* dead.

He gazed at Rietz through eyes bearing a remarkably bovine expression, even for Maschinenobergefreiter Schauroth who'd never been a particularly imaginative man. It occurred to Rietz in that first appalling moment of partial recognition that his lot was always, it seemed, to be considered irrelevant when under scrutiny by the dead. Navigator Grutner had stared at him in very much the same disinterested manner a few weeks before.

After the *Campbeltown* had exploded, that had been. And before the upper part of Grutner fell off his pedestal.

The greatest difference between the dead Schauroth and the dead Navigator Grutner was that – other than having been laterally bisected, of course – Grutner had come through the experience of getting himself killed for Führer and Fatherland relatively unmarked, whereas Schauroth hadn't.

Which explained why the recognition had, in Rietz's case, been of necessity partial. And once again, perfectly excusable.

Normally people recognize other people by a combination of several factors – height; build; voice; some previously familiar trait or manner – but essentially by their facial characteristics.

That wasn't so easy, not even for Rietz who knew all his men well as a good German officer should . . . and certainly not when trying to identify the corpse with the articulated sock as being *unquestionably* that of Maschinenobergefreiter Schauroth towards whose well-being he, Rietz, was supposed to owe at least a certain duty of care.

'Ohhhh, Christ!' Rietz muttered, momentarily sickened. Death observed from a U-boat generally presented a more remote threat to one's equanimity.

The heavy calibre bullet which had entered the back of Schauroth's head had exited taking most of the front – normally the most useful contours for purposes of identification – with it. Now only Schauroth's forehead and eyes maintained their original configuration. Along with that curiously indifferent expres . . . !

Rietz felt the hair beginning to creep at the back of his neck . . . because *were* the eyes staring at him? Or was the corpse of Maschinenobergefreiter Schauroth still trying, in its helplessly mutilated way, to TELL him something?

Ever so carefully Rietz turned, following the dead man's gaze further down the length of the engineering store with the muzzle of the now tremendously presented gun; ignoring the sweat pouring heedlessl . . .

'Ohhhh, JESUS Christ!' he said again.

For that was the moment in which the Captain found himself reluctantly endowed with at least *some* small capacity for deduction. Not only to the extent of being able to hazard the precise calibre of bullet which had killed Schauroth, but even to establishing its origin.

It had been a 9mm standard Kriegsmarine-issue Parabellum round.

Furthermore, should the matter ever reach consideration by a U-Bootwaffe Court of Inquiry, which – in view of the prospect for survival of anyone becoming overly preoccupied with the mechanics of murder within the engineer's store of the *Stralsund* – did seem increasingly unlikely, then potential Witness Kapitän-leutnant Rietz would also be able to confirm that the round had been fired by a German Navy Luger Model Po8 pistol; almost certainly one of those issued earlier that same morning to each man in his crew.

He could afford to be pretty emphatic about that. As positive, in fact, as he could now be in identifying the man who'd actually SHOT Maschinenobergefreiter Schauroth . . . ! Sweat-blurred vision or not, Rietz could clearly make out what was becoming the inevitable run-of-the-mill Luger still held by the *second* inhabitant of the engineer's store.

The greater difficulty, he felt bound to concede when his heart stopped pounding, would arise out of attempting to deduce WHY?

Because, judging by the rapidly glazing indifference in that second Trojan horseman's fixed stare, it seemed that not only had Rietz finally discovered the whereabouts of his missing First Lieutenant – but that young BECKER was dead as well!

Once again the Captain was spared the need to summon a sleuth's expertise to establish why his First Lieutenant had ceased to be. Becker had either bled, or choked, or simply horrified himself to death when he realized what had been done to him.

Someone had quite evidently cut the young officer's throat.

The Captain's initial revulsion began to give way to a terrible anger. But measured; tightly controlled as always in crisis coupled with a cold realization that his duty – more than that: their continuing prosecution of the whole mission against the British dry dock – demanded he learn as much as he could of what had taken place down here in this hellish store of dead men.

But how much longer could he afford to delay before the *Java Star* nudged the two-mile prerequisite which would initiate Juggernaut? Which would, in turn, trigger Oberleutnant Rohde to launch his torpedoes, unaware of the gruesome drama that was developing aboard the *Stralsund* . . . ?

Or *was* their consort commander so unawa . . . !

Rietz knuckled his brow savagely. One thing *was* bloody certain: there wasn't time to waste on THAT repetitive and unhelpful speculation! Come to that, he didn't even know if

Rohde WAS still the decision maker out there, or whether von Strelow had taken command . . . he didn't even know for certain that he *had* seen the Fregattenkapitän sailing anonymously within what was rapidly becoming an ever more sinister company.

Glancing hurriedly at his watch, he tried to visualize the respective positions of the two closing merchantmen right at that moment – he had, say, six or seven minutes left at most . . . ? Before Rohde's torpedoman reached for the firing button and he, Rietz, became well advised to either make his peace with God, or run like hell . . . !

Rietz prudently checked that his exit was still clear. Through the open storeroom door he could gaze wistfully down the internal alleyway, past the galley door to the main deck suddenly more inviting than ever before.

The Captain returned to frowning at the scene of the crime without really being too sure of what an investigating officer was supposed to look for. Starting a jigsaw puzzle was easier, and he wasn't even competent at those. All he really knew about jigsaw puzzles was that you began with one piece, then gradually fitted all the other pieces to it.

He glowered uncertainly at the two dead men. With murder, it seemed one had little option but to confront the whole picture, then try and break it down into its component parts . . . hope to Christ you could isolate some improbability: some anomaly – some *anything* which would lead even the most inept criminologist to shout 'Eureka!'

And all within six *minutes* . . . ?

Leutnant Rudi Becker had slumped to a sitting position, fair head lolling marionette-like against the far bulkhead, eyes locked on to a line of sight – or would a proper detective more accurately think of it as a line of, well, of *sightless*ness, Rietz couldn't help digressing – which encompassed both the exit to the world beyond, and Maschinenobergefreiter Schauroth: neither hardly astonishing in the circumstances.

No more than was the blood surrounding Becker. There were further blood smears on the steel bulkhead, descending in a vertical grue to a point abaft the Leutnant's shoulders. Again much as one might expect from a man slithering helplessly on fast draining legs to adopt Becker's final attitude, Rietz decided without a great deal of conviction.

He looked more closely at the gun. It had actually slipped from Becker's nerveless hand and lay beside him. Rietz also noticed absently that Becker's fingernails were bitten to the quick, which surprised the Captain even if it didn't advance his murder enquiry very far: he'd never thought of young Becker as the nervous sort.

A sea bigger than the others rolled the *Stralsund* to starboard. Schauroth's loosely articulated foot fell away to starboard in sympathy, as did Becker's loosely articu . . . ! The steel compartment door banged shut, then creaked open again, and Rietz suddenly became conscious that he was risking his life – more importantly, deserting his primary duty – in hunting for something he wouldn't have the wit to recognize even if he found it.

As a last resort he picked up the Luger and sniffed it vaguely. He'd seen a motion picture once, in the Fleet Cinema at Kiel, where a policeman had done that. If memory served him, that single curious act had solved the crime.

To Rietz it smelt exactly like a Luger pistol. The stench of gun oil overpowered everything else.

THIS, Rietz thought, by then totally at a loss and beginning to feel faintly hysterical, is bloody *ridiculous*!

'So try logic, *Dummkopf*,' his compressed anger roared. 'Clues? You wouldn't know what a clue was if you collided full ahead with one in the middle of the night, Rietz. On the other hand you *are* a professional killer yourself: you do have the capacity for cold, detached analysis – see how Schauroth's face is blown away: how his brain was exploded; ceased to function in the split second he was struck down . . . ? Doesn't THAT tell you *some*thing about the sequence, about the cause and hideous effect of this bizarre blood bath, you fool . . . ?'

'Five minutes left – no more!' Rietz's instinct for survival interjected uneasily, cautioning the flow of his rage.

At the bottom of the ship the engine bravely continued to sigh and chug and exhaust on what little steam remained, encouraged perhaps by the knowledge that, whatever happened now, it would never be completely abandoned by men after all. That, in the bleak gallery above, two watchkeepers would sag in blank contemplation of each other while keeping it company until the very end of time.

'THINK, Rietz!' Rietz urged, sweating as his watch ticked steadily. 'It's staring you in the face, man. The only logical solution. All there, in the contact of a 9mm bullet with a man's skul . . . !'

He tensed; frowned, not really believing his own gut feeling at first. Could he really be capable of attaining such heights of previously undreamed-of rationale? Of suddenly solving a riddle which had persistently eluded him for six days?

Of deducing, merely from the wounds inflicted on that gory tableau the identity, no less, of the *Stralsund*'s enemy within?

Oh, admittedly still not supported by any indication of *why* anyone, remote-controlled assassin or out-and-out madman, should not only have attempted to take the life of Leo Fischer but, the mute evidence now suggested, had fully intended to murder *every* officer associated with Operation Juggernaut.

But nevertheless: 'EUREKA!' the Captain felt well justified in exclaiming.

Positive in his own mind that, irrespective of motive, the traitor simply *had* to have been . . . Maschinenobergefreiter Schauroth!

I am considering a mutually destructive confrontation between two men, Rietz had reasoned. Assuming one corpse to be that of the victim, then surely the other, by definition, has to be that of the aggressor?

Yet it was clear that Schauroth had died instantly, probably before he even hit the deck, having been shot in the back of the head when making to leave the compartment. Certainly the engineer rating could never have cut Becker's throat *after* the young officer had fired. Not with such extensive brain destruction as that – more catastrophic, in fact, than anything Rietz had previously envisaged as being caused by a single 9mm bullet.

Ergo, Rietz concluded, Schauroth MUST have attacked Becker first. However appalling the premise, Becker must have lived just long enough *following* his receiving his mortal throat wound, to aim, and squeeze a trigger.

Knowing he really shouldn't delay his withdrawal a moment longer, he still replaced his now superfluous pistol in its holster then crouched before Becker and ever so gently closed the boy's once-blue, now pitifully dulled eyes for what would be the very last time.

It struck him then that he really hadn't been a very good commanding officer. They'd never talked together. He didn't even know whether young Becker had a mother, father . . . even a pretty girl back home who would cry for him.

But he harboured an uneasy suspicion that he, Paul Rietz, would. Eventually. When he had the time.

'Even though you couldn't sing *Deutschland Über Alles*,' he said softly, 'you knew how to conduct yourself as a German Officer. On behalf of the Führer I salute you, Leutnant Becker!'

. . . Rietz sensed, rather than heard the movement behind him. Followed by the creak of the compartment door moving on oil-begrudged hinges even though, at that precise moment, the ship wasn't rolling with sufficient energy to induce such a curious phenomenon.

He was still whirling, still fighting to regain his balance; still clawing to recover his weapon yet again from its bloody *holster* and realizing far too late that everything he'd assumed had been based on a complete misconception – that he'd ever been anything MORE than a bloody awful detective – even as the heavy steel door slammed shut!

Trapped as he now found himself in the soon-to-be coffin of the *Stralsund* with two dead men as his only ship's company, Kapitänleutnant Rietz did not require the perception of a sleuth to deduce the significance of the *next* sound.

The quite unmistakable rattle of a door's outer locking pin driving home.

Chapter Eleven

Rietz could derive bleak comfort from knowing that he'd been at least *partly* correct – that someone aboard the *Stralsund* DID intend to kill every officer associated with Operation Juggernaut . . . it was merely that Rietz's Someone hadn't actually turned out to be Maschinenobergefreiter Schauroth.

Though it's a bit bloody LATE, he thought bitterly as the first seeds of panic flowered within him, to dwell in retrospect on my *other* elementary oversights.

Hurling himself at the steel door he yanked without any anticipation at all at the rusted handle. For the second time since venturing into that hellish prison his gut feeling was proved right – nothing did happen!

The Captain wiped a tremulous hand across his forehead, nerve already disintegrating before what was fast becoming a guilt-obsessed memory of his surface action against the steamer *Oberon*: the long-drawn-out dying of her captive seaman more than ever threatening now to adopt the nature of a self-fulfilling prophesy.

He booted the door furiously and roared 'BASTAAARD!' at the top of his voice, not even sure of whether such immature pique was directed against the still anonymous killer or his own inexcusable complacency, then took a deep breath and tried to think.

How long DID he have left before the sea climbed aboard to welcome him? Three – not more than four – minutes . . . ? Dear God but he'd taken longer than *that* to consume the last of the Frontboot-marinaded ham with which they'd celebrated the dubious victories of their last patrol.

Immediately after despatching the *Obero* . . . !

Abruptly Rietz decided against thinking too much, and applied himself to devising more productive means of escape. But there was little to suggest a course of action in the engineer's store; only crumbling, sparred racks and oil-black wooden boxes containing rusted spare parts. He'd already noted there was no other way out – not unless a salt-encrusted ventilator shaft through the deckhead counted, but only if you were a sea-going rat: its diameter wasn't much greater than the splay of a man's hand.

Feeling a bit lost he stood frowning at the dead rating by the door. Something kept niggling him: something not quite right about the way Schauroth had died. He couldn't think of anything more constructive to do, so – as an alternative to simply curling into a foetal ball and sucking his thumb – he decided to at least satisfy his curiosity.

Picking up the Luger lying by Leutnant Becker's already pallid hand he thumbed the release stud below the trigger guard. The magazine ejected against his palm and he withdrew it fully from the butt to examine it.

Rietz's expression, already bleak, became hard as flint.

He knew immediately that he wasn't holding the pistol originally issued to Rudi Becker. Whoever shot Schauroth had subsequently exchanged weapons – and, more significantly, magazines – presumably to forestall any connection being traced back in the event of an ammunition check . . . and pointing even more certainly to his being no aimless madman. The *Stralsund*'s traitor had, in fact, just proved himself to be calculating, resourceful and utterly without morality.

He'd also given Kapitänleutnant Rietz a further pointer to one final hope for survival.

Rietz raised his own Luger: it was indeed a beautifully balanced weapon, the ultimate union of Swiss design and solid German engineering – and took deliberate aim at the body of Maschinenobergefreiter Schauroth.

Then squeezed the trigger. Seven times! Coldly, and with measured precision.

*

The Captain had decided against using Leutnant Becker's substituted pistol to kill Schauroth seven more times. He should have realized earlier that the engineer rating's initial head wound couldn't have been caused simply by a standard military pistol round. Such appalling destruction could only have resulted from the explosive exit of a dumdum: a bullet that had fragmented on its passage through Schauroth's skull because the killer had first cut an indented cross to weaken and splay the projectile's snub nose.

Rietz had recognized that vicious modification as soon as he glanced at the remaining cartridges in Becker's magazine. They had been bastardized with a callous disregard for the Geneva Convention: even possession of such obscenities was a court martial offence in the Kriegsmarine, and they weren't even bloody necessary.

No more than it would have been for the Captain to inflict any greater damage on the already unfairly maligned Schauroth than was absolutely unavoidable – but Rietz, already at extreme risk, knew how unpredictable a ricocheting bullet would be within a steel box. And it had nothing to do with rank: merely with logic. Compared with the slender corpse of his First Lieutenant, the portly Maschinenobergefreiter's capacity for beer and *Leberwurst* had offered him as the most absorbent mass in the engineer's store.

Such chilling pragmatism highlighted yet again the dangerously complex machine that war had created out of a peacetime passenger ship officer. While Paul Rietz, the man, could feel repugnance at the use of an illegal round, a great many Allied seamen would have vouchsafed that U-Bootwaffe Kapitänleutnant Rietz, when circumstances demanded he be detached either in the prosecution of his duty to his Führer or to ensure the survival of himself and his crew, could be very cold and very detached indeed.

The seventh expended cartridge ejected from the pistol and tinkled brassily across the soiled deck while the staccato detonations still reverberated within the compartment. Rietz stopped firing, retaining the eighth and final round in the Luger's chamber. Being practical again. Just in case whoever heard the

131

shots and reopened the door proved to be that same someone already harbouring intentions other than the succour of his Captain.

If anybody *did* hear them this time. If not . . . ?

Rietz squatted and waited to see whether rescue or the Atlantic Ocean would arrive first. He relaxed with his back against the bulkhead beside the dead boy and fastidiously beyond the spread of Leutnant Becker's slowly congealing life force. There wasn't anything more he could think of doing to pursue the continuation of his own.

He recalled Leo Fischer's assertion that singing kept one's spirits up.

Largely for Becker's sake, he began to hum *Deutschland Über Alles*.

Lookout Schadt actually opened the door thirty seconds later: still looking a bit like an ungainly penguin.

Correction, Rietz decided, hauling himself wearily to his feet. Now more like an apprehensive, ungainly penguin.

He'd never seriously considered Schadt for the role of the *Stralsund*'s on-board killer, so he didn't use his eighth bullet. Which was just as well because Schadt more or less proved he wasn't by throwing up on the spot, and no one with such fine susceptibilities, Rietz knew, would ever have cut a dumdum.

On reflection, no one like Schadt should have been on Juggernaut at all.

Leo Fischer followed: forcing brusquely past the unhappy seaman with HIS common-or-garden Luger drawn and grimly presented. But Fischer had already been hit on the head and had learned, before Rietz, not to trust empty compartments in the *Stralsund*.

'What the FU . . . ?' the normally imperturbable veteran snapped, unable to conceal his anxiety – then saw Becker and Schauroth and, turning pastry white, muttered, 'Ohhhh, the *bastards*!'

Rietz frowned a little at that. It seemed an odd thing to say. For one thing, Leo apparently assumed that *he* hadn't committed the crime himself, despite appearances. For another – though the impression could merely have been a fleeting indiscipline of his own already fevered imagination – didn't Leo Fischer show more the look of a man not so much surprised as . . . well, as having just confirmed some worst fear? Which was quite ridiculous because surely no one, other than the butcher himself, could have anticipated *this* bizarre slaughter?

Rietz shook his head, savagely uncaring they might detect the dislodged proof of fear-sweat hazing under the glare of the fly-blown lamp. What the hell was HAPPENING to him that he even suspected his most trusted shipmates . . . ?

And anyway, it so happened that Leo Fischer was the one man aboard – apart from Bootsmaat Landgraf – who COULDN'T have killed Becker! Both Landgraf *and* Fischer had constantly been with Rietz on the bridge from the moment that young Becker had hastened below to recover the confidential books.

'There's nothing you can do for them, Schadt. And not a word to anybody when you get back on deck – understood?'

Schadt wiped the back of his hand across his mouth: made a brave attempt to come to attention.

'*Jahwohl*, Herr Kapitän!'

'Good man.' Rietz swung urgently. 'Whereaway the *Java Star* now, Leo?'

Fischer also put considerable effort into regaining the insouciance Doktor Goebbels would have expected of a fighting German officer. He looked creditably bored again.

'Still three miles on the bow, dear boy, and holdi . . .'

But Rietz was already running.

At least the violence which lay ahead promised a rather more familiar dimension of horror.

Taking the bridge ladder two steps at a time, he kept to the port side to avoid causing more speculation among his crewmen waiting by the boats than necessary. One relieved glance had told him the British ship was still distant enough for such eccentric behaviour to remain shielded from curious eyes.

First thing he did was check the shaft revolutions on the

battered wheelhouse counter, confirming with relief that Masch-inenobergefreiter Schauroth had gone to meet his death in the engineer's store only after he'd tended the boilers. Though slowing, the *Stralsund* still retained steam pressure enough to refrain from coasting to an embarrassing – to say nothing of highly suspect – stop during the next critical minutes.

He turned, sensing Landgraf's perplexity. Stolid as ever at the wheel, the Bootsmaat nevertheless made it clear he viewed his Captain's explosive re-emergence from below with certain reservations, but, to Landgraf, the progressive abandonment of the *Stralsund*'s bridge deck by all three officers, one after another, must have come as a traumatic diversion from the pre-action scenario *he'd* been led to expect.

'Don't ask, Bosun.' Rietz forced himself to slow: to readopt his actor's role as the Man of Iron looking forward to the novelty of being torpedoed. 'Just keep her steady as she goes.'

He experimented tentatively with an appropriately sardonic grin.

'. . . and think of the Führer, naturally.'

As soon as the Captain compressed his eyes into the rubber cups of the Zeiss he could tell that destroying her, even as the price for the British dry dock, was going to cause him pain. Stout-funnelled, with beautifully proportioned upperworks and a sheer to her deckline as graceful as any yacht, their soon-to-be Trojan horse pushed a great white, trusting bone in her teeth as she continued to close with the *Stralsund*'s apparent neutrality.

Rietz permitted his gaze to rise skywards before searching further for the calling card of Oberleutnant Rohde on which everything now depended . . . Dammit, he just *had* to look up at the sky. Just for a few blessed moments.

There were the most exquisite cotton wool clouds over his head. And an infinity so clear and blue . . . The Captain inhaled a great breath of sea air, diluting the residue of terror still sour within him. Suddenly the day seemed ineffably sweet. Even, should the worst come to the worst, for swimming.

Rietz went back to combing the two and a half miles of sea which still separated them . . . and THERE IT WAS! He tensed, caressed the focus wheel as the sweep of his Zeiss detected the first sign of Rohde's U-boat positioning for the . . .

Rietz shied from the obvious connotation then shrugged: grinned tightly. *Bugger it . . . positioning for the kill!*

The boy was doing well. Just the briefest of tactically unavoidable betrayals: a five-second cut-feather of white foam some eight cables to port and almost lost in the two metre swell. But then Rietz would have expected little else under these conditions. The *Stralsund*'s steady approach was intended to offer Rohde all the elements required for a text book evolution. Just as the freighter *Oberon* had offered herself up to Riet . . . !

Rietz stopped grinning. Even tightly.

Only a couple of minutes left. He could easily have been down there with those in the U-boat, the way he could visualize, hear, sense . . . almost smell the atmosphere as she prepared her attack.

She'd be rocking gently now, nudging ahead under the whine of E-motors, disciplined by her trimming planes: a weapons platform in suspension. Rohde would be crouched tensely, hands poised above the rotating handles of the gleaming oil-bright periscope; white cap . . . Rietz did smile again at that – at the thought of Rohde's so openly coveted white commander's cap. *Christ* but he'd been an envious little prick . . . ! Still, white cap ostentatiously flat aback and snapping orders to his wooden-featured acolytes in the coming sacrifice that other, more assured Frontboot captains would speak with measured authority.

Tubes one and two prepare for underwater firing. Flood tubes – open bow caps . . . Steer course . . . !

Beside Rohde, stopwatch in hand, Navigator Grutner would be sweati . . . Rietz frowned. Grutner was victoriously dead, of course: meticulously subdivided by a Tommy destroyer – well, whichever unfortunate young officer *did* now hold the dubious appointment as Rohde's scratching post. Whoever he was, Rietz hoped for his sake he'd learned the Party salute at the heel-clicking classes . . . AND the words of *Deutschland Über Alles*.

Boat balanced, Herr Oberleutnant. Depth – twelve metres thirty! his new Chief would be reporting.

*Engines slow ahead – Tower! Stand-by to check TARGET bearing
... Quickly, now!*

JAWOHL, Herr Oberleutnant . . . 'Go PISS yourself, Herr
Ober-bloody-leutnant . . . !'

Report hydrophone bearings, Stem . . . No – NOT Stemmler!
Stemmler was here, aboard the *Stralsund*: listening for radio
warnings from the Tommy . . .

Rohde's current sound man then. He'd be picking up the
underwater resonances created by both ships: crouched there in
his booth the size of a coffin, headphones clamped over lank
hair, sweating, concentrating. *Distant propellor echoes on Red two
five and closing, Kapitän! Target . . .* That's *me*, that target. Me –
RIETZ! Rietz realized, suddenly feeling a bit outraged . . .
*Target noises still moving left, sir: bearing zero-two-zero, loud and
increas . . . !*

Leo Fischer arrived on the wing, breathing heavily. 'Rohde?
You can see him?'

'Over there. Eight cables.' Rietz pointed. 'At least he's read
the Doenitz book on how to be an invisible U-boat Kapitän.'

Leo picked up the two heavy, old-fashioned lifejackets lying
in readiness on the deck and handed one to Rietz. He couldn't
help looking troubled, but Fischer hadn't had enough time to
be a detective, even a lousy one.

'Put this on. Might save you from being a dead U-bo . . . Oh,
dammit, Paul – Becker and Schauroth. What *happened* down
there?'

A couple of minutes left? Rietz thought, trying hard not to
make it too obvious that he was already consciously flexing his
knees, preparing to absorb the impact if the deck should buck
under the force of the explosions . . . *maybe only one minute now!
maybe LESS than one?*

'I found them like that. My guess is someone lured Becker
from my cabin to the engineer's store – then cut the boy's throat!'

'And Schauroth?'

Two miles! Rietz judged, eyes locked on the British ship.
She'd reached the critical two mile separation – *Christ, Leo, why
can't you concentrate on more immediate horrors. Like us both being
fused into charcoaled bloody particles in the nex . . . !*

'Heard Becker scream, maybe? Innocently turned up to investigate: tried to beat a retreat – got himself shot on his way out.'

'Any idea who?'

Dead bloody nonchalant all of a sudden.

Tubes one and two – prepare to fire. Range . . . !

Rietz kept his frown concealed within the rubber cups of the Zeiss. In company with his irritation. Wasn't Leo being just a bit *too* bloody stoical, even for Leo? Or did he harbour some greater concern? Wasn't Leo Fischer rather more preoccupied by what had already taken place than what was about to . . . ? Yet, if so – why? The Dead were dead. What Rietz thought: what he surmised about the cause and the perpetrator of such chilling slaughter was hardly of . . .

Fire Tube One . . .

Rietz imagined he saw the feather again. Just where he'd have placed it had it been his attack. The muscles began to really knot around his spine . . .

Fire TWO!

The U-boat would be recoiling perceptibly from the squid-like expulsion of the tubes. Starting to bow lift at the abrupt loss of trim. They'd all be listening for the *click* of Grutn . . . the *Navigator's* stopwatch: loud as a hammer within the tense silence of the boat.

Both torpedoes running . . . Tightly, from Sound.

'Any idea who killed them, Paul? Who locked *you* in, come to that?' Fischer persisted.

Rietz finally lowered his binoculars and swung, nerves stressed to the limit: 'Christ, Leo; can't you drop it for now? I mean, *I* don't know, DO I? I can't even match two pieces of a bloody *JIGSAW*, dammit . . . ! The only thing I *AM* sure of is that whoever it *was* dropped poor bloody Schauroth with a dumdum round!'

Fischer took an involuntary step backwards at that. Rietz could actually see the colour drain from the veteran's cheeks, which did seem a bit of an overreaction. However chilling its implication, the choice of weapon could hardly have come as a greater shock than the actual murders of two shipmates!

'The incompetent little TURD!' Fischer snarled quite inexplicably.

'Beg pardon?' Rietz muttered, thoroughly lost by then, incompetence being the last quality he would have attributed to the *Stralsund*'s killer. And anyway, he thought bemusedly, surely such disparagement would be more properly directed at her bloody Captain – me!

The Captain's confusion became further compounded when an inexplicably galvanized Leo grabbed his sleeve and began to drag him forcibly from the extremity of the wing. As Rietz resisted, tottered uncertainly, his outraged glare fell upon the surface of the heaving sea a half cable outboard.

He stopped resisting, and began running instead.

'Ohhhh, the INCOMPetent little *shit* . . . !' he bellowed in full concurrence: black-furious at this, the very last straw of an already appalling morning.

It being a pleasant, sunny sort of day the effervescent track of the inbound torpedo wasn't at all difficult to detect, even without the aid of binoculars and even though it wasn't quite following the angle of attack meticulously laid down in the Opord. Not streaking towards the *Stralsund*'s hull as it NOW was.

Homing to explode, not on her stern as prescribed – but precisely amidships. Right below where they stood!

Chapter Twelve

◄═◉═►

'You *do* appreciate, I trust,' Fischer claimed modestly, 'that my lightning reflexes almost certainly prevented you from sacrificing your life for Germany there and then, and for little tactical benefit? Always remember when bent on heroics, dear boy, that Goering, Himmler, Ribbentrop . . . all that pseudo-divine crew who strut in the anteroom of the Wolf's Lair and demand our allegiance: they aren't so much concerned with us lower orders giving of our blood valiantly, as giving of it profitably.'

But that unabashed, to say nothing of disconcertingly subversive conceit, only came later.

In between nightmares.

Rietz had almost made it as far as the wheelhouse door by the time Rohde's first – and only remotely effective – torpedo became masked by the overhang of the bridge, intent on blowing the belly clean out of her.

The second one missed altogether. Even sprinting on wings of sheer desperation, Rietz still caught an astonished glimpse of the remaining half of Rohde's salvo shaping to pass a good fifty metres AHEAD of the *Stralsund*'s bow.

Which, on the positive side, did encourage him to feel reassured that no deliberate intention to sabotage the mission on Rohde's part had existed – nor, more importantly, on the part of Fregattenkapitän von Strelow.

Or whoever else was pulling the Führer-child's strings.

*

It's strange, he'd found himself debating in the few seconds left for the torpedo to complete its course, how such a short time can seem such a long time. How one can muse on so many things, and of such rich variety – Maschinenobergefreiter Schauroth, for instance . . . Now *he'll* be grinning a knowing grin at this precise moment.

Then Rietz remembered that Schauroth hadn't been left with the necessary flesh, bones and teeth with which to smile: not even the rictus-induced grin which was the natural right of the dead, and drew a terrible fortitude from that reflection. Determined himself to survive this coming hazard if only to execute the Iceman capable of doing such a dreadful thing to a brave and simple comrade.

He even had time to accept that such black ambition would carry a price. For, by striking the *Stralsund* amidships in the supposedly safe haven where all hands had congregated, Rohde's miscalculation was almost certain to cull a few more from his already diminished band of Trojan horsemen . . . and thereby confront him, Rietz, with what would unquestionably present the most bitterly resented irony to have so far spawned from this bedevilled parody of war.

That in the very last, long anticipated moment before U-Boot-waffe Kapitänleutnant Rietz finally WAS blown up by his own U-boat and should have been interceding for his own salvation – he would find himself capable only of formulating a quite bizarre prayer.

. . . that, however many of his men *were* about to be selected by the gods to go down with Becker and Schauroth, trapped in the bones of the *Stralsund* – the traitor wouldn't be one of them!

The Captain didn't actually get very far with his grim supplication before four hundred kilos of high explosive impacted more or less under his feet.

He lived through it, and continued to function after it. That was the sum total of his achievement. That, and a wry appreciation that his own particular survival had nothing to do with the gods and everything to do with Fischer's early warning. Had Rietz remained, unexpecting as he was, at the extreme end of the port wing, then he would certainly have been disjoined or incinerated or very probably both, which would have cured his paranoia but done little to resolve the sinister chain of events causing it.

Even the fleeting impressions of cataclysm which *did* remain etched on his memory were gleaned largely because Rietz himself succumbed to a conflict of logic. While base instinct compelled him to hurl himself full length towards the illusory cover of the wheelhouse at the moment of impact, he still found himself twisting with masochistic deliberation – hands clasped rigidly over his head, elbows drawn forward and together to protect his face – to observe just what being on the receiving end of one of his own G7E torpedoes was really like.

It was to prove a disappointingly fragmented endeavour.

To claim that he heard the missile detonate, any more than he smelt or saw or tasted the violence of it, would have been to exaggerate: to imply that the experience remained within the constraints of tolerance to which human senses can respond.

Which it didn't.

His entirely false impression was that the *Stralsund* blew up in slow motion: a leisurely affair between mechanical things which provided him not so much with any sense of personal involvement as with an oddly abstract entertainment. Rather as if he were once again watching events unfold – albeit, this time, from the very front row normally allocated to junior rates – of the Fleet Cinema in Kiel.

First the outboard end of the bridge snaked upwards, propelled on a rising sun of superheated gas. Then the largely wooden structure began to separate into component lengths of tread-worn teak planking which continued to ride the crown of the fireball. Other, lower, parts of the ship caught up; began to jostle for place in that vertical redistribution, each endowed with the same lethal momentum which had so abruptly ended Navigator Grutner's war. Rivets, iron plate, awning spars, rail sections, fairleads ... some already smoking or glowing in their high temperature excitation.

Next followed the sea itself; sucked into a great towering

waterspout reaching for the clouds: brown tainted with spent explosive, black streaked with atomizing coal dust from the *Stralsund*'s gutted port bunker. Rietz watched with detached interest as the whole of number three lifeboat lifted bodily from its davits at the forr'ad end of the port boat deck before it, too, disintegrated like an exploding cask . . .

Good Lord, he thought dazedly. Did I do this to *other* ships? Inflict such wounds? Cause them so much pain . . . ?

That the Captain considered it normal to direct his compassion towards the structures he'd crucified, rather than the Allied seamen who'd sailed in them, betrayed the extent to which the strains of being conscripted to war had corrupted his early misgivings. Had persuaded whatever part of his mind that sat in judgement on the actions of Civilian Rietz, to substitute what were no more than sacrificial idols in place of human beings, and so enable the Military Rietz to live with the otherwise unbearable revulsion he would have faced at wantonly destroying his fellow seafarers.

It was Rietz the ex-merchant seaman's anaesthesia, his psychological defence: the engine which drove his Duty-dominated singleness of purpose and made him such an efficient enemy. He *had* to cling to it because he had nothing else to sustain him: close his mind to the dark unease that such argument was morally corrupt – as fallacious as claiming that the killer of Schauroth might also be absolved from guilt providing he could lament if not for what he had done to his victim, then at least for the distress he had caused to the bullet.

Certainly it demonstrated that Admiral Doenitz had chosen well when he selected U-Bootwaffe Kapitänleutnant Rietz to press home the Führer's directive irrespective of its cost in casualties. 'Casualties' meant, in human terms, his own men: his own kind. He admired, and felt privileged to lead, every one of them – apart from one. He cared deeply for them all – apart from one. He would unhesitatingly lay down his own life if it would ensure the return to the Fatherland of any one of them . . . apart from ONE.

But *only* after the exigencies of war, the premiums in deaths and mutilations considered viable by the Reich to press home Operation Juggernaut, had extracted the necessary price.

. . . which explained why, even as the blast overtook Rietz, bowled him helter-skelter into the wheelhouse to join Landgraf, his concern had once again crystallized around steel and wood rather than flesh and blood. Directed, not so much towards what the torpedo was doing to his crewmen, as to what it was doing to the *Stralsund* herself: in particular to her starboard lifeboats.

His was a dispassionate anxiety . . . a simple pragmatism.

Whether or not his Trojans would still be left with the means to launch as planned, and thereby to smuggle sufficient arms aboard the *Java Star* to secure their final vehicle to the target.

The coldly Objective Kapitänleutnant Rietz brought up hard against the grimly Subjective Bootsmaat Landgraf at much the same time as most of the port-side windows.

Landgraf had already hit the deck under the steering position: now both of them hugged its scarred, grimy planking as shards of blast-propelled glass whirled and tinkled about them.

The hanging column of spray lost its spine, began to hiss back across the ship. Glass stopped falling out of the shattered frames. Landgraf stirred uncertainly, causing razor splinters to tinkle prettily again, a bit like Chinese chimes, as they slid from his shoulders.

'Fucking GREENHORN!' Landgraf muttered; a reference directed more, Rietz charitably assumed, towards Rohde than himself. Either way, he decided it was hardly the moment to task Landgraf with Conduct Prejudicial . . . for one thing Landgraf was as shocked as he: for another he considered the Bosun's comment more than generous and, last but not least, he suddenly became aware of blood running down his arm.

'SHIT!' he blurted, feeling scared and faintly hysterical.

'He's that too, sir. But then, the Herr Oberleutnant's ALWAYS been one,' the Bosum pointed out reasonably from beside him: clarifying the thrust of his previous criticism.

'Pardon?' Rietz said, even his own voice sounding hollow through the fuzzle clamping down over his hearing.

The roar of escaping steam still managed to penetrate his consciousness. But other than that, and the odd tinkle of glass, a silence had seemingly descended over the stricken ship: a curious unreality. A macabre sensation of time in suspension.

Trying very hard to think, the Captain tentatively explored the source of his own sympathetically escaping blood and found what looked like a fairly superficial gash opened clear from left shoulder to elbow. Well, superficial compared with the cut inflicted in Leutnant Becker, anyway.

'Shit!' he said again, his alternative being to sob with relief. Then, feeling reassured, even managed to eye Bootsmaat Landgraf severely, challenging him to push his luck.

Seemingly Landgraf hadn't been shocked enough to lose *all* sense of proportion. The Bosun just returned an amiable, slightly drunken grin through the soot and blood which now masked his face.

Fischer came running downhill from the starboard wing. He appeared to be mouthing, but no words penetrat . . . !

DOWNhill . . . ?

Jesus, but we're turning turtle . . . going OVER! Rietz realized dully, the cobwebs of lethal inaction still clogging his mind. His inability to do anything about it worried him because he wasn't too stunned to appreciate that the *Stralsund* must have a hole the size of a railway tunnel in her port side by now, most of it below the waterline. And he was *very* aware that ships with railway tunnels through them tended to sink rather more quickly than operational plans, even those sanctioned by the Führer, had anticipated.

Dear Lord but he felt sick. *Get a bloody GRIP on yourself, Rietz . . . !*

The deck leaned further . . . ten degrees . . . fifteen . . . The sound of someone shouting began to penetrate as if from a distance; coal dust blew in suffocating eddies through the ruins of the wheelhouse: coal dust and whisping steam all mixed up with the bitter-sweet stench of exhausted high explosive.

It turned out that Fischer was the one who'd been shouting, just as Rietz had thought. He grabbed Rietz's arm to haul him to his feet.

144

'All *hell's* broken loose on the boat deck. We've got to get DOWN there, Paul . . .!'

Rietz heard himself scream with agony and Leo let go as though the limb was white hot – which it bloody well FELT!

'Lord but I'm *terribly* sorry, old boy,' Leo blurted, comically polite. Then the *Stralsund* lurched again, shook herself hugely back to the near vertical as the weight of water in her belly temporarily stabilized. The last of the glass fell out of the windo . . . !

Rietz whirled, grateful for the detonation of pain which had at least cleared his mind . . . He'd even forgotten the *Java Star* – the sole justification for this nightmare!

'Go down and take charge of the boats, Leo: I want to see how the Tommy's reacting.' He fumbled awkwardly with blood-slippery hands to confirm that the Zeiss were still suspended, by some miracle, around his neck. 'You go with Kapitän-leutnant Fischer, Bosun. Get everyone aboard and start to lower . . .'

'*That's* what I'm trying to bloody TELL you – *if* we've got any boats LEFT to launch! Rohde's managed to blow our funnel away too: toppled it across the starboard side boat deck!' Fischer looked bleak. 'It trapped some of the crowd when it fell, Paul.'

The Captain sagged. Men trapped. It seemed he was to be haunted yet again by the macabre sinking of the Steamer *Oberon*. Suddenly he felt deathly tired and inadequate. Broken glass began to tinkle gently – funny: how he could detect glass singing yet he still couldn't hear a thousand tons of water ingressing just below them.

The little bits of glass slowly slid from other bigger bits as, quite perceptibly, the *Stralsund* began to keel over to port once more. Rietz knew it would be for the last time.

'Then either you haul them clear in sixty seconds flat,' he retorted brutally, 'or pray to GOD they're dead already!'

He couldn't step out on to the port wing any more: there simply wasn't one. Aboard the *Stralsund* the shipmaster's God-given right to walk his own bridge ended in shattered, amputated teak planking one unwary step past the wheelhouse.

Instead he had to hook his uninjured arm around the splintered frame in order to look down into the gash which now carved his stricken command from double-bottoms clear to her bridge deck. He hung there momentarily, assessing the thundering cataract of seawater pouring into her; hesitating in its bedlam occupation each time the ship rolled sullenly, temporarily back to starboard with pulverized timbers; boxes; straw matting; dunnage ... all swirling crazily in a black sludge of coal and oil and dislodged rust – half a century of bilge collectings and neglect – before spewing finally from her sundered bowels as she heeled unsteadily to port again, a little further each time: twisted, exploded frames and tortured hull plates impacting: digging monstrously below the surface to detonate a further flurry of foam and spray ...

The Captain pulled back hurriedly, his unpleasant duty satisfied. She was only coasting now; making bare headway. Rohde's ineptitude had achieved what Maschinenobergefreiter Schauroth had been so brutally prevented from doing – stilled the beat of her heart for ever. The loyal old *Stralsund* was already dead.

'And regrettably for we who would, in less fraught circumstances, wish to mourn your passing, Ship,' Rietz observed bleakly, 'your interment *also* promises to be uncomfortably imminent.'

He winced as he lifted his binoculars but there wasn't time for weakness. There really wouldn't be time to accommodate any physical pain, any personal feeling from now on.

The British freighter was doing exactly what he and Fischer had predicted she would do all those weeks of planning ago, while St-Nazaire still burned and Adolf Hitler's rage at the destruction of the Normandie Dock had first compelled him, Kapitänleutnant Paul Rietz, to embark upon his voyage of the already Damned.

Less than two miles away, and spurred by what she'd seen happening to the mysterious neutral, the *Java Star* was already shying away under full rudder with the white water kicking high under her counter: shaping to evacuate the area like the proverbial bat out of hell.

Courage didn't enter the equation, only brutal reality. Compassion had foundered in mid-Atlantic along with the first enemy rescue ships once the greatest sea battle of all had been joined. Now such weakness was exploited to the full by Rietz and his fellow hunters. No longer could any Allied master afford to offer his command as a sitting duck by stopping to recover survivors in the certain proximity of a U-boat. The Frontboot crews expressed a cynical appreciation for the few reckless ones who still did. They called them *die Knochensammler* – the Bone Collectors!

Bone Collectors usually died very quickly as well. An unprofitable exchange for conscience.

The *Stralsund* shuddered: leaned a little further. Rietz could hear more distinctly now – even listen to the sound made by the ship's exhausting lungs. Air, compressed by flooding seawater, was beginning to wail from her engineroom ventilators with an eerie, ever increasing cadence. The *Stralsund*, adaptable to the misfortunes of war even to the end, was composing, and playing, her own death march.

Rietz lowered the Zeiss to search the sea between the two merchant vessels, waiting. The next few seconds were vital.

'Come on,' he urged, only vaguely aware that blood had begun to drip freely from his elbow. 'Come ON, you useless little bastard – do *something* righ . . . !'

. . . a white feather glistened, elongated to a twinkling knife blade of spray cutting the sun on the water. Rietz refined the focus wheel as the periscopes came clear of the swell. Then the swirl several metres ahead of them; the saw-tooth net cutter which presaged the emergence of the black bow itself, steeply angled, travelling fast, exploding forth in a froth of white sea to embrace the light of day . . .

Rietz heard the rumble, saw the jets of oil-laden fumes explode astern as the main engine exhausts came clear and the U-boat's surface diesels roared into life.

Her tower began to show movement even while the sea still threshed and abandoned in frustration below the rusted guard rails: the bridge crew swarming through the hatch to take up lookout and gun positions . . . Rohde's white cap commanding centre stage: arrogant somehow, even at that distance; bright-

147

reflecting as its wearer moved with imperious urgency for the curve of the spray deflector to appraise the fleeing British merchantman – Not even a bloody glance in our direction! Rietz noted bitterly – then realized his anger with Rohde was clouding his objectivity: the Oberleutnant was only acting in this instance as he himself would have done; looking first to the enemy.

Though perhaps that's what I *am* doing anyway, come to that, he suddenly recollected with bleak misgiving. Even as I stand here admiring my own kind; my own compatriots . . . perhaps I am indeed looking towards my most dangerous enemy of all!

. . . but for all that, for all his uneasy acceptance that nothing concerning Operation Juggernaut might be quite as it seemed, the next manifestation – the waterspout – came as a total surprise, even to Rietz.

It must've shaken the absolute *shit* out of Oberleutnant Rohde!

The Captain sensed, rather than glimpsed, the puff of white smoke from the British ship's stern. He certainly heard the high-pitched rising shriek of displacing air – he definitely *saw* the detonation in the sea close alongside Rohde's boat and watched, eight times magnified through the salted lens of the Zeiss, the column of water which climbed high above their Frontboot consort before collapsing back across her foredeck.

Good Lord. Rietz blinked with a certain professional admiration, laying aside his sinister misgivings – even briefly overlooking the absolute certainty that his *own* ship was about to sink under him at any second. The Tommies are actually SHOOTING at him!

A second seemingly innocuous puff of cordite smoke, instantly dissipated by the wind of passage which whipped the enemy's Red Ensign into an illusion of defiance above her poop gun platform: her stern chaser.

Almost certainly some ancient cannon salvaged from a Royal Navy yard where it's been lying since our previous war, Rietz speculated deprecatingly. Manned no doubt by a scratch guncrew of bloody-minded Brit merchant seamen in the charge of the Second Mate . . .

Then the *Java Star*'s second shell exploded close enough to

Rohde to encourage every head, notably including the one wearing the white cap, to duck unhappily for the cover of the U-boat's armoured bridge and Rietz decided instead that he was watching well trained gunners serving a meticulously calibrated four-inch weapon.

So don't respond, Oberleutnant, he urged tightly, becoming anxious. Stick to the orders *I* gave you! Don't let the misapprehension that you're some kind of Nazi invincible lead you into taking on an adversary you're neither experienced enough nor man enough to tackle. That's ten thousand tons of punishment-absorbing steel there, whereas you only need to take one round on the casing and you're finished – she's too big and too good for you: gun for gun she'll outshoot you on the surface, while you haven't got the underwater speed to overtake her and deploy your eels . . . and anyway – apart from the proven likelihood that you'll bloody well MISS her – we *need* her. Stick to the bloody PLAN, dammit!

Tightly he concentrated on the heads reappearing above the glistening spray deflector. And then he smiled, albeit grimly because Rietz was first a German officer and U-boat man himself, for Rohde's white cap positively emanated the fury born of humiliation . . . Rietz could sense, almost taste the sweetness of the Oberleutnant's discomfiture. The Führer-child would be mortified, would make his crew suffer for his spitefulness – but was nevertheless doing exactly what he'd been bloody well told to do.

Run away!

The U-boat's diesels roared and spat a throbbing, oil-charged truculence as she swung away to settle on a reciprocal course which took her in the opposite direction to the British ship. The shark, ignominiously sent packing by the dolphin.

Rietz was still smiling: still appreciating this very latest irony – that Rohde's operational task would have constrained him to turn tail and be seen to break off the action whether or not the *Java Star* was defensively equipped and resolute enough to prove it – when the deck suddenly shivered and he heard a rumble from deep inside the ship which shocked him into revived awareness of his own precarious situation. It was the overture to the *Stralsund*'s death rattle; a bulkhead, a boiler – some vital part of her carrying away . . .

Yet, oddly, Rietz didn't move immediately, nor did he permit his concentration to falter. Not even when the sea lapped excitedly over the fo'c'slehead and his nearly finished command fell five degrees further on her side.

He wasn't smiling any longer, either. Not even grimly. The whimsical humour of Rietz had just abandoned the *Stralsund* along with any lingering trust he'd harboured in those who had conspired in her counterfeit murder.

Even when the Captain *did* finally whirl with his ship breaking up under him and Death just a little too close on his heels, and began running for the boat deck, he wasn't concerned so much with what he might find – as what he'd just discovered.

There could be no room whatever for doubt *this* time.

. . . one of the heads he'd seen on the bridge of Rohde's dutifully retiring U-boat out there was *unquestionably* that of Fregattenkapitän von Strelow.

Chapter Thirteen

◆

They moved like monstrous disciplined phantoms through the angled murk, the Kapitänleutnant's horsemen. Even the sun had deserted the *Stralsund*'s starboard boat deck: now only puce-tinged rays penetrated; cast giant hurrying shadows against a swirling fog of steam and smoke and clinker ash and coal dust roaring and tumbling from the seat of her amputated funnel. Seawater invading her fireboxes was exploding the furnace linings, forcing pressurized gasses into volcanic eruption . . .

My God, Rietz thought as he slid numbly, careless of the wound in his arm, down the bridge ladder for the last time. Am I mad, or have I created this Inferno?

First he looked urgently towards the davitheads; saw that both lifeboats still appeared to be relatively undamaged, and uttered a silent thanksgiving. Now only whatever reprieve the ship would allow them before her increasing angle of list made launching impossible, remained in question.

He was surprised to realize that so little time had apparently elapsed since the hit – maybe it had just *seemed* longer up there, all alone on the bridge? So far only number one boat had actually begun to lower jerkily to the accompaniment of squealing blocks. The arms detail were still loading camouflaged sub-machine-guns into the second boat – concealed within a rigid canvas stretcher frame in the company of a convincingly nervous-looking Matrosengefreiter Jakobi acting the part of dummy casualty . . .

'DON'T DROP 'IM . . .!' Bootsmaat Landgraf's own special brand of reassurance carried clear above the din: 'Hold *on* to the after fall, Number Two! Get that fuckin' snarl-up cleared NOW or you're on a CHARGE, Fittkau . . . !'

The Captain swung, frowning through the steam towards the wreckage of the funnel just as Leo Fischer appeared from the gloom, iron-grey hair matted with filth, eyes hard as black marble.

'The Chief's still trying to get bolt cutters into two tons of impacted scrap. Two dead so far. Rohde should be bloody court martialled!'

'He'll be hanged with piano wire if I get my way. Who have we lost?'

'Scherdel and Mainzer. Pulverized. They'd taken cover under the lee of the funnel deck when it came down.'

'They're dead – leave them!' Rietz snapped harshly. 'Sinder-mann's too bloody important to the operation to play undertaker: he should be moving to his boat.'

'I said *so far*, Paul.'

Rietz stayed expressionless even though the demons of his recurring nightmare instantly began jeering, '*Oberon* . . .'

'Who else, Leo?'

'Young Schadt. Trapped and smashed to hell.' Fischer looked tired: a lot older somehow. 'Worse, Paul – the boy's still fully conscious.'

Sindermann glanced up but didn't stop cutting as the Captain approached on the run. The Chief's features appeared more skull-like than ever behind his beard; white-drawn despite the mask of carbon dust.

'Did Schauroth get out?' he asked flatly.

Rietz just shook his head: it was hardly the time to discuss murder. Sindermann shrugged. Chief Engineer Sindermann had already used up all his grief. 'He was a good U-boat man: a good *Maschinenobergefreiter*.'

Rietz slipped his lifejacket off and squatted.

'Well, *you've* got yourself in a pretty pickle, Schadt,' he said conversationally to the boy under the funnel.

The *Stralsund* shuddered again, and the rumbling carried even louder from below. The Captain and the Chief Engineer's eyes met. Schadt had very little time left.

Sindermann put on an extra specially reassuring grin for Schadt's sake. He hadn't run out of compassion. 'Typical deck sailor, eh, Kapitän? Does this to himself, then relies on us engineers to get 'im out've the shit as usual.'

Schadt tried very hard to smile bravely, but only managed to squeeze a tear from a bewildered and terrified eye. He was slipping into shock, but not fast enough. Rietz crawled in beside him under the overhanging round of the funnel and said briskly, 'Right, let's have a look then!'

Schadt's right leg had been torn off at the knee, the left smashed into a pulp of flesh and bone. A coke-encrusted angle iron had penetrated the boy's groin – Rietz didn't even want to guess how deeply . . . He got up, casually dusting his hands and wondering how in PITY'S name God could allow such a terrible thing to happen to a nice kid like Schadt when he'd been merciful enough to kill the others properly.

And the real horror of Schadt's crucifixion hadn't even begun.

'The Chief's wrong about seamen, Schadt – you're the smart ones. You put on an act, then quote regulations to me.' He shook his head mock severely. 'Well, don't expect *me* to excuse you rowing once we've got you in the boat. A few nasty bruises don't count.'

Schadt did smile at that. And gained courage from its implication. The Captain looked at Chief Sindermann through the swirling fog, and jerked his head meaningfully. Sindermann squeezed the boy's arm, and grumbled, 'Bloody cutters! Wouldn't slice bread . . . I'll nip down an' get a proper set.'

As soon as he'd gone Rietz casually put his hand inside his jacket. 'Fancy a cigarette?'

Schadt sniffed. 'I don't smoke, sir. Mum always told me not t . . . !' His back arched and he began screaming as the pain finally caught up with him.

The Captain surreptitiously withdrew his hand from his jacket. 'Shush, son. Your Mum'll be upset if you let her hear you crying.'

The boy's eyes opened wide in wonderment. Just for a moment he stopped screaming. 'Mother, sir . . . ? *Here?*'

Rietz ever so gently took the pallid hand which reached out to her: was glad that Schadt could draw such comfort from the illusion he'd created.

The ship sagged further by the head and water began to blow from the ventilators forward.

'There she is, Erich. Over there – by Kapitänleutnant Fischer . . .'

He squeezed the trigger of the concealed Luger just as Schadt turned his face away in joyous greeting.

Not at all frightened any more.

It's a funny old world, Rietz reflected dully. One irony after another. Take that shot I just fired – that was my eighth and last bullet, and if I hadn't been so unprofessional a fighting man I'd've reloaded long before now. It's almost as if it was *meant* for Schadt. I nearly used it on him earlier, down in the engineer's store . . . when he saved my life!

So maybe it wasn't such an old campaigner's myth after all: that every bullet really *did* carry someone's name on it. The Captain couldn't help wondering where his might happen to be, in that case. Probably in some thoroughly bored Tommy sentry's Lee Enfield magazine. In Southampton.

If the gods even allowed him to get that far.

He'd ejected the empty clip and was methodically palming home a fresh one ready for the *Java Star* – he HAD to cling to the conviction that he'd at least be proved correct in his assessment of the *enemy's* next move – when Leo came over at the run. His eyes narrowed when he saw Schadt.

'I tried to leave him enough to smile with,' Rietz remarked almost apologetically. Not that he expected Fischer to understand.

'Both boats in the water. We're ready to abandon, Paul.'

The Captain nodded and stood up stiffly, painfully. There were fragments of Schadt spattered across his discarded life-jacket. He decided to leave it where it was.

'Did Stemmler pick up any general U-boat warnings from the Tommy?'

'Ohhhhh *shit*!' Leo muttered, looking embarrassed. But his

usually precise mind had been addled by being blown up for Germany too, even if the experience hadn't, in Fischer's case, been so much a result of the Führer's directive as an oversight on the part of the *Stralsund*'s on-board assailan . . . !

'Ohhhh SHIT!' Rietz endorsed, starting to run aft towards the radio room, fear already mounting that Funkgefreiter Stemmler – as vulnerable to attack at his lonely listening post as ever Schauroth and Leutnant Becker had been – might have become murder victim number three . . . Number FOUR, he corrected savagely, quite unjustifiably, but nevertheless plagued by what he'd just done to poor Schadt.

Fischer caught up with him. 'He's my responsibility. I screwed up the head count, old boy . . .'

The *Stralsund* began to sag forward and sideways all at the same time. Rietz could hear, above the screeching of the breaking ship, the distant thunder of water pouring in over the foredeck bulwarks.

'Shut up an' get the BOATS away!' he roared over his shoulder. 'Go ON, Leo – *I'm* her Captain! It's MY bloody privilege to leave when I'm ready . . .'

I was right the first time. This *is* the Inferno, created by the paranoia-distorted cells of my brain, he decided as he raced heedlessly through the steadily canting fog of regenerated steam and ash roaring from the funnel deck.

Then he realized he was being silly, and that there had been nothing imaginary about Maschinenobergefreiter Schauroth's evacuated skull and Leutnant Becker's slashed throat, and the Mark G7E torpedo which had killed three more men unnecessarily.

Nor, as from his confirmation of only minutes – or had it been a lifetime? – ago about Fregattenkapitän von Strelow's utterly illogical but nevertheless very real presence aboard the U-boat which had launched it . . . ?

Rietz frowned so hard at that point that he very nearly stopped running. Very nearly: but not quite. Being mad and being plain suicidal wasn't quite the same thing.

. . . but he really couldn't afford to sidestep FISCHER'S

never entirely convincing appearance aboard as a hapless stow-away any longer. Precipitated, according to the laconic Kapitän-leutnant, by a minor head wound which had knocked him unconscious until too late to return him to shore?

A remarkable escape indeed? the new ultra-suspicious Rietz thought bleakly. And particularly so from the hands of a killer who'd since put such store in making certain his victims remained permanently mute that he graduated from clumsy weapons like chain stoppers to carrying knives scalpel-honed enough to slice through throat tissue and muscle at one slash. And to cutting *dum-dums* . . . ?

Rietz *did* stop then as the full implication hit him. Momentarily. Whether or not the bloody ship WAS sinking.

'Dear Jesus,' he echoed, stunned. 'Surely there can't be TWO KILLERS? Each slaughtering independently. Each without the knowledge of the *other* . . . ?'

And each – unless their names just happened to have been Schadt, Scherdel or Mainzer – about to pull away in the boats? Still-anonymous cancers working within the body corporate of his surviving Trojan horsemen?

Rietz changed his mind. He was very firm about it.

I'm not mad – I'm *dead*. Well, I HOPE I'm dead . . . that Rohde's torpedo killed me outright and that this IS proper Hell. Because I really don't think I can cope with any more of this and *then* have to look forward to dying at the end of it!

There came a horrendous CRACK from forr'ad. The whole bloody ship swayed drunkenly to port as the *Stralsund*'s foremast started to fall over the side . . .

The Captain had only begun to run again – just in *case* he wasn't actually dead – when a hugely distorted figure loomed through the murk, steaming full ahead the other way.

Of course Funkgefreiter Stemmler, being Stemmler, slammed to rigid attention as soon as they'd sorted themselves out after the collision. The rating's regulatory servility lost something in its execution, however, as Rietz clearly heard a tooth being sucked, which showed his hearing had become fully restored if nothing else.

'Sorry, sir,' Stemmler snapped with wooden derision. 'My fault entirely, Herr Kapitä . . . !'

He had guts, Rietz was bound to concede. For all his resentment of authority, Stemmler did have guts.

'DON'T,' he snarled anyway, fed up with everything, 'be so fucking *cheeky*, Stemmler. Just follow me an' get the hell off this ship!'

He didn't really think they would, though. Not by then. She was literally poised to slide into the Atlantic bow-first, angling more and more to port. Deep below them her bulkheads were collapsing in sequence; imploding with reverberating explosions: shaking the whole bulk of the *Stralsund* as her Leviathan cadaver finally succumbed to the seas which had coveted her for half a century . . .

'STARB'D SIDE!' he shouted above the growing cacophony. 'TRY FOR THE STARBOARD RAILS, STEMMLER . . . !'

But neither of them could *reach* the outboard side all of a sudden. She was canting too hard, gravity compelling them downhill as the boat deck fell away . . . fifteen . . . twenty . . . twenty-FIVE degrees! A vegetable locker tearing loose from its mountings and sliding crazily, lethally, downhill. A fine mist of spray being forced from the bursting hatch covers forward and beginning to haze across the tormented ship . . . Rietz and Stemmler weren't even *running* for their lives any more, they were barely making headway: skidding and scrambling for purchase along the 'V' formed between the base of the angled funnel deck housing and the blood-slippery planking of the boat deck itself. German blood – Lookout Schadt's blood, and that of Scherdel and Mainzer who had all embarked on Rietz's great adventure prepared to shed it heroically for the Fatherland, yet had ended by sacrificing it under a pointless avalanche of corroded steel.

Even Stemmler looks scared at last, Rietz noted with savage, thoroughly unworthy satisfaction. Stemmler looks every bit as terrified as *I* am now . . . !

He'd just got himself mentally resigned to dying all over again when he glimpsed the discarded rope fall angling, as the *Stralsund* angled, from the now vacated davithead of number two boat.

157

Its hauling part was hanging free: steadily inclining towards them . . .

'The FALL, Stemmler,' he roared, throwing himself full-length sideways across the tilting deck, stretching vainly to grasp the end just too far away to touch. He rolled on to his face, lying virtually uphill now, with feet jammed against the housing as the ship continued to list remorselessly on top of them.

'Shin up my back! Try to reach the FALL, MAN . . . !'

Stemmler's seaboot ground into his hip. Rietz bit back a grunt of pain as a second foot smashed agonizingly into his injured shoulder, levering against his prone frame for purchase . . .

Stemmler hung there for a moment; abseiling between life and death: looking down on the helpless Rietz while clinging to the rope which offered them both at least a fighting chance of making it over the side.

It was then that the Captain experienced a whole new dimension of fear: went deathly cold as he registered Stemmler's expression. There seemed to be something holding his Radioman back: restraining him from grasping Rietz's desperately extended arm – a hesitation. Almost an indecision . . . ?

The deck began to vibrate convulsively as the sea flung talons of spray high above the defeated ship: roared in triumph as it finally raced aft, overrunning hatches and winches and by now howling ventilators to detonate monstrously against the forward face of the *Stralsund*'s centrecastle. Rietz could sense her gathering herself: beginning to slide ever faster, and suddenly he knew he was very sane indeed, and really did want so desperately to live despite all his earlier disparagement of the condition.

'*Please*, Stemmler?' he implored silently, refusing to betray his true depth of terror even then by screaming the plea out loud. He was, after all, a German officer.

More than that – wasn't he U-Bootwaffe Kapitänleutnant Rietz, the Chosen Sword of the Führer? Rietz, the Man of Iron?

Rietz, the bloody FRAUD?

'Please, Stemmler . . . HELP meeeee?'

Chapter Fourteen

'You know, if you really *must* persist in keeping this Man of Iron myth alive much longer,' Rietz upbraided himself later, when he had a spare moment in between terror, revulsion and exhaustion, 'you're not only going to have to get a grip on yourself but, from a purely practical point of view, you're also going to have to learn to *trust* people. No individual can capture a ramship, unmask a traitor *and* blow up a British dry dock in isolation.'

'But how CAN you trust people,' his Paranoia retorted with unsettling logic, 'when those same people keep KILLING each other behind your back? And what about Stemmler – you were utterly convinced a few moments ago HE wasn't going to grab your hand. AND Leo Fischer – now you've even slotted HIM into your scenario of gloom and skulduggery as a sinister player . . .'

'Now look,' Rietz said to himself. 'You've got to the stage where you imagine malice in everybody – every one of your key men. Fischer, Stemmler . . . you'd even decided Maschinenoberge-freiter Schauroth was the killer – until somebody KILLED him! It really isn't the sort of attitude Ulysses would've allowed himself to adopt, otherwise he'd never have managed to select enough trustworthy heroes to put *inside* his bloody horse in the first place . . . !'

His Paranoia frowned doubtfully. 'I suppose,' it muttered uneasily, 'one can always look on the bright side. You've still got twenty men left alive and hopefully about to board the British freighter – IF the Tommies do what you're banking on them doing, of course – and only one of your chaps . . .'

'Well, maybe two, Rietz conceded, thinking back to his latest bout of rationalization. 'I admit that there are maybe TWO traitors and assassins within my group – excluding von Strelow, of course. Who might only be taking a sea voyage in a U-boat for the improvement of his health.'

'OK! Two possible traitors at most,' his Paranoia agreed, not quite sure by then of where the thrust of the argument was supposed to lead. '. . . which STILL leaves you with eighteen utterly trustworthy, thoroughly reliable fighting men on whom you CAN depend!'

Maybe even nineteen, Rietz reflected hopefully, feeling better. Stemmler *did* grasp my hand in the end . . .

'Don't EVER do that to me again, Stemmler,' the Captain had snarled, still shaking, when the radio operator finally did reach out and hauled him up the canting deck to the starboard rails.

'No, sir, I promise I won't,' Stemmler said grimly. And looked, for once, as though he meant it. The only uncertainty Rietz then had to consider was, well, whether Stemmler meant he wouldn't hesitate again – or wouldn't offer another helping hand if eve . . .

. . . but that was before Rietz had confronted, and devastated with reasoned argument, his inner suspicious about everybody concerned with Juggernaut.

'Ohhhhh, *Christ*,' Stemmler had subsequently added without any ambiguity at all when, clinging precariously to the rail, they both turned to face outboard.

And downwards!

The *Stralsund*'s slab side yawned below and ahead of them: no longer vertical as in the orderly geometry Rietz had come to expect of a ship, but sloping away now like a great steel toboggan run to where white seas, agitated by the rising displacement of her massive and capsizing starboard bilge keel, pounded and boiled and jostled and thundered to fill the void of her going.

Barely beyond the maelstrom, pressing their own safety to the limit, waited the two ship's boats. But right at that moment they lay a whole death-slide away ... as impotent to help as any straggle-legged water beetles they emulated.

Rietz felt the blood drain from his face; felt his hands close vice-like around the rail now behind him – for the life of him he couldn't even remember having clambered through it, out on to that lunatic perch – and thought wistfully of the old adage impressed on him as a boy sailor: 'Don't leave the ship till the ship leaves YOU ...'

Then realized fear was the most dangerous conspirator in his own self-fulfilling prophesy. That the *Stralsund* wouldn't leave him: no more than the British *Oberon* had relinquished her grip on *her* human cargo – the suction of her foundering alone would be fierce enough to drag him and Stemmler down along with the now admittedly careless corpses of Schadt and his other two German heroes squandered under the funnel ... Schauroth and young Leutnant Becker would be going anyway, already entombed for ever in their flooding execution cell.

Thirty degrees ... Thirty-FIVE degrees ... The whole ship bellowing behind and below them as she rolled further and further to port!

'GO!' he roared to Stemmler. 'Go NOW, man. Before it's too LATE ...!'

'I can't,' Stemmler mouthed, ashen-faced. 'I can't LET MYSELF ...!'

FORTY BLOODY DEGREES ... FORTY-FIVE ...!

'Back at Base they say you're a homosexual, Stemmler,' the Captain remarked casually, conversationally.

'Beg pardon?' Stemmler echoed, thunderstruck.

FIFTY DEGREES AND STILL ROLLING ...! Rietz summoned his very best officer-quality sneer.

'Are you, Funkgefreiter – a nancy boy? An original Golden Rivet?'

Stemmler let go of the rail and lunged for Rietz, black with rage ... then understood.

'With respect: you're a bastard – SIR!' he shouted as he launched himself down the cresta run.

'Just so long,' Rietz roared back, following him, 'as it IS with respect, Stemmler ...!'

*

'Whereaway the *Java Star* now?' he coughed painfully, trying to get up from the bottom of the boat. It seemed he was *always* having to ask where the bloody target was. In between crises.

'Hull down somewhere over there, old boy,' Fischer pointed vaguely south with his free hand. They couldn't see very much at all from the height of eye in the lifeboats: only peaks and troughs of seas which now shouldered them with moderate tolerance. Leo eyed Rietz accusingly. 'Still steaming for the horizon, I might add. And leaving the distinct impression that they've never read the parable of the Good Samaritan.'

'I don't suppose,' Rietz defended waspishly, 'they've read your Mrs Beeton either. So they've still no reason to suspect they're our rabbi . . . !'

He coughed again, and retched convulsively. A lot of coal dust came up: all mixed with the salt-filth from his lungs. In the eyes of the boat Funkgefreiter Stemmler was doing much the same thing. But then, they wouldn't have been there at all had it not been for the courage of their comrades at the oars allied with Kapitänleutnant Fischer's superlative boatmanship: the steadiness with which he'd steered her calmly into the maelstrom to snatch them both from the suddenly not-so-proverbial jaws of death.

'And Rohde?'

Leo changed hands on the tiller, waving equally vaguely northwards with the other one. 'Making off and giving his best imitation of a Frontboot that's fired its last eel and is heading back to Base to re-ammunition. Personally I'd consider him a safer bet if he actually had . . .' His eyes went hard. 'And that's speaking as one who happens to be on the same side!'

'She's going, sir,' one of the rowers called with a note of awe.

The Captain struggled to his knees, gripping one of the thwarts. No one was able to assist him; they were still rowing urgently to place as much distance between themselves and the *Stralsund* as prudence, and the vortex she was about to create, demanded.

She rolled completely over until her barnacled, weed-fouled

double-bottoms and keel lay embarrassingly awash, with the seas creaming and threshing to climb atop her even in that final indignity. They could hear vast weights plummeting inside her: a kettledrum booming a final pandemonium of destruction across the all-too-narrow intervening gap – even the old main engine which had steamed her for countless miles would be tearing free of its corroded mountings; smashing hugely through her once-decks, compelling itself without any steam at all to reach the bottom of the Atlantic Ocean before her.

. . . and then she sank. A bit of an anticlimax really. Quietly, and without fuss, just as she had lived. The most curious warship there ever was.

And there was only a swirl of bubbling air and gouting sea fingers to mark where she'd been, from which odd, floatable things occasionally tore free – an empty drum; a locker; a grating rising to dip morose farewell before swirling back into the grue. Once a whole wooden awning spar speared clear from the agitated grave to soar quite high in the air before buoyancy gave way to gravity and it, too, relinquished its short-lived independence.

And then there was nothing. And the gallant old *Stralsund* had gone with her cargo of fresh dead men, and her ghosts of seadogs past.

'Ach, she was a hell of a ship anyway,' Stemmler grunted.

'Yes, Stemmler,' Rietz said. 'She was a *hell* of a ship.'

There was no point in rowing. Rietz didn't intend them to go anywhere.

Bootsmaat Landgraf brought his boat alongside, and they loosely secured the painters to keep them from drifting apart. Then drifted.

The sun got hotter. The waves calmed even more now their appetite was briefly satisfied. And their father, the Atlantic, grew ever larger and more lonely. Rietz still decided against breaking out their fresh water. They were well over a thousand miles from land, and he wasn't *that* sure of the British.

The two counterfeit stretcher casualties, one in each boat, began to cook gently in their makeshift strait-jackets.

'Let's have a cabaret: make a proper cruise of it,' Rietz said. 'Do your striptease, Jakobi.'

Matrosengefreiter Jakobi pulled a few concealed knots inside his contraption: simpered: '*Voilà!*' – and it all fell away like magic to reveal the three Schmeisser sub-machine-guns.

'The sight o' *them*'ll give the Tommies more to get excited about than the ass of any Hamburg whore,' Landgraf grinned.

Everybody laughed; especially now the torpedoing was over.

Well, everybody but one.

But nobody had expected Chief Sindermann to laugh anyway.

Every now and then they were reminded of the *Stralsund*.

A part of her would wander by and bob acknowledgement. Usually something small. The wheelhouse grating followed their drift like a faithfully persistent dog, for instance. Almost as if it had been trodden on by seamen all its life, and couldn't bear to face the world alone.

A pair of spare underpants, a galley kettle and a saloon chair came by.

Rietz fished the underpants out and held them at fastidious length. The men loved it.

'Kriegsmarine issue. And judging by the outrageous size of the crotch,' their Iron Captain hazarded, 'I'd say these belong to *you*, Bootsmaat Landgraf!'

Landgraf beamed; much complimented. 'Like a small bet on it, sir? They'll have a tally on 'em.'

Rietz looked. The tag showed *Msch/ob/gftr SCHAUROTH H.*

'No name tag,' he said. And threw them well away from the boat.

It began to develop into a game. *Flotsam an' Guess'em* someone christened it. As soon as an object was sighted they tried to guess what it was before its origins became obvious.

Rietz didn't discourage it: kept them cheerful even though he, himself, was becoming more and more concerned that his faith in British resolution had been sadly and – considering he'd cast them adrift in two chips of boats a month's sailing from anywhere – suicidally misplaced.

Of course, there was always Rohde. He would be back once

the ploy had been tested . . . but that, of course, depended on Rohde's ability to find them again and Rietz harboured an uneasy recollection that Rohde's navigation had been as pin-point as his marksmanship . . .

Kapitänleutnant Fischer, entering into the spirit of the thing, proved he could wax lyrical, generate enthusiasm for even the most humble artefact.

'It's only a bloody light bulb,' Matrosengefreiter Leinweber grumbled, by then getting a bit pissed off with kids' games and probably feeling seasick, as most of them were beginning to.

'*Only* a light bulb, Leinweber?' Leo echoed, monstrously taken aback. 'Only a LIGHT bulb . . . ?'

'Yeah, well, we been watchin' it f'r half an hour, Herr Kaleunt. Bit disappointing when it turns out to be nothin' more than a light bulb. Sir.'

'Ah, but that's the view of an unimaginative man,' Fischer chided gently. 'Appreciate its wonders, its strength of character before you condemn it to obscurity, Matrosengefreiter Leinweber. Does it not strike you as significant that, while the ship it came from sank to the bottom of the sea – the light bulb still survives? That the lowly light bulb may well passage from coast to coast; ocean to ocean; through typhoon and storm-wrack and hazard, young Leinweber: while all around great vessels fall prey to the elements . . .'

'There's something else – two points on the starb'd bow!' Rietz interrupted gratefully, pissed off as well. Shortly he proposed to upgrade this rather childish diversion to one more appropriate to total war: order them to keep watch for much larger things approaching at eighteen knots from the still empty horizon.

'And if *that* pastime fails,' he thought bleakly, 'we play at being real sailors. Hoist the scraps of standing lug sails both lifeboats carry, and embark on what will be the longest and most harrowing game any of us have ever conceived of.'

There was a saying in the U-boat Service. *Um so länger war die Fahrt, desto besser war die Kameradschaft* – 'The longer the voyage, the better the crew spirit.'

'Suggesting we'll all be *bloody* good friends by the time THAT trip's over!' Rietz decided wryly. He'd never been entirely con-

vinced of the saying's validity, anyway. One thing was for sure –
it wouldn't prove the case for any crew commanded by Oberleutnant Rohde.

. . . the general concensus was that the object the Captain
had sighted would turn out to be either a mattress or a canvas
bag of something.

Jakobi suggested it was a sack of potatoes and started a heated
argument about the floatability of potatoes before they stuffed
him back in his stretcher and told him to shut up.

Certainly it was lumpy and formless, and not drifting much
faster than the boats themselves, only slowly overtaking them,
which suggested that – like the wheelhouse grating – the wind
had little effect on it.

Eventually those who'd opted for it being a canvas bag of
something were proved the winners, but only on a technicality.
The canvas bag actually contained cork blocks, and proved to
be a Swedish Merchant Marine lifejacket. The corpse wearing
it looked just like a spreadeagled penguin . . .

'More like a penguin than ever,' Rietz considered bleakly.
'With his legs amputated like that.'

He didn't have to call a halt to the game after all. No one
showed much enthusiasm for continuing it after that. On the
other hand, Lookout Schadt seemed perfectly content to stay
with his shipmates now he'd found them again, having successfully torn himself from the embrace of the funnel. But there
were too many unpleasant things weaving like tendrils in the
water around him for morale to benefit from his presence, and
Rietz decided enough was enough. They'd left Shadt once: they
would have to again.

He shrugged as he met Leo Fischer's hard eyes above the
tiller. It was the sort of eventuality one tended to overlook when
planning an operation.

'Let go the boatropes,' Fischer said. 'Out oars . . . Give way
together!'

Rohde did find them ten minutes later. Or Rietz assumed it was
Rohde: one periscope was very much like another when its parent
craft was running submerged.

It began to circle the two boats slowly.

'The bastard'll be counting heads,' Fischer grunted. 'See how many of us made it despite him.'

Rietz couldn't help wondering which bastard Fischer actually meant – Rohde or von Strelow. But then, Leo didn't know about von Strelow.

Did he?

He couldn't help also thinking how like a shark's dorsal fin the periscope seemed; particularly when viewed from water level. Sharks circled their potential victims first, before they moved in for the kill.

The Captain shivered even though the Atlantic wind was still warm. What made him think in terms of sharks and victims, when they were all a part of the same great German endeavour?

Chapter Fifteen

Rietz was sorry he'd lost his trusted Zeiss lenses when he and Stemmler had abandoned the *Stralsund* in such an unseemly fashion – they'd finally been wrenched from his neck and he hadn't even felt them go – but as it happened he wouldn't have needed them to win the final round of the game. The horizon distance seen by a man of average height standing in a lifeboat is something less than three miles anyway and, as a veteran Frontboot commander, the Captain's eyes were as attuned as any sea eagle's to looking out for prey.

Admittedly the Mannesmann tube derrick he'd warned Becker to look for at her foremast gave him an unfair advantage over the others. Helped him to be first to positively identify the ship heading straight for them even while she, herself, was still hull down.

So the *Java Star* HAD come back to rescue them despite the increased risk to herself: a calculated risk made acceptable only by Rohde's apparent withdrawal. Rietz had gambled entirely on that one assumption.

'The first rule of war, old boy,' Leo Fischer had said. 'Know thine enemy . . .'

Not only is it a truism, it also makes fighting that same war easier from my point of view, Rietz reflected without any great self-satisfaction. Knowing I have the advantage of fighting it against an enemy weakened by compassion.

*

'Remember your section leaders, and stay close to them while heading for your designated key point,' he called quietly as they waited for the rabbit to steam under their piecrust. 'The Chief will lead the engineroom assault. Funkgefreiter Stemmler *must* secure her radio shack before she can shout for help. Kapitänleutnant Fischer has now taken over the duties of Leutnant Becker, and will take charge of the deck while Landgraf and myself make our run for the bridge . . .'

Apart from Leo – and young Schadt, who would certainly keep the secret – none of them knew about Becker. Or Schauroth. Only that they went down as casualties of the torpedoing.

Then Rietz remembered there *was* at least one other who knew exactly how Schauroth and Becker had died, and wondered grimly which assault party he'd detailed HIM to.

'I emphasize once again – other than where resistance is offered, there will be NO unnecessary killing,' he added, unintentionally icy: almost certainly being unfair to the others. 'Once the *Java Star* is in our hands you will treat the Tommies with the respect due to prisoners of war.'

He looked over the faces turned towards him from the boats. Stolid, unemotional, brave faces. German men – the Führer's men. *His* men! He wanted to tell them that: tell them he saluted them.

But he was Rietz. And they expected him to act like Rietz: speak as Rietz would. The games were over.

'Anyone who does contravene that order will be formally charged with murder, and court martialled immediately on return to U-Bootwaffe Service . . .'

He permitted them just the ghost of a smile then.

'Now, all get off your backsides – and bloody well WAVE!'

She came so close they could hear the splash of the seas parting under her forefoot, and detect the steady rumble of twin engines deep inside the elegant, grey-painted hull.

Rietz noted the extra look-outs posted on her bridge and at her bow and stern. The four-inch naval gun on her poop was trained fore and aft but still closed up: most of its seaman crew standing watching in charge of a uniformed officer – the Second

Mate? – while one still sponged out what was probably an already gleaming barrel. The *Java Star*'s crew were obviously very proud of, to say nothing of modestly expert with, their little vixen. It all suggested that, while her Captain may have been a brave man, he wasn't entirely reckless.

Or no more so than was the Good Samaritan, Rietz reflected wryly. 'When he stopped and trusted in the Lord to ensure that the thieves really *had* departed from the scene of their crime . . .

Though Rietz felt bound to concede that the Good Master had been careful not to place *total* reliance on the Almighty's vigilance alone. U-Bootwaffe Kapitänleutnant Rietz – having seen the inhuman things he'd seen through his target marker, and done the things he'd done to ships with his torpedoes – was the first to appreciate that simple Faith must have been stretched monstrously taut for any Allied shipmaster engaged in the Battle of the Atlantic by mid-1942.

In fact, Rietz granted that the enemy Captain had only over-looked one military precaution he might still have taken; quite understandably he was assuming U-boat attack to present his only threat at that juncture – no one was manning the twin anti-aircraft machine-guns mounted on either wing of her sand-bagged bridge deck.

Rietz was fervently grateful for that natural oversight. They could just as easily be deployed to cover the foredeck and boat deck. He caught Fischer's attention and lifted an eyebrow imperceptibly. Leo glanced up, and smiled a tight acknowledge-ment. Rietz felt reassured that no British heroes would live long enough to fill in for the Almighty before he stormed the *Java Star*'s bridge.

. . . but other than that, and the heads of men standing by the boarding net ready unrolled over her forr'ad well deck bulwarks, she could have been any merchantman belonging to any nation making an unscheduled stop on passage. She could just as easily have been German. Two or three off-watch crew-men leaned interestedly on the rails outside the crew quarters aft: a couple of engineers in white boiler suits watched idly from the head of the engineroom fiddley on the main centrecastle deck . . .

Deep inside her an engine telegraph jangled, whereupon the throb of the idling diesels suddenly mounted. White water began to thresh and whorl forward from under her counter as her Old Man brought her briefly astern. When the way fell off the telegraph jangled again, and the rumble died.

An officer with silver hair and four gold rings leaned out over the bridge wing as Rietz stood up in the boat.

'Please hurry,' the *Java Star*'s Captain called. 'My Chief Engineer informs me there are less stressful ways of spending an afternoon . . . can you manage to pull to my boarding net?'

'God bless you for returning, Captain,' Rietz shouted. 'I have two injured men, both in the stretchers as you see. My others are shocked but otherwise well.'

'Ready oars . . . ? Give way *together*,' Fischer said in a low voice. They would be the last orders, the last words to be spoken in German, until Rietz gave the signal – he would not do that before every last man had gained a foothold on the British deck.

Landgraf's boat bumped heavily alongside, followed by the Captain's. Heaving lines snaked down from above and the stretchers were made fast . . . Rietz couldn't help a wry and somewhat belated twinge of concern. The Tommies were about to discover that Swedish merchant seamen were pretty damned heavy!

'Hurry, lads!' a tightly measured voice called from above. 'Quick as you can!'

More heads peered down, silently urging them to greater effort. Arms reached down to help the first of Rietz's Trojans over the bulwark capping. There was a tension in the air, tangible: oppressive. This was the bravery of the sitting duck. The *Knochensammler* . . .

'Easy does it, mate,' an English voice said as Jakobi's stretcher was gently eased inboard. 'Soon 'ave you fixed up.'

'Who wants a fag?' another Tommy called. 'We got fags, hot cocoa, an' if you speak nice to the Chief Steward 'e might even manage a drop o' rum . . .'

'What the hell's a *fag*?' Rietz whispered to Fischer, breaking his own rule as a Captain was entitled to do. Leo grinned broadly as he turned to grasp the boarding net.

'In this instance, a cigarette. Just consider yourself fortunate this is a British ship, old boy – and not a Yankee!'

Kapitänleutnant Rietz was still trying to figure *that* cryptic remark out even when he began to climb . . . !

Rietz had never met his enemy face to face since the war began; not his living enemy. It was a strange experience; unsettling. The man who greeted him at the bulwark could well have been a mirror image of himself.

Early thirties, lean, with an air of quiet authority: a little more wind-tanned than Rietz, who'd never quite lost his submariner's pallor. He wore a reefer uniform and the British Merchant Navy's summer zone white cover to his cap. His three faded gold rings marked him as the *Java Star*'s Chief Officer.

'Afternoon. I'm Bill McGregor,' he said, as easily as if playing host at a dinner party. 'And you, sir, are . . . ?'

Rietz looked round quickly. His men were playing the part well; standing uncertainly, some looking nervous, others dazed . . . he wasn't even sure himself of whether they were acting or not. Certainly their make-up was authentic. Every one of them showed creases of strain ingrained by a now sweat-glossy patina of filth from the *Stralsund*'s shattered boat deck.

But the Tommies were moving among them; kindness was a dangerous disease. Stemmler was calmly accepting an English cigarette – a very cool Stemmler again: not the Stemmler who'd briefly betrayed his terror just before the *Stralsu* . . . !

Rietz tensed. A portly officer wearing Chief Steward's rings and a concerned expression was moving purposefully towards Jakobi, now lying in his canvas restraint on the deck and protected to some extent from scrutiny by a huddle of the Trojans. But the Chief Steward was moving far too close for comfort . . .

Rietz put his hand inside his jacket and pulled out the Luger.

'Kapitänleutnant Paul Rietz,' he said, feeling faintly ridiculous. 'Of the Sixth German Flotilla, *Befehlshaber der Unterseeboote!*'

McGregor stared at the gun and muttered, 'Bloody *hell*!'

Someone else announced disbelievingly, 'They're not Swedes – they're fucking JERRIES!'

172

The horsemen were all pulling Lugers now: whirling towards the stretchers where Jakobi and . . . and WHO? Rietz couldn't remember the second Matrosengefreiter's name for the *life* of him right at that moment! – where Jakobi and who*ever* he was, were desperately fumbling at concealed releases which wouldn't relea . . . !

The British Chief Officer lunged for Rietz's gun. Leo Fischer hit him a glancing blow on the side of the head with his own Luger. McGregor spun away with an oath and cannoned into Bootsmaat Landgraf, clawing doggedly for possession of *his* weapon. Landgraf shot him twice in the stomach, more in surprise than anger, and the mirror image of Rietz doubled up and sank to his knees before lifting his head to stare dazedly, rather reproachfully AT Rietz . . . until blood came out of his mouth and he slumped to the deck.

Jakobi's canvas strait-jacket finally flew apart with an oiled gleam of machine pistol barrels. Stemmler, Landgraf – Leinweber who didn't think much of light bulbs – each seized a Schmeisser . . . a big British seaman, clearly a seasoned barroom brawler with a several-times broken nose and roaring now with outrage, kicked Matrosengefreiter Jakobi viciously under the chin even as he tried to scramble erect from the stretcher. Rietz heard jawbone shatter clear above the rattle of cocking handles and Jakobi gurgled horribly as he arched backwards, a perfectly genuine casualty.

Kapitänleutnant Fischer took controlled aim and put one round clean through the Tommy's head. The fat Chief Steward began to bolt aft, heading for the centrecastle ladder and bawling 'Send a distress; send out a distr . . .'

Rietz thought savagely, Ohhhh *fuck* it: this wasn't supposed to happen! and pulled his trigger vaguely in the fleeing officer's direction. The Chief Steward went down in a Catherine wheel of untidy arms and legs, squealing with a Kriegsmarine 9 mm parabellum somewhere in his groin.

Rietz hoped Fischer could handle the mêlée on the well deck: roared hugely, 'GO – SCHNELL . . . !'

. . . and took off for the ladder himself.

*

He found himself ticking the deck levels off on a mental plan, recalling them from precise details von Strelow had produced of the *Java Star*'s superstructure . . . forr'ad well deck ladder to centrecastle deck, leaping over the writhing figure of the caterer: leading a clattering convoy of running feet now shaping course for the main starboard alleyway . . .

Heads leaning right out over the bridge dodger: staring down in horror. The British Master's voice roaring, quite unbelievably, 'Get off my BLOODY SHIP . . . !'

And then in under the shelter of the overhang. Smart green-painted deckheads and war-grey rails; clean-scrubbed wooden decks: a well husbanded ship.

'A good First Officer . . . McGregor, wasn't it? Should've been a passenger trade man,' Rietz considered as he whirled for the next ladder up towards the promenade deck. 'Or perhaps not. A bit hot-headed for passengers . . .'

Chief Sindermann's black gang parted company there, continuing to race aft towards the engineroom. Sindermann had taken personal charge of the Schmeisser . . . Rietz noted the Chief's eyes as the bearded lips parted in farewell, and hoped none of the duty watchkeepers caught down below would consider token resistance to Sindermann a matter of patriotic principle. He didn't want the blast from a bomb dropped on Cologne to spark a fury of cold-blooded execution in mid-Atlantic . . .

The promenade deck – '*Schnell, schnell, SCHNELL* . . . !'

Rietz blinked, faltered involuntarily as his eyes rose above deck level – a white-jacketed and pigtailed Chinese steward was running shrieking, mad-eyed towards him . . . *Chinese*, he thought numbly. A Liverpool *China*man? Jesus, the British use all sorts to fight their wa . . . ! Then he caught sight of the red fire bucket raised above the berserk Oriental's head, poised to smash down on his own, and fired in panic . . . yet the banshee *still* kept COMING!

Rietz fired again: twice. Desperately. He could SEE the bloody rounds hitting the white jacket: exploding crimson flowers against the snow . . . STILL the man kept coming! Rietz was far too late in attempting to duck as the heavy metal arced into its homicidal deployment . . .

174

The racketing yammer of a Schmeisser just behind and only slightly to starboard of him shocked Rietz's nervous system almost as much as the bucket. Expended brass cartridge cases tinkled and bounced down the ladder pursued by the bucket while the Chinaman's whole chest exploded, propelling him monstrously, bloodily, backwards. Rietz noticed absently that there was a bright yellow bow on the corpse's pigtail, and wondered if it held any significance . . .

'My compliments, Funkgefreiter,' he growled shakily.

Stemmler's grin showed sardonic through the gunsmoke.

'That's us square,' he said.

'*Sir*, Stemmler! This isn't the Wild West,' Rietz reminded him.

'SIR!' Stemmler bellowed.

Someone began firing a sub-machine pistol aft in urgent bursts from somewhere down on the main deck.

Rietz remembered the seven man crew and the Second Mate at the poop gun, just as the pandemonium clamour of emergency alarm bells detonated throughout the *Java Star*.

The Captain started running again.

They sub-divided yet again at the foot of the starboard bridge ladder: Stemmler and young Leinweber sprinting aft in the bright sunshine, breasting the shadows of swung-out and war-readied lifeboats etched black against the funnel deck casing; heading for the vital radio room at roughly midpoint.

Rietz suspected Stemmler wouldn't allow the *Java Star*'s operator the benefit of any doubt – if the British Sparks *was* already transmitting in panic, then every additional key stroke would be a stroke nearer to alerting Southampton to danger.

He was right . . . Funkgefreiter Stemmler was firing even as he kicked the door in!

Bootsmaat Landgraf was sweating, breathing heavily; the Schmeisser barrel wavering with every puff as he moved beside Rietz to ready himself for the last hurdle.

'If I'd needed this kind've exercise I'd'a joined the bloody Wehrmacht,' he growled.

'Too much beer,' Rietz grunted. 'Too many women, Bosun.'

He swung to stare up at the ominously silent bridge wing looming above them, hoping there would be no further need for killing. Merchantmen in these latitudes prepared themselves against sophisticated, remote-controlled destruction. Few were likely to carry small arms on their bridges: the days of storybook adventure were over. Pirates simply didn't swarm aboard from small boats in the middle of the Atlantic . . .

Then he remembered the Chinaman.

Rietz still launched himself up the steps two at a time.

But with a little more prudence.

The *Java Star*'s master met him as he breasted the rise.

The British Captain was standing facing him, unafraid, in the open wheelhouse doorway. In the same moment Rietz saw the diminutive apprentice's face, white with huge apprehensive eyes, through the starboard windows, and knew why the Captain wasn't resisting.

A Fourth Officer barely out of his teens – roughly the same age as Leutnant Becker had been befo . . . and a stony-faced Quartermaster stood warily, truculently, by the wheel; also obviously constrained by orders to surrender to the inevitable.

'Hold fire!' he called sharply to Landgraf.

'I came back because I believed you needed help,' the Captain said with contempt. 'In return, you exploit the cover of a neutral Flag to murder my crew in cold blood.'

'Correction – in the pursuit of war!' Rietz snapped. 'This isn't some damned British gentleman's game we're all playing.'

'My last ship was torpedoed in mid-winter, and without warning,' his enemy retorted icily. 'Thirty of my crew went down with her. Sixteen others froze to death on the rafts before the surviving few of us were picked up . . . I don't need any Nazi thug to lecture me on gamesmanship!'

Nazi thug . . . ? My God – he means ME! Rietz realized bitterly. Yet surely he understands that I, too, am a seaman? One of HIS kind . . . ? That I, too, am merely doing my duty . . . ?

He stiffened. 'In that case, you will be disinclined to jeopardize further lives to no avail. You will hand over the key to your confidential book safe, and order your crew to cooperate!'

'I'm *damned* if I will,' the Bulldog growled.

Rietz shrugged indifference.

'That's your choice.'

U-Bootwaffe Kapitänleutnant Paul Rietz knew then that his would be a bitter victory. It was a much more difficult thing to do than to simply fire a torpedo.

Pushing roughly into the wheelhouse, he seized the terrified apprentice while Landgraf's Schmeisser swung to cover the officer and quartermaster. Expressionlessly Rietz placed the muzzle of his Luger against the boy's temple.

'. . . but THIS young man,' he said in a voice alien even to himself in its brutality, 'will most assuredly be damned if you *don't*!'

Chapter Sixteen

As soon as Leo Fischer reported the decks secure and that his team were working their way through the accommodation, the British Master and his watchkeepers had been escorted with set faces from the bridge. It was a practical psychology.

Cut the head from the octopus, Rietz thought, and you command the tentacles.

He watched them go, feeling curiously drained of emotion. Only the capture of the merchantman's engineroom now remained to be confirmed. He wasn't overly concerned for the outcome. He didn't think Chief Sindermann's martial resolve likely to falter.

Enemy casualties had proved lighter than they might have been – five of the *Java Star*'s crew had died, including one of the gun crew from the poop deck who'd tried to rush Fischer's team, and her Radio Operator who had, according to a studiously laconic Stemmler, 'offered resistance'. Her Chief Officer, McGregor, was expected to die soon. Rietz was sorry about that: his had been an unprofitable gallantry. He suspected that the portly Chief Steward he himself had shot would also be unlikely to survive what was certain to prove an endurance test for the fittest in the Tommies' coming voyage.

On the whole, Matrosengefreiter Jakobi's smashed jaw did seem – other than to Matrosengefreiter Jakobi, of course – a modest price for the successful conclusion of Juggernaut's penultimate phase.

Rietz found a pair of British Barr and Stroud binoculars in

the bridge box. He was surprised at how clear things appeared without the salt bloom he'd come to accept as a part of his U-boat life. He still missed his faithful Zeiss, though. Just as he missed what shreds of self-respect the war had so far left him with. Prior to the moment when he'd seized the boy apprentice . . .

The Captain levelled the glasses to watch as Rohde's U-boat blew her way to the surface in a flurry of spray to wallow, no less black and menacing despite the sunshine, barely a pistol shot from the *Java Star*'s bridge.

Immediately she closed up for surface action. Even as the bridge team took station, her foredeck and anti-aircraft gun crews were clambering from the hatches and running to their posts. Smoothly, threateningly, her cannon began to swing: train on the captured merchantman's bridge where Rietz stood as soon as its layer slipped into his still-dripping metal seat and ground his cheekbone into the sponge cup of the gun sight.

Further forward, the loading hatch clanged open and men began to drag an inflatable raft on deck, ready it for launching over the saddle tanks. The specially wired detonators came next; carefully passed up from below . . . Rietz stirred: fighting the weariness which followed action. One of his more immediate tasks must be to check the *Java Star*'s stowage plan: hope to God von Strelow's Abwehr intelligence reports would prove correct about her carrying a part ammunition cargo. Being forced to undertake a ship-to-ship transfer of torpedoes sufficient to destroy the Tommy dock would be both laborious and time-consuming: expose them longer to risk of enemy counter-attack.

He swung the Barr and Strouds, anxiously scanning the seemingly empty sea beyond their consort. It wasn't impossible that they were already under somewhat bemused surveillance. Onkel Karl's boats weren't the only subsea predators operating in the Atlantic.

Landgraf came out of the wheelhouse and saluted, grinning.

'Chief's just telephoned up to report the engineroom secured, Cap'n. Sounds fit to spit nails – the Tommy black gang give 'im a bad experience when he stormed down there.'

'He met resistance?'

179

'Nossir – I meant they give up like lambs. Di'n't offer Chiefy a single excuse to shoot none of 'em.'

Rietz felt grateful for that. In the long run it would be better for Sindermann.

Then saw the demolition packages being transferred to the raft now gyrating in the surge of the U-boat's displacement, and shrugged inwardly. If Sindermann *has* much of a run left at all, he qualified dispassionately. In common with the rest of us!

'Post a lookout on the port wing. To cover the sector we're blanking from Oberleutnant Rohde's view . . . and, Landgraf?'

'SIR?'

'Before he boards his lifeboat – *give* their Fourth Mate his bloody WATCH back!'

He stayed on the starboard wing for a further minute after Landgraf had gone.

The Barr and Strouds afforded an intimate survey of the heads on the distant conning tower. For the first time there was no funnel smoke, no vagrant steam, no *Stralsund* eccentricities to interrupt his searching for aspects familiar.

In close up Rohde appeared as young, as handsome, as arrogantly cocksure as ever, leaning importantly over the spray-shield. Remarkably so, Rietz conceded – for a youth who'd just killed three precious men by his ineptitude.

He didn't recognize any other face, apart from one. And that only by the compressed slit of a mouth which showed below the U-Bootwaffe issue lenses which were, in turn, closely examining him.

He took great care to keep his own expression stony, uncommunicative, as he turned from the wing.

Rietz guessed he wouldn't have very much longer to wait anyway. To discover precisely *why* a Fregattenkapitän of B-Dienst should display such high risk interest in the capture of an ordinary Allied freighter?

He would have preferred to set them adrift in their own boats, but that was impossible. The *Java Star* had to appear as whole, as unremarkable as possible when challenged by the Southampton guardships.

'I regret that operational necessity requires you to take passage in such cramped accommodation, Captain,' Rietz said, feeling ridiculously disadvantaged. 'None the less, the *Stralsund*'s boats are seaworthy. They are also provisioned and watered enough to ensure your men, with prudent rationing, the means of survival for thirty days.'

'Do you *really* expect us to show gratitude?' the British Master said.

'Perhaps some small relief would be appropriate,' Rietz retorted bleakly. 'Had I been following my usual vocation and simply torpedoed you, Captain, you may well have found yourself without time to even launch boats.'

'Go to hell,' the Bulldog offered uncharitably.

Rietz smiled. It was a very dry smile. 'Your wish may well be granted sooner than you hope. In the meantime, I have provided each boat with a sextant, charts and a note of our present position – I suspect my advice on which course to set for land would not be well received.'

The older Captain hesitated. 'My Chief Officer has just died. If you possess any kind of honour you will ensure that he, and our other dead, are accorded a dignified sea burial.'

'If it is within my power, I shall, Captain,' Rietz nodded. He saw the boy apprentice watching him, still with great round apprehensive eyes that reminded him of his own when he, too, had been an innocent. For all his fear, the boy had never uttered a whimper under the threat of Rietz's gun.

'What's your name, *Jüngling*?'

'Thomas, sir,' the boy said. 'William Thomas.'

On an impulse Rietz pulled the Iron Cross from his own neck and handed it to the youngster.

'Take this, Wilhelm. Show it to your children when that day comes. Tell them you won it for your courage.'

His eyes rose involuntarily to the long black U-boat which courted them with such sinister attention. There was more activity on her bridge suddenly. A flurry of movement.

Rietz smiled at the boy reassuringly.

'. . . when you fought the Nazis,' he added.

*

It seemed a long climb, back up to the *Java Star*'s bridge. Funkgefreiter Stemmler was waiting for him.

Rietz directed a quick glance over the dodger to see the two boats pulling away, packed with men. Their faces stared silently, bitterly towards him. Rohde's inflatable carrying the infernal exploding machines was also beetle-legging its way across the intervening gap. He didn't have a lot of time to waste.

'Stemmler?'

'I can't find a copy of the British war call signs for merchant ships, sir,' Stemmler said. 'They must be with the sailing orders in the Master's safe. I ought to keep 'em handy in the radio room in case we get a route diversion signal or whatever.'

Rietz frowned. 'Don't they usually keep their own call sign prominently displayed in front of the operator?'

Stemmler looked bland. 'They do. But they aren't bullet-proof . . . I made a mess of this one.'

The Captain looked at him curiously: dispassionately.

'But it still made you feel good – using a machine-gun, Funkgefreiter? Seeing the whites of the enemy's eyes?'

'Isn't that why we all volunteered?' Stemmler shrugged awkwardly. 'Until now I've just been able to listen to the bastards, haven't I?'

'I didn't quite catch the last part, Stemmler,' the Captain grunted.

'Sir!'

'I'm going down to search the safe now,' Rietz said. 'I'll let you know if I find what you want.'

The Master's day room of the *Java Star* was roomy and full of light: a world apart from the *Stralsund*'s foetid, cluttered cell. Stepping over the coaming from the alleyway leading to the boat deck, Rietz could immediately see forward, through big square armoured windows and out past the foremast clear to the so-far empty horizon.

A framed photograph was jammed securely into the bookshelves. An attractive, dark-haired woman standing self-consciously behind two children – a boy and a little girl, both staring earnestly into the lens. Rietz felt a momentary regret that his enemy contemporary hadn't been permitted time to take it with him.

He knelt before the safe and opened it, ignoring for the moment the Naval Control books she carried on routing and communications; lists of codes and war lights and convoy signals and contingency instructions to merchant masters: a treasure trove of Allied secrets which would be passed over to Rohde's safekeeping before they went their separate ways, for eventual transfer back to Berlin.

Von Strelow will be professionally interested, he reflected absently. Or *would* he . . . ? Rietz had thought a lot about von Strelow – particularly since Schauroth had lost his head and Leutnant Becker had gurgled his life away through a severed windpipe – and had found it hard to avoid the conclusion that Fregattenkapitän von Strelow might just have been pursuing interests more pressing than intelligence gems from a captured British freighter.

He found what he wanted and moved to the desk to examine them. The cargo manifest was easily handled, but he had to unfold and spread the multi-coloured cargo stowage plan that Chief Officer McGregor had prepared so assiduously during the ship's loading, before the war caught up with him, too.

It covered the whole desk top. Every hold space, every stowage compartment neatly colour-coded in greaseproof pencil blocks with that particular cargo's destination – mostly Southampton, with coastal for Sunderland· before she discharged completel . . . !

He blinked. Checked against the pages of the cargo manifest, then sat back and chewed his lip thoughtfully.

Abwehr had been wrong about the ammunition. There was over two thousand *tons* of it! Five-hundred-pound aerial bombs; incendiaries; four-inch artillery shells; naval depth charges; ball and tracer rounds . . . all stowed, according to McGregor, in the upper tween decks of number one.

So it seemed that the Führer's vengeance would indeed be terrible: that they'd captured themselves an Aladdin's cave of potential destruction. Nearly three times the explosive power anticipated. Enough to blow a hole in the King George V dry dock as big as . . . Rietz smiled without a great deal of humour – as big as Southampton itself?

And coincidentally widening, even further, the area of blast those of his men who survived the initial ramming would need to clear within the all-too-few minutes of grace the time fuses would allow . . .

Time!

He rose and left the cabin, moving urgently to the meticulously sand and canvas scrubbed teak rail overlooking the foredeck. The U-boat's inflatable had already bumped alongside their vacated scrambling net: Fischer's deck party dropping stout lines, preparing to hoist the detonators aboard.

Rietz experienced a twinge of irritation. Considering the perilousness of their situation, Fischer himself appeared to be displaying a degree of *sang froid* remarkable even for Kapitän-leutnant Fischer. Instead of supervising the military activity he'd wandered to the forward area of the well deck where he was now laconically inspecting the doors to those compartments situated under the break of the *Java Star*'s fo'c'slehead.

'Kapitänleutnant FISCHER!'

Leo turned, showing the grace to look at least mildly startled, and waved acknowledgement.

'According to the plan, the ammo's in number one upper,' Rietz shouted. He noted the upturned faces and added his usual hint of iron. 'The gods on the side of the Third Reich are smiling on us for a bloody change, gentlemen. Not only have the Tommies given us full measure; they've been considerate enough to oblige us with easy access.'

'More to the point, old boy: are our particular gods smiling broadly enough to guarantee that easy access extending as far as Southampton *Water*?' Fischer called back to laughter from the men.

It's curious, Rietz reflected, watching the veteran Lieutenant-Commander walk unhurriedly back to take charge of his work party. They – I myself, come to that – draw such strength from Leo's imperturbability . . . so why did I never, during all those days of the *Stralsund*'s voyage to this meeting, feel inclined to mention von Strelow's suspected presence aboard Rohde's boat to him?

Or had that simply been Rietz's Paranoia?

He frowned, returning his attention for no particular reason other than that his Paranoia suggested he should, to the break of the fo'c'sle which had seemingly acted as the focus of Leo Fischer's interest. The compartments in there, entered by water-tight steel doors, held no particular significance, being mostly allocated to domestic stowage – access to the cable locker, for instance. Usually a paint and rope store; a bosun's store; often a lamptrimmer's cuddy.

And, traditionally – a . . . ?

'No,' Rietz muttered. 'No way. No possible *way* . . . ?'

But he still swung from the rail abruptly. And headed uneasily back to the Master's cabin.

He found what his Paranoia had told him to look for.

Quite clearly marked on the stowage plan spread before him, and further confirmed by the *Java Star*'s cargo manifest.

But that *had* only resulted from his Paranoia putting crazy arguments to his brain again. And this time his Paranoia's thesis simply couldn't hold up to practical scrutiny.

Admittedly it did suggest a not by any means original motive for killing two men in cold blood. Or half a dozen men, come to that. Murders most foul had been committed throughout history for very much less.

. . . it also – if one stretched one's credulity just a little further – suggested why a high-ranking Intelligence officer from Berlin might . . . just *might* have been given cause to ponder over a spy-net report on one particular British freighter with more than routine interest, out of a hundred Abwehr reports to pass before him daily. It might *even* explain why such an eccentric operation as Juggernaut, with its Trojan horses and Judas goats and ants and owls and wolves and – Go on, think it . . . and *sharks*? Rietz thought grimly – why IT had been conceived in the opportune wake of the British attack on St Nazaire . . . but tailored to suit not so much the Führer's demands for retaliation, as to . . . ?

Rietz's Paranoia ran out of steam then. From that point conjecture had to proceed through improbability into the realms of sheer fantasy. It simply wasn't possible to encompass the scale of skulduggery which would involve a FRONTBOOT – a whole fighting *U-boat* and fifty of a crew – just to . . . !

Not UNLESS . . . ?

He was still sitting behind the desk, frowning ferociously by then at the cargo plan, when Funkgefreiter Stemmler appeared at the cabin door. As soon as the Captain lifted his eyes he guessed Stemmler hadn't come for the codes.

'You killed Leutnant Becker and Schauroth, didn't you, Stemmler?' he confirmed calmly; a bit too bloody late as usual.

'Yes,' Stemmler said. Then grinned. 'Sir.'

Rietz wasn't surprised. Not any more. Even as a failed detective and jigsaw puzzler he'd been able to deduce *that* much.

The instant he'd noticed the Luger in Stemmler's hand.

Aimed very purposefully at his forehead.

Chapter Seventeen

Stemmler moved quickly across the cabin and placed the muzzle of the pistol hard against Rietz's cheekbone. 'Keep your hands just where they are,' he warned. 'On the desk!'

The Captain thought how brave the British apprentice, Thomas, had been. He hadn't cried out once when Rietz the Nazi Conqueror had done much the same thing to him. He'd earned his Cross of Iron.

Stemmler removed Rietz's pistol from its holster inside his reefer jacket and stepped back. Rietz pointedly eyed the two guns now in the rating's hands.

'I always said you were a cowboy, Stemmler.'

Stemmler grinned again. 'You always kept ordering me to call you "sir", as well. Now you can't.'

'Sir!' Rietz reminded him.

'*Sir*!' Stemmler barked automatically.

'Thank you,' Rietz said. 'How long *have* you been a traitor, by the way? Conspiring with Fregattenkapitän von Strelow?'

'You're on to him, then?' Stemmler shrugged. 'It's academic anyway as far as you're concerned, but after they called me up from the Merchant Marine I worked on his staff in Intelligence.'

'Until you were court martialled for theft of a comrade's gear and transferred into the U-Bootwaffe,' Rietz supplemented, irritated with himself. 'I held your service record, remember? I just never put two and two together regarding your previous posting . . . so now what, Stemmler?'

Stemmler shrugged again. 'So now I kill you.'

'Humour me on one account before you do – why did you help me to the rail before the *Stralsund* capsized? It offered you a perfect opportunity: no suspicion on yourself.'

'There won't be this time. This is an enemy ship. All it needs is one rogue Tommy still aboard who surprised the Kapitänleutnant: shot him with his own gun – and I'll be the one who swears I saw him run away to hide again. I'll be gone before they figure it.'

'A getaway aboard Oberleutnant Rohde's boat? Positively Machiavellian, Stemmler. Can't begin to imagine how you're planning to work it – but you haven't answered the question.'

'You weren't scheduled to die until after we took this ship. Only Leutnant Becker . . .' Stemmler looked blank. 'Anyway, you tend to be a survivor. I don't take chances.'

Rietz thought grimly about the dumdums, and agreed that Stemmler was definitely a belt and braces man.

'Still not good enough. You locked me in the engineer's store after the killings – *that* wasn't for the good of my bloody health!'

Rietz sensed there wouldn't be many more answers when Stemmler began to dart anxious glances at the open cabin door. The man was losing his nerve again. Yet Rietz needed to ask so many more questions.

'The Leutnant bled a lot,' Stemmler admitted finally, looking embarrassed. 'I had to gain time to clean myself up before going back to the radio room. I guess I panicked a bit.'

Just as you did at the rail – just as you're about to do again NOW! Rietz reflected bitterly. And I actually HELPED you get clear of the *Stralsund* – yet another bloody irony!

Though he was almost certain by then that it wasn't one spawned out of war this time. That the killings, the whole nightmare so far, had nothing to do with the war. Not if fantasy, and the *Java Star*'s cargo manifest, were correct.

'What about Kapitänleutnant Fischer, Stemmler?' he snapped urgently. It was the one thing he *had* to know. 'IS he a part of the plot? Or did you really try and kill him, too?'

But Stemmler just grunted, 'Oh, bugger THIS . . . !'

The Captain saw his Sound Man's finger curl, whiten as it took up first pressure on the trigger.

'You were right about *one* thing, Funkgefreiter,' he surrendered philosophically. 'I am a survivor.'

Then shot Stemmler cleanly. Through the head.

Rietz would have been the first to admit it hadn't been a particularly honourable thing to do. But then, Funkgefreiter Stemmler had always hated officers and supposed gentlemen anyway. It gave him the best reason of all now; to resent them even more.

Apart from removing the back of Stemmler's skull, the round had smashed a scorched, ragged hole through the cargo plan concealing the Captain's second weapon – the Luger he'd taken from young Becker's corpse. The one still loaded with Stemmler's own dumdum clip.

It was a pity: to damage the plan like that. It had been a really professional work of art. A tribute to a brave enemy.

But one had to learn from experience: take heed of one's previous weaknesses. Like trusting people. And what had happened so far – what was *about* to happen, he suspected, in those calm Atlantic waters – had simply gone to reinforce Rietz's view that people weren't reliable. Not like ships were.

So Rietz, too, had learned the hard way never to expose himself to the hazards of empty shipboard spaces.

Not without being prepared for visitors.

His next visitor was almost predictable: it was getting to be a habit. Leo Fischer came running again; clattering anxiously up the ladders from the main deck at the sound of the shot. It seemed Leo was *always* being triggered into action by the sound of a shot from Rietz.

A bit like an Olympic sprinter: I fire – he runs, Rietz thought humourlessly, still disappointed at being forced to execute Stemmler before Stemmler had fully explained how on earth he and von Strelow could have hoped to get away with what they'd planned.

And how, in particular, they'd persuaded Oberleutnant ROHDE to join them. Rohde was a fully programmed Nazi officer. The Führer commanded Rohde's only allegiance – Rietz had sailed with the youth for long enough; was fully convinced of that. So how the *hell* . . . ?

Kapitänleutnant Fischer went full astern in the doorway, and blurted, '*Christ!*'

Rietz was more prepared this time. He was watching Leo's expression very carefully. There *was* something more there than a simple reaction of horror. But still not enough to be sure.

'Stemmler killed Becker and Schauroth,' Rietz said. 'He probably tried to kill you, too. On our first night out?'

It appeared to be time for Fischer, too, to fall into the by-now standard format. In Leo's case, a curious apprehension? He'd just started to ask, 'Did he *say* anythi . . . ?' when Bootsmaat Landgraf arrived at the double steering his Schmeisser.

Landgraf ground to a halt, took one shocked look at the exploded brain tissue which contained Funkgefreiter Stemmler's remaining secrets, and grated, 'Who DID IT?'

But Stemmler and Landgraf had been shipmates and drinking partners on runs ashore for a long time . . . Rietz had to be careful there. He couldn't afford to overlook that fact.

He said bleakly, 'I can only ask you to believe me for the moment, Bosun – Stemmler was no friend to anyone on this operation's mess deck.'

He decided to resist the temptation to ask where the other elements of Juggernaut were . . . that really *would* have pushed post-mortem routine into the realms of the farcical. Instead he laid Becker's gun on the desk and appraised the seaward situation for himself, through the big armoured windows.

The *Stralsund*'s two British-manned boats – Surely the most bizarre Lend-lease arrangement of this war? Rietz brooded irrelevantly – had pulled away to some five cables, half a mile, off the *Java Star*'s port bow. Now their crews, with typical British Merchant Service phlegm, had begun to make what little sail they could muster, and settle in for a grim and lonely voyage.

But not as lonely as they imagined. The exigencies of Operation Juggernaut couldn't allow that: couldn't risk even the unlikely event of their being detected by an Allied vessel during the next few days, and thus giving the game away. So Oberleutnant Rohde carried Doenitz's orders to provide the *Stralsund*'s fragile boats with a Cyclopean shadow; track them constantly until sufficient passage time had elapsed to enable the *Java Star* to reach Southampton, and compromise became a superfluous concern.

And if they should be sighted, a move made to pick them up in the meantime before Rohde broke away to make for his next appointed, if somewhat improbable coastal rendezvous with those of Rietz's group who escaped the ramming?

Rietz the U-boat man caught sight of his own slightly wistful image reflected back from the window . . . well, *then* the Führer would be presented with a bonus on his retribution, and Rohde with another sitting duck – or perhaps, in this Noah's Ark Oddessy of intrigue, a Judas goat suggested a more appropriate expression? Either way, a second opportunity to get it right. To practise his marksmanship on a real enemy: a *Knochensammler*. On yet another Bone Collecto . . .

Rietz tensed suddenly as an unsettling thought struck him: swinging to search for the U-boat itself. That final task of Rohde's had been a part of the *original* Juggernaut plan – the strategy approved by Doenitz and Godt . . . whereas Rohde had been flown to Berlin since then for a further, secret briefing.

By Fregattenkapitän von Strelow!

Rietz was dimly aware of Fischer's low tones addressing Landgraf in the background, and Landgraf's still dazed replies. But by then he was more preoccupied in watching the long black silhouette of the U-boat.

Frowning.

She had unexpectedly begun to forge ahead; to leave her station close by the *Java Star*: her foredeck hands still hauling the recovered inflatable aboard, while the exhaust from her grumbling diesel motors rose to hang like a shroud astern of her before being caught and frayed by the rising wind.

Yet Rohde's orders specifically required him to stay in close company until released on Kapitänleutnant Rietz's authority as Mission Commander . . . ?

He began to call, 'Leo – do *you* know why Rohde's started to bloody well pull ou . . . !' when he felt a familiar sensation at the base of his skull.

'Don't move suddenly, Paul,' Fischer's voice carried quietly: dispassionately. 'Don't force me into executing summary justice.'

Rietz stayed very still. And went very cold.

Already intimately qualified to recognize the caress of a pistol barrel. And having completely run out of spare Lugers himself.

Eventually he turned. Very slowly.

'Justice?' he blinked. 'What the HELL are you talking about, Leo?'

'Being found once with a gun in your hand and two dead crewmen in an otherwise empty compartment may well have implied ill fortune,' Leo said bleakly. 'Being surprised twice in that situation, Paul, *must* be considered to exceed the bounds of coincidence.'

Rietz looked incredulously for support from Landgraf, still standing over Stemmler's body with an expression of tortured confusion on his leathery features. The Bosun was a simple, uncomplicated man and Rietz felt for him. He knew how this dilemma must have been tearing the old seaman's loyalties apart.

But Landgraf knew nothing of the circumstances other than the evidence before his eyes. The Navy had conditioned him to obey orders without question – and Landgraf had obviously been given an order. The Schmeisser was now trained, woodenly but nevertheless determinedly, on Rietz.

'You will remain under open arrest in these quarters, Paul,' Fischer growled, 'until we part company with Oberleutnant Rohde's task element and no further liaison with outside agencies is possible. On the conclusion of Juggernaut, assuming you survive, you will be returned to Germany for court martial.'

'Don't,' Rietz appealed earnestly, 'be *bloody* silly, Leo.'

But if Leo Fischer did feel silly, he wasn't betraying it. The veteran submariner had come ominously to attention. There was no insouciant twinkle in the grey eyes: no hint of previous camaraderie.

'Until then, as senior German officer present, and under the Military Powers invested in me by the Third Reich, I must formally charge you, Kapitänleutnant Paul Georg Rietz, presently on special detached duty from the Sixth Flotilla *Befehls-haber der Unterseeboote* . . .'

Yet Fischer KNEW . . . Fischer bloody well *knew* he wasn't guilty. That his, Rietz's, arrest was farcical: the likelihood of his return to Germany a mockery; a practical nonsense.

'. . . with the triple murders of Kriegsmarine Leutnant Rudi Becker; of U-Bootwaffe Maschinenobergefreiter Heinrich Schauroth – and of U-Bootwaffe Funkgefreiter Karl Stemmler. All of whom were serving under your command at the time of their deaths.'

Chapter Eighteen

—◆◉◆—

'I can't stay long,' Leo said. 'I'm only sorry to have had to do it, Paul.'

'No, you're not.'

Rietz stared grimly around the cabin that was now his delegated prison. Pantomime concentrated the mind wonderfully, it seemed. He'd even begun to acquire a somewhat belated facility for putting together jigsaw puzzles. Not exactly a triumph of deduction, admittedly: having been virtually force-fed with even the basic pieces.

'No more than you are for having ordered my own crew not to enter into conversation with me, Leo. Or having placed young Leinweber, who's thick as two short planks and would charge a bloody battleship if a Kapitänleutnant told him to, outside my door with further orders to shoot me if I even open it . . . ?'

Rietz shook his head bitterly. 'You parade the term justice – then perpetrate a particularly cynical travesty of it. Christ, man, YOU know Stemmler was the *Stralsund*'s killer as well as I do. *And* you lied to me about the reason for your being in the hold when the *Stralsund* sailed!'

Fischer hesitated. 'Just be damn glad you're still alive,' he said grimly.

Rietz glowered: it hardly seemed *that* much of an achievement under the circumstances.

'I offered much the same comfort to that British Master out there. Before I set him adrift in the middle of the Atlantic on a matchstick.'

194

'Which you used to do with commendable regularity and no more bloody sense of guilt than the rest of us when you were a U-boat commander. So where's the difference?' Leo turned abruptly for the door. 'This is getting us nowhere, and I have to go. Landgraf's placing the fuses on his own; it's a tricky job even for an ex-torpedoman.'

But even Rietz had worked it out by then. He knew Leo wouldn't be back. That Leo Fischer was never going to come back.

He indicated the spread of the cargo plan: playing his last desperate card from a still largely incomplete pack.

'As tricky as blowing, say . . . a strongroom door, Leo?'

Fischer froze with his hand on the handle.

'It's all there on the desk, isn't it?' Rietz pressed tightly. 'The reason why you've used – or should I say *ab*used – the system, with the express purpose of effectively isolating me?'

'The system?'

'The German sailor never questions an order from a superior officer: we both know that. Landgraf's a classic example – oh, he'll suck a tooth or give a wooden look, but he'll still carry it out to the letter. Whereas you've gone one better, haven't you? You've given an order made so plausible by the apparent evidence that even my own men consider it justified.'

Leo turned slowly to face him. 'Look, this all seems a bit melodramatic to me. Damned if I can see what you're getting at, laddie.'

'I'm *getting* at your having capitalized on events to keep me out of the way during the next critical phase,' Rietz growled. 'Before Rohde's boat does finally part company . . . but with Kapitänleutnant Leo FISCHER aboard. As he's always intended to be!'

Fischer's challenge came hard. Whiplash hard.

'You claimed *reasons* why, I believe?'

Rietz grabbed the stowage plan with the ragged hole in it and waved it furiously, even childishly.

'All right – you want a *reason*? Then I'll GIVE you a bloody reason . . . ! How about an item of cargo which DOESN'T have anything to do with military objectives, Leo? The one that's in the forr'ad strongroom according to the manifest, and which a certain Fregattenkapitän von bloody Strelow KNEW would be aboard this ship even *before* the St-Nazaire raid?'

For a long moment Leo Fischer eyed him speculatively. Then relaxed; grinned a resigned surrender as if relieved that the need for subterfuge was over.

'Shit,' he conceded wryly. Ever so much more like the old Leo.

'The one consigned from the United States Government to replenish the coffers of the British War Treasury, Leo?' Rietz completed, breathing heavily. '. . . the one and a half metric tonnes of GOLD?'

'We *are* talking about piracy, aren't we? A private venture?' Rietz gloomed once his pulse rate had subsided to ordinary furious. 'I mean, you're not going to claim this is an act of war, or anything mundane like that?'

'No. I would modestly argue it's anything but mundane,' Leo confirmed, producing a cigarette absently.

Rietz said, 'I'll have one too,' and accepted a light.

'You don't smoke,' Fischer pointed out reasonably.

'YES I bloody do,' Rietz snapped. 'As from now!'

Rietz inhaled deeply, disregarding the acrid bite at the back of his throat. He didn't bother walking to the window to update himself on what was happening outwith his local nightmare. It seemed such operational trivialities didn't much matter any more.

'Von Strelow *is* behind this, of course?'

Leo raised an eyebrow.

'You've seen him then? Was he playing sailors, feeling the wind on his face?' Fischer grinned humourlessly. 'He's an arrogant bastard. Been Fregattenkapitän and Party privileged too long. I warned him you were a hawk: to keep his head down.'

'But he conceived it? Presumably he'd been looking for a way to exploit Abwehr's reports on routine Allied gold shipments for some time? Eventually he got lucky with this one. The Tommy raid on Nazaire gave him the perfect excuse to propose retaliation to the Führer under the guise of capturing a Trojan horse.'

196

'More an eleventh-hour decision, I gathered. Von Strelow's nothing if not an opportunist. Most of the middle echelon Nazis are,' Leo shrugged. 'Mongrel cunning: he saw his chance and took it.'

. . . which explains why the Fregattenkapitän was so vague in his planning, yet so precise in the detail, Rietz thought bitterly. Didn't quite have time to figure out how the capture could be effected. Which was where we of the U-Bootwaffe came in, namely Leo and I as two of Doenitz's bloody ants – only it now seems that *one* of us aspired to join the Owl!

'Why did he do it? He had a future. Hitler's patronage. Captains of desks in the *Tirpitz Ufer*, particularly those with Party connections, have never been noted for going short of luxuries.'

'He considers the war already lost,' Fischer said harshly. 'He's a rat leaving a sinking ship before it actually hits the iceberg. He's a realist without loyalties, Paul: anticipating a future where German officers will become criminals by definition anyway.'

Rietz stepped back as though Fischer had struck him. 'Not POSSIBLE! The Führer has decreed it: the Third Reich will last a thousand years . . .'

'Jesus, you're naïve,' Leo growled. 'The Führer's a MAD-MAN, laddie. Only tunnel-visioned patriots like you, or Nazi-programmed fanatics like Rohde, can't see it . . . whereas von Strelow's an Intelligence expert: the man's a turd, but by GOD he's trained to read the writing on the wall – knows this war will be won or lost at sea, and that we can all forget the *Tirpitz* and the *Scharnhorst*. Hitler's surface fleet's a joke: it's we of the U-Bootwaffe alone who've sapped the Allied strength so far, and at what hellish cost? Kretchmer, Gunther Prien, Schepke, Lemp – they've gone. Frontboot losses are catastrophic: three boats failed to return to base in the week the *Stralsund* sailed . . . the tide's turned against us, Paul. Even *you* sense that Doenitz is losing the Atlantic battle for ALL your stubborn bloody idealism.'

Rietz rounded on the veteran, shocked to the core by his defeatism. But they'd been friends for all Fischer's new treachery. He HAD to know the answer.

'But you're no rat leaving a sinking ship. It still doesn't explain why someone like *you*, Leo, previously a gallant officer and gentleman, should sink to conspiring with scum to commit piracy . . . and cold-blooded MURDER, dammit?'

Fischer glared back: eyes steel-bleak, narrowed with hurt.

'NEGATIVE, laddie – *not* murder! Not of my own kind, and outwith even the barbaric excesses of war. Stemmler either acted on his own psychopathic initiative, or on von Strelow's orders. I sincerely believed the Funkgefreiter was aboard for one reason and one reason only – because he was a *radio* man! It was all a part of von Strelow's distorted genius. He'd provided Stemmler with the Juggernaut codes. Why do you think no signals were ever passed to you querying our mutual disappearance, eh?'

Rietz blinked. Of course! – *Stemmler* had been his only link with Doenitz's Headquarters. Which, by definition, had placed Stemmler in the unique position of being able to weed all incoming signals: decrypt and withhold those which would have raised questions, clamoured for answers even from a detective as dense as he . . . !

'Stemmler killed Leutnant Becker without your prior knowledge?'

'You have my word, Paul. If you still give it any credence.'

'Why?'

'My guess is that Stemmler was instructed to make damn certain neither you nor young Becker, as the mission officers, could object to the transfer of the gold when the time came. Your unfortunate Maschinenobergefreiter Schauroth probably surprised him in the act, and took a dumdum for his pains.'

Leo's eyes failed to conceal his contempt for those he'd become involved with. And almost certainly his belated regrets.

'It was an unnecessary cruelty. A needless overkill. *My* part in this was to neutralize your authority while we blew the strongroom doors: keep you and Becker from making awkward protests – only, I hasten to add, by virtue of my rank and incontestably superior capacity for dirty tricks – until the transfer took place . . .'

Leo braced abruptly. 'Which, by the way, it still must do, for all our frank digression, Paul. Time is pressing; the charming von Strelow will be tapping an impatient foot, and we're all at risk as we sit quiet in the water. The quicker I conclude my distasteful business of criminality and take apprehensive passage with Oberleutnant Rohde, the quicker you can continue with your Odyssey of self-sacrifice for the Fatherland . . .'

The veteran's mouth twitched at the surprise on Rietz's face. 'Don't worry: by the powers invested in me by the Third Reich,' Fischer looked sardonic, 'my last official act as Senior German Officer will be to lift the mark of Cain from your innocent head before I go. All an embarrassing mistake. Your crew will believe me because they want to believe me. They don't like what's happened, Paul: they're good Germans. Chief Sindermann needs you to help him kill Tommies, while Landgraf's sick as a parrot . . . he'll be delighted to have you back to kick him around again.'

Rietz stared after him. There were still so many questions . . . one and a half tons of gold, for a start! How the hell did von Strelow expect to get away with it? Where was he intending to *head* for in a world consuming itself in the flames of war . . . ? But that still didn't explain how in *God's* name he'd succeeded in persuading the Führer-child Rohde to become an accomplice – even more incredibly, to recruit Rohde's entire CREW . . . ?

Nor, more importantly for Paul Rietz, why Leo FISCHER had ever joined forces with animals like Stemmler and von Strelow in the first place . . . ?

'He'll kill you, of course,' Rietz called urgently. 'Once you cease to be of further value to him. The measure of von Strelow's loyalty is the sightless eyes of another fellow German officer, Leo. Already drifting accusingly in the company of a simple man in the engineer's store of the *Stralsund*.'

'Then I'll be no worse off.' Fischer smiled faintly. 'I burned my boats the moment I faked my own kidnapping. Were I ever to be returned to Germany, Konteradmiral Godt will personally hang me from a meat hook if Doenitz doesn't claim the pleasure for himself. And quite rightly so.'

'You can still come to Southampton, Leo,' Rietz said quietly. 'Redeem your honour . . . ? Even if you do survive the final adventure – which, as we now appear to carry two thousand tons of ammo forr'ad, by the way, is becoming increasingly unlikely – you'll only get as far as a Tommy prison camp.'

'Where my U-Bootwaffe POW peers will court martial me – and THEN hang me from a meat hook!' Leo snorted derisively. 'You asked for reasons, Paul. Well, here's the why and wherefore of the fall of Leo Fischer ... I fought one bitter war for the Kaiser while you were still a child: and then loyally served my so-called Fatherland through a dishonourable peace, rebuilding the Navy, preparing for the day when Germany could lift her head again – and to show her gratitude, she's turned me into a bloody office boy: a planning vegetable! Because I was injudicious in my criticism of Hitler when he came to power, of all his filthy retinue of sycophants, they took me out of the boats I loved and passed me over for promotion. I owe the Third Reich NOTHING, laddie – she's wrung me dry and damn well thrown me on the scrap heap!'

Rietz gazed at his friend silently. He wanted to show how much he felt for him: understood his pain, but he didn't dare. Time was too pressing, and too many questions still remained unanswered.

'But the Führer hasn't thrown *Rohde* on the scrap heap, has he? That's the part I really can't understand. Rohde simply hasn't *got* a mind capable of encompassing treachery. The boy's an utterly dedicated disciple of the Party, Leo. Adolf Hitler, for all your contempt for him, has given Oberleutnant Rohde a sense of direction: a pride of country, a big shiny U-boat, and *carte blanche* to hunt the seas and slay dragons for Germany ...'

He broke off uncertainly. Now LEO was frowning. Looking somewhat taken aback.

'But Rohde isn't IN on this, dear boy. I'm surprised you ever thought he was ... ? Lord, no – Rohde knows absolutely nothing of von Strelow's intentions. Oberleutnant Rohde, as you so correctly pointed out, wouldn't know his arse from his elbow, metaphorically speaking. Not unless it had a swastika stamped on it.'

Rietz felt his jaw drop vacantly. Dammit, the gold had to be spirited away somewhere. Therefore Rohde HAD to be an accomplice, a traitor too. This was the middle of the Atlantic Ocean. There was no *way* . . . ?

He heard his Paranoia launch into peals of mocking laughter. If Leo was deliberately holding back on that most crucial issue – then had *everything* Fischer claimed been nothing more than a cynical manipulation of the pieces of the jigsaw? Did Leo hold him in such contempt that he took him for THAT much of a fool . . . ?

But he had to hear it plainly. Unambiguously. Even at the expense of being forced to resort to sarcasm.

'I see. So Rohde is merely carrying out orders as does any other U-Bootwaffe officer? You are actually telling *me* that the Führer – supported by Admirals Doenitz, Godt, and the whole bloody infrastructure of our *Operationsabteilung* – has *personally* authorized von Strelow to use the Kriegsmarine in pursuit of a criminal activity on his own behalf? To employ one of his desperately needed front-line U-boats as . . . as a PIRATE SHIP . . . ?'

Leo grinned ever so broadly at that. More like the old Leo than ever.

'In a nutshell, old boy . . . ? Yes!'

'*Christ*!' Rietz muttered.

Knowing in his heart that Fischer wasn't lying.

As it happened, there wasn't any more time to listen to his Paranoia, which immediately panicked into voicing a whole new range of sinister fantasies. Or even to tell it to bloody well shut UP!

Because that was the moment when both men detected the unmistakable echo of distant gunfire rolling across the sea towards the waiting *Java Star*.

Kapitänleutnants Rietz and Fischer hit the door at the same time; exploding into the alleyway and running for the bridge.

. . . and the HELL with Matrosengefreiter Leinweber's sub-machine-gun!

Chapter Nineteen

—◆●◆—

'What in God's name is he doing out there?' Fischer muttered blankly.

'I thought you *knew* Rohde was moving: getting under way,' Rietz snarled, lunging for the Barr and Strouds in the binocular box. 'Christ, it's YOUR robbery. *I'm* only the Mission Commander . . .'

But that was the Iron Rietz responding; the Ordinary Rietz was fighting a revulsion already burning acid in his gut. As soon as he'd heard the measured, staccato bursts of gunfire he'd guessed what they implied. The earlier and only vaguely registered preparations taking place on Rohde's bridge had instantly assumed a horrifying significance in retrospect; the very stuff of nightmares.

He'd rejected his Paranoia's unease at that time: paid little attention, too preoccupied with salving his conscience by giving the British apprentice, Thomas, a medal. To prove to the kid he'd been wrong about Nazis.

Only it now seemed – he hadn't!

The blue haze of expended cordite from heavy calibre machine-guns mingled richly with the diesel grey of the slowly cruising U-boat's exhausts. The whole acting as a filter to the rays of the evening sun: imparting to the lenses of the Barr and Strouds a soft, rather pretty – almost surrealist – quality as the Captain's finger coaxed them tensely into focus.

These really *are* excellent optics, Rietz thought numbly. Eight magnifications. Night-coated. Capable of turning matchstick enemy seamen over half a nautical mile distant into perfectly recognizable . . .

'Oh my GOD!' Leo Fischer the New Buccaneer, the Senior German Officer present, concluded ashen-faced beside him.

. . . into perfectly recognizable, exquisitely detailed, macabrely jerking, hideously disintegrating PUPPETS!

Rietz could have said many things to Fischer then. Terrible things. Unforgiving, whiplash-savage, utterly vitriolic things.

But he spared one glance at the eyes of the man who stood by his shoulder, so haunted yet so determinedly erect in his misery – so damnably *tortured* . . . and voiced none of them.

The *Stralsund*'s lifeboats, her last tangible legacy, had faded from sight by then, sunk to the level of the sea and awash; planking riddled, buoyancy tanks perforated; their very description a mockery. Now only a single mast fouled by a shroud of canvas sail still projected to point shocked and woeful accusation at the arrogant sea pariah which slid slowly between them.

While all around the warship drifted aimless hummocks in the sea. Swirling, revolving, eight-times-magnified dead men in kapok-exploded affront: bobbing in grotesque convoy, giving eventual cause for the shrieks of half a hundred widows, and the sobs of children barely fathered.

And the tears of at least one mother.

Among the conquered enemy, nosing them callously aside, the U-boat still trailed its growling haze. Crewmen were spaced, legs astraddle, along its rapier length. Each man now held a sub-machine-gun; the heavy work was done. Von Strelow's angular form appeared to be missing from the tower, but perhaps such front-line intimacy was not to his taste. No, it was Rohde's moment. A time for the Oberleutnant with the White Cap of pride to be expansive, to invite his heroes to take the sea air: to celebrate victory, Rohde-style.

Through the apertures of the Barr and Strouds, Rietz watched expressionlessly as sometimes a hummock moved in dazed supplication before jerking, cavorting strangely, bobbing even more frantically in soundless mime. Such bizarre visual warning made

Rietz better prepared than his fellows to anticipate the time-delayed gunshot carrying eventually to the *Java Star*.

Invariably a single shot. It seemed there was little sport to be gained from a whole nine-millimetre burst . . . and they were also killing time.

The Herr Oberleutnant striking his first devastating blow for Germany in the Battle of the Atlantic, according to his lights? Rietz reflected grimly, long past feeling. While waiting for Kapitänleutnant Fischer. To blow a strongroom!

But Kapitänleutnant Fischer wasn't in the mood for buccaneering right then. The anger, the savage contempt, burned in steel-grey eyes which never flinched from the scene ahead. Rietz didn't offer him the glasses. Leo Fischer's nightmares would be graphic enough without his, Rietz's, help.

With measured care the Captain replaced them in the bridge box, not wishing to jar the seating of the lenses. He was glad he hadn't recognized those sporting shipmates of Rohde's, notwithstanding that some might well have sailed with him; faced crushing death shoulder to shoulder in that very same killing tube.

All said and done – so had Funkgefreiter Stemmler.

The horsemen had clustered silently, uncertainly at the port side break of the fo'c'sle when the firing had begun. Even Landgraf had abandoned his delicate work among the ammunition stowages; clambered urgently from the forehold to join the ratings in shocked contemplation.

Rietz sensed the anger about the ship, their common revulsion, and felt damnably grateful for that.

'Get back to your duties!' he still roared harshly, for his part was that of grim-jawed Captain, and murder and massacre and piracy couldn't be permitted to interfere a moment longer with the war task of their prize. 'I'll want names, Bootsmaat Landgraf – the name of any lookout not attending to his sector in one minute from NOW!'

Landgraf swung, startled, and immediately the leathery glare of his fury at Rohde softened, changed to satisfaction when he saw Rietz back in his element. He still hesitated though, quite properly, and looked to Fischer.

Rietz cocked a sideways look as well.

'Time to bite the bullet, Leo? Understand me clearly. For as long as I live, I'll somehow contrive to see von Strelow and Rohde – every last man aboard that obscenity which claims to be a warship – taken back to Germany to face trial for murder. Doenitz will be the first to convene a summary court. You, for your part, will never see one ounce of British gold. So, if you *do* propose to order my crew to shoot me . . . ?'

Fischer stirred, dragged his gaze finally from the slaughter pool on the bow.

'DON'T be bloody silly,' he retorted for all his emptiness. Then leaned over the front himself. 'You heard the Kapitänleutnant, boys? Then bloody well go TO it!'

Matrosengefreiter Leinweber appeared at the top of the ladder porting his Schmeisser uncertainly.

'And put *that* away, laddie,' Leo growled spiritedly. 'We've seen quite enough of those . . . Can you steer a ship? Stand a trick at the helm?'

'Yessir,' Leinweber jumped smartly to attention. Utterly relieved.

'Then stand to the wheel.'

He turned to Rietz. 'Go *on*, then, Ulysses. You've got your Trojan horse and the pirates are carousing and off guard. Sail her against England while you've got the chance.'

'What about you?' the Captain asked softly.

'I told you. I burned my boats when I turned my back on Germany; sold my allegiance to a monster and his fool. But, by GOD, the one thing I *do* still have choice in – is the manner of my dying.'

The veteran smiled faintly. Wistfully.

'. . . and Southampton really *will* be the adventure to end all adventures, won't it, old boy? One hell of a way for a chap to go.'

'Slow ahead starboard . . . St'b'd the wheel.'

The *Java Star* trembled, began to swing, present her stern to the distant haze. Rietz looked aft and saw his old command coming under the shadow of a Red Ensign fluttering above the deserted poop gun, and thought what a *crazy* situation they were in.

'Midships. Ring straight through for full ahead both, Kapitän-leutnant Fischer.'

He crossed to the engineroom telephone. Sindermann could prove a problem: he'd need all of Sindermann's hate to press home his final attack, and Sindermann could hardly be expected to understand why they should be deserting Rohde.

Sindermann's flat voice answered immediately.

'I'm going to need all the turns you can give me, Chief,' the Captain called.

'We're off at last, then?'

There *was* a truculence there, clear in Sindermann's tone.

'Affirmative,' he hesitated. 'By the way, we're in dispute with our support element. Could be we'll have some very angry U-Bootwaffe men on our tail. Don't ask why.'

'I saw! Part of the Opord we weren't briefed on?'

So *that* was what was wrong with Sindermann.

'If you want to make a comment, Chief: bloody well make it.'

'You called 'em U-Bootwaffe, Kapitän. Most of us would resent that. They're filth back there.'

Rietz found himself frowning at the phone. Sindermann had lost everything to the British. Sindermann had smiled his bearded death's-head smile every time an Allied freighter went to the bottom: had watched a tanker burn, and positively hungered for the smell of Tommy pork.

'The Oberleutnant destroyed the enemy, Sindermann,' the Devil's advocate in him snapped in automatic defence of a fellow officer, simply because the system demanded he should. 'Isn't that what we're all trying to do?'

'If we have to do it Rohde's way, then . . .' The Chief's voice faded: came back fiercely, defiantly. 'Then God forgive me, Kapitän, but I'm glad my kids'll never have to live in the new Germany!'

So it seems you WERE alone, at least on this messdeck, after all, Stemmler? the Captain thought. Even Sindermann feels SOME compassion. Still knows the difference between an act of war, however savage, and a brutal atrocit . . . !

Rietz didn't get any further with his deliberations on the goodness and the evil in men.

For that was the moment when the wheelhouse *windows* suddenly blew in on him again.

. . . f'r the SECOND bloody time that day!

Leutnant Becker was screaming a terrible chilling scream, while Maschinenobergefreiter Schauroth had suddenly begun to shout.

Which really is *very* odd: his being able to scream like that, Rietz considered solemnly, seeing how Becker's windpipe is severed clean as an assassin's conscience . . . on top of which, Maschinenobergefreiter Schauroth can't *possibly* go around shouting when – thanks to von Strelow's treachery and Stemmler's psychopathic avarice and Ober-bloody-leutnant Rohde's still God-knows WHAT motive for becoming a pirate – Schauroth hasn't got a face to even *smile* with! And anyway, they're both keeping watch in slime two thousand fathoms deep by now, along with Lookout Schadt who even takes his mother to sea: all three of them, and another two of my Trojan horsemen who now, if my memory serves me right, live in the *Stralsund*'s funnel – all *five* of 'em down there and no doubt looking forward to the company of another three-score hummocks sinking down and down, and ever so slowly down, with hair splayed like jellyfish tendrils and bubbles drifting from vacant mouths and eyes staring blankly, reproachfully about them at this very minute.

There'll be a language problem, of course.

And a bit of explaining to do . . . especially to the hummocks.

But Rudi Becker can always translate f'r a start. He's damn proficient in English, Leutnant Becker. Which is a bit of a liberty, considering he can't even sing '*Deutschland Über Alles*'.

. . . mind you, the hummocks can always pick up a bit of German. After all, they *have* got till the end of Time itself.

Haven't they?

. . . Matrosengefreiter Leinweber was actually the one who was screaming. And Fischer and Landgraf doing the shouting.

Why had Landgraf come to the bridge without permission?

Bootsmaat Landgraf never acted without orders, and Landgraf had his own task down in number one, setting fuses.

Rietz opened his eyes and noticed Leinweber's hand. And then shifted his frown to the *Java Star*'s wheel grating maybe three metres away – and saw Leinweber's other hand!

The one still attached to Leinweber.

The Captain tried to move, and the tinkle of glass shards played an ominously familiar accompaniment.

'. . . first bloody round clipped the WING!' Leo was bellowing, beside himself with rage.

'Eh?' Rietz muttered.

He was splashed with blood, but most of his bits seemed to have remained in place, and a lot of the blood appeared to be Leinweber's. Landgraf was shouting at the wounded seaman to stop bloody WRIGGLING while 'e gotter tourniquet secured PROPER . . . !

'Jesus,' Rietz thought as consciousness flooded back. 'Some-one's shooting at *us* now. Heavy stuff. Primary armament stuff. Luck of the Devil – first damn ROUND must've clipped our port wing.'

'That's what *I* just SAID,' Fischer snarled. 'Rohde's opened fire on us, laddie. He's half a mile astern and giving chase . . .'

Rietz was already dragging to his feet, carelessly shedding glass, stumbling on an already stumbled course through shattered eyeless doors, slumping to support himself over the after rail of the shrapnel-scarred bridgedeck.

The U-boat was following precisely down the straight white lane of their boiling wake. He found himself weighing her professionally: for him a wholly original victim's eye view present-ing, incidentally, a much smaller target than previously imagined. Just a vertical stick of tower above the wider rounded turn of her saddle tanks. Too far astern still to make out, without glasses, the crew manning her foredeck cannon . . .

But that was a premature detachment; a brief stirring of Rietz's periscope syndrome, the Captain's natural affinity for the trade of widow-making. He was still addled, still thinking in far too simplistic terms to cope with the convoluted progress of Operation Juggernaut.

'Rhode can't. He wouldn't dare!' he heard his shocked denial. 'God dammit, Leo: you an' I – we both *outrank* him!'

It sounded ridiculous. Even to Rietz.

Which made it all the more curious when Leo Fischer just shrugged an equally ludicrous qualification. 'Then bear in mind that von Strelow outranks us all – a Staff Fregattenkapitän with nothing to lose.'

A second shell ripped the sky between themselves and the racing U-boat, exploding close alongside and drenching the bridge with spray.

'I *was* being unintentionally facetious,' Rietz growled peevishly. 'I wasn't really proposing all this could be resolved by simple reference to the Navy List and a discussion on the powers of military bloody command.'

'Take it from me, laddie – it's *all* about that!' Leo shook seawater from his hair. 'Rohde is carrying out his orders just as earnestly, just as damn stubbornly, as YOU are!'

'That's crazy,' Rietz muttered. 'My orders came from the Führer: from Karl Doenitz and Godt – YOU know that. Target, Southampton Water at whatever the cost . . . Operation *Juggernaut*, Leo – NOT Operation Self-destruct!'

'Christ, you're so gullible; so bloody artless. ROHDE'S orders come from Adolf Hitler *too* . . . ! Can't you see it YET, laddie – that Oberleutnant Rohde is acting under the same authority YOU did when you sailed with the *Stralsund*? That he's doing what he believes is his duty for Germany under precisely the same terms of reference that *you* were given . . . ? Which – at this moment – is to hunt us down and pound us into a burning wreck: stop us dead in the water? For the greater glory of the Third bloody REICH!'

Rietz stared at Fischer incredulously. Had the last explosion driven him into total insanity? Completely scrambled his brains?

Had Leo, in fact, become a casualty of war?

'At least, he will unless . . .'

Fischer paused, looking more bleak than ever and not at all like a case of battle fatigue.

Rietz became conscious of the rail vibrating under his hands, runnels of blood from his reopened shoulder wound shimmering

209

and waltzing with each other along its length, agitated by the excitement of the chase . . . he looked quickly away, knowing he *had* to concentrate.

Appraise the situation, Rietz: switch into periscope mode, dammit!' he thought wryly. Rather more practical than passing out . . . A U-boat *could* overtake them eventually, running on the surface throughout the night. He, better than any of them, knew that Rohde did command the sophisticated means to ultimately bring the *Java Star*, any hapless freighter, to heel.

The Captain's enforced dispassion began to falter: deviate.

. . . and thus allow Rohde to board, and expropriate the gold at leisure?

And then hand it to von *Strelow*?

All, it seemed, by order of the FÜHRER . . . ?

'Unless – *what*?' he ground, suddenly recalling Leo's challenging pause. Still not understanding how such a question could even have come to pass. Already anticipating the answer.

Fischer's hard gaze dropped very deliberately to the unmanned British gun on the *Java Star*'s poop.

'No way,' Rietz snarled. 'There's no WAY, Leo, that I'm going to fire on a U-BOAT!'

Chapter Twenty

———◦———

Rohde's third round detonated against the after end of the centrecastle and the *Java Star* shuddered in agony. But she was a big ship, and could bear such pain for long enough presenting, as she did, little area of hull to hole.

But she would succumb eventually to the process of high explosive attrition. And Rohde would keep it up remorselessly: all through the night if necessary. Rohde enjoyed killing ships. He'd stay up late, just to kill a ship and win a medal. He'd never be as good at it as Rietz was, but he didn't need to be. Not against a running freighter.

You didn't have to be a marksman to work in a slaughter house.

'I rather think,' Leo said, 'the time has come for another story, young Rietz . . .'

'Once there was an industrious Ant,' Leo began, 'who had great, if somewhat misplaced, respect for the Wise Old Owl: a bird who – history might just conclude – may not have been quite as wise and omnipotent as the Ant fervently believed . . .'

Kapitänleutnant Fischer lit an unhurried cigarette then blew a most elegant smoke ring, piercing it before it was destroyed forever by the wind of their headlong retiral.

All very reminiscent of a previous discussion in a wooden shed in St-Nazaire, Rietz gloomed resignedly. Leo had been equally obscure and irritating then.

'Now it so happened that the Ant commanded an Ant submarine. And sank a lot of ships because the ships were sailed by Bulldogs who had earned the displeasure of the Wise Old Owl.'

'Oh, bloody well get ON with it!' Rietz growled waiting tightly, apprehensively, for Rohde's next shot.

'. . . until one day the submariner Ant was sent for by an Admiral Ant, and told that *he* had been selected to perform a very important task for the Wise Old Owl – to blow up both himself *and* one of the biggest kennels the Bulldogs happened to own . . .'

Leo cocked an eyebrow then, and squinted at Rietz.

'. . . and THAT, dear boy, was where a middle-ranking Ant, a Fregattenkapitän Ant, came into the story. To brief the submariner Ant on just how to go about making – ah . . . dare I say *monkeys* out of the Bulldogs? And he did indeed describe a clever ploy. Like pretending to be one of their horses.'

Rietz saw the puff from the black U-boat astern and tensed; fought to stay in control. When the waterspout rose close along-side, the Captain felt his concentration span for small talk rapidly diminishing. 'Fish in a barrel,' Sindermann had once said. 'Like shooting fish in a bloody barrel . . .'

'The interesting thing about the middle-ranking Ant,' Leo continued, but with a definite snap to his tone, 'was that he had a *personal* directive from the Wise Old Owl that placed him, too, one stage above God – and everybody, even the Admiral Ant, jumped to do his bidding. Didn't protest, even knowing a lot of very small Ants would die . . . Didn't even bloody *question* the authority he carried. And why not . . . ? Because they all, each and every one of them, had their ORDERS!'

Rietz swung. 'Are you telling me von Strelow DIDN'T carry the Führer's authority to give those orders?'

'Don't be silly,' Fischer said mildly. 'We all know he did. The Führer's letter commissioning von Strelow as his coordinator was perfectly genuine. Come on, old boy – they gave you the *Stralsund*, didn't they? A U-boat? All the facilities you de-manded?'

'So?'

'So what were your orders. What was *your* target, Paul?'

'You were at the briefing. You know bloody WELL what my ord . . . !'

Rietz stopped there. Abruptly.

'Say you'd been an even smaller Ant, Paul?' Leo asked softly. 'Say you'd been a newly promoted *Oberleutnant* Ant? And a senior ranking Fregattenkapitän Ant – even more impressively, a fully fledged Party member Ant – recalled you importantly to Naval Headquarters in the *Tirpitz Ufer*. Showed you his authority signed by Adolf Hitler; bearing Hitler's seal . . . and then briefed you personally. Detailed your own Most Secret Annexe to the operational plan being prepared for the Führer's approval?'

'You mean . . . ?'

'Exactly!' Fischer's eyes were hard as flint. 'A change to the Opord which neither Doenitz nor yourself knew anything about. No more than was the Führer himself going to.'

Rietz finally did understand then. All about Operation Juggernaut, and why Becker and Schauroth had died. And why Stemmler and von Strelow had been so confident they would get to South America or anywhere else they damned well chose.

Even as the next shell smashed into the *Java Star* and razor-steel splinters shrieked and whined about the bridge, and a ragged hole appeared like magic in the great funnel above them while Bootsmaat Landgraf came dodging and growling black-faced with outrage, fed up to the bloody TEETH with this, the greatest U-Bootwaffe fuck-up of all time . . . !

Even in *that* most frightening moment, Rietz worked out precisely why Oberleutnant Rohde felt it incumbent to try and kill his mission commander.

. . . and why it suddenly didn't matter a DAMN whether or not that mission commander fired back!

'Muster a gun crew at the stern chaser, Landgraf,' the Captain roared above the echoes of the ship's increasing agony. 'ON THE *DOUBLE* . . .!'

The British four-inch shell slid into the greased barrel at the punch of Landgraf's fist. As golden and gleaming and lethal as any fashioned by Krupps.

Rietz felt nothing now as he stood by the gun, Barr and

Strouds fixed intently on his U-boat – on the TARGET, dammit! Think ship killing. Just a ship. Any ship! He could see the white cap above the sprayshield . . . Rietz directed the gun on the white cap. It made a good aiming mark.

Fischer had slipped into the layer's seat. Rietz didn't mind that. Fischer had been denied a decent war up to now. Now the Kapitänleutnant's eye was glued to the gunsight, hands caressing the elevating handles.

'Elevation line . . . Angle of sight . . . *Range* . . .!'

By guess and by God. Shooting by the seat of the pants. No rangefinders, no fancy fruit machine calculators here. This was still Nelson's Navy; the British merchantman's cannon – wet the finger and hold it to the bloody wind to judge deflection.

'Lay! Range, nine HUNDRED . . . Mark!'

The U-Boat fuzzed in smoke again and Rietz found himself staring down the line of fire. The incoming shell hung like an angry, eight-times-magnified hornet in the glasses for a split second, then scorched overhead with a high-pitched whistle to hit the starboard side of the radio room before ricocheting, buzzing, into the Atlantic.

'Armour-piercing,' Rietz thought absently. 'They'll have to do better than that.'

It seemed quite bizarre – engaging in a surface duel against a *Frontboot*.

Particularly one manned by dead men.

Because Oberleutnant Rohde *was* dead. As was every last man in his crew. No matter how successful an operational patrol they completed once they'd finally parted from von Strelow; no matter how many broomsticks denoting victory the Oberleutnant grandly boasted from his tower as he re-entered the Nazaire lock way he – they – were still all dead!

. . . it was just that nobody had told them yet.

The really hurtful thing about it all, the Captain recalled bitterly as the gun's breech block clanged shut, is that I'd actually put my finger on the solution myself. Up there in the master's cabin, when I lectured Leo Fischer on abusing the military system to contrive my arrest? Orders are orders in the Kriegsmarine: even more unquestionably, in Oberleutnant Rohde's case, when they're given by a Fregattenkapitän. For any junior officer, come to that. Look at me – I got an order. *I* never doubted its veracity. And I'm *still* doing my damnedest to get to Southampton and blow myself up, no matter what . . .

Rohde must have *loved* HIS order from von Strelow. Given on behalf of the Führer, of course. A scenario straight from the pages of a Hitler Youth adventure comic – with, perhaps, the hint of a Cross of Iron by the hand of Adolf Hitler, once all had gone well . . . ?

A Top Secret mission within a mission. Take aboard von Strelow before sailing to rendezvous on that first evening with the *Stralsund*. Shut down all radio communication, both incoming and outgoing: something to do with enemy deception signals – you don't ask a Fregattenkapitän to justify his order: especially not when you're an obsequious little Nazi turd with ambition to become an obsequious *big* Nazi turd . . . then onwards in company to the very heart of the Atlantic, to intercept the *Java Star*.

. . . but by then ROHDE believes – because von Strelow and the Führer have decreed it – that there are *two* tasks to be accomplished; not merely one of pressing home an attack on Southampton as prescribed by the Juggernaut Opord. Task Number TWO is all about a consignment of gold. The Führer feels it would be a matter for regret should it go to the bottom along with Kapitänleutnant Rietz and his gallant horsemen, by then hell bent on Suicide Plan One. The Third Reich needs gold as much as any nation fighting a war of righteousness – where and why . . . South America! To help turn the neutrals; the already fence-sitting pro-Nazis. The banana spies . . . Not too arduous a voyage. Just land Special Ambassador von Strelow ashore in some remote paradise, then resume your patrol. Don't bother with Southampton and rescue. The Führer regrets the heroes *en route* to Southampton must be considered expendable . . .

Sail back to France to collect your medal, of course. When you've accomplished your deeds of derring-do against the halt and the lame and the weakly escorted convoys, young Attila.

Return arrogant and proud once you've run out of eels – and Schmeisser bullets!

. . . then start wondering why the Gestapo and the boot-faced SS troopers are waiting to meet your victorious landfall with such bleak, inhospitable faces . . . ?

. . . Rietz gazed at the white cap surmounting the ship of already executed dead men astern, and felt nothing. Not even dislike.

He couldn't even *blame* Rohde. He'd have done much the same himself. They were all programmed to obey. He, like Rohde, would even have been prepared to fire on his own comrades – if he'd believed, as Rohde undoubtedly believed, that the comrades had turned traitors: made off with the Führer's gold.

He'd have acted without question. If a Fregattenkapitän had ordered him to.

And he did have to salute von Strelow's initiative, if not his morality. It wasn't every Intelligence officer who borrowed Karl Doenitz's U-Bootwaffe. To fund his emigration.

'Target ON!' Fischer shouted from the layer's seat, hand poised on the firing lever.

'FIRE!' Rietz bellowed.

Rohde's U-boat blew up in a great blinding flash.

There was a very long silence on the *Java Star*'s poop deck.

A very reflective silence.

'Well, fuck me,' Bootsmaat Landgraf said eventually. Mystified.

Not surprising really: the Bosun's unease.

Considering Kapitänleutnant Fischer had never actually *fired* the gun.

Chapter Twenty-One

Rietz kept going over and over it in his mind as they steamed the short distance back to where the U-boat had sunk.

One moment Rohde's boat, and his gun crew and his bridge watch – and von Strelow almost certainly, plus nearly fifty other men below – had been trailing them like a black bat out of hell . . . and the next moment there had been a sort of blinding convulsion, a white light, a freezing of the sea around the U-boat . . .

And then she'd simply detonated in a great blinding flash, with her rapier bow and her fine-trimmed stern parts rearing from the Atlantic. And midships – just where the bridge had been – a climbing, hissing column of spray and steel and parts of men and . . . !

'Stop engines,' Rietz called quietly.

'Stop engines, sir!'

Rietz and Fischer walked out to the undamaged starboard wing and gazed down at the wreckage fifty feet below them. It was beginning to get dark: not a good time for searching for survivors.

Not that anyone expected there to be many.

Not that anyone was all that bothered. They'd all watched Rohde's idea of mid-Atlantic rest and recreation. Or had it been von Strelow's?

'Lifejacket light over there,' Leo said, pointing.

Rietz focused the Barr and Strouds. He was beginning to

prefer them to his old Zeiss. Admittedly they hadn't had as much harsh treatment: weren't ingrained with U-boat salt.

'Get the boarding net over, Landgraf,' the Captain called down to the foredeck. 'Keep a sharp eye out for anyone else.'

There was oil mulch-thick on the water. And a few scraps of wreckage. A couple of mattresses, a wooden bench from the motor room and half a dozen corpses. None of them had lifejackets, of course. They wouldn't stay afloat as long as poor bloody Schadt.

There seemed to be a deathly hush over the sea. And all around the ship. Weird. Unsettling. Probably the oil, Rietz thought uneasily. Like a blanket, muffling the sounds of living things.

He kept wondering how in God's name she'd managed to blow up like that. What kind of accident could have sparked such a holocaust. A faulty fusing; some careless error in the torpedo compartment . . . ?

'One survivor aboard, Kapitän . . . think he's an officer. Badly shocked an' covered in oil.'

Rietz looked at Fischer and raised a speculative eyebrow. The veteran shrugged. They'd find out soon enough.

'Keep searching!'

The Captain leaned over and checked the water aft, then allowed his eye to roam further afield. After a moment he said, 'Leo?'

'Yes?'

'I think I know what happened to Rohde.'

'What?'

It was Rietz's turn to point.

'*Jesus*,' Kapitänleutnant Fischer muttered.

Rietz had reached the stage when he really didn't care any more.

'New "T" Class. Fifteen hundred tons displacement; nine knots submerged,' he said. 'British, of course.'

They all look the same: just as evil, Rietz decided as they watched the submarine settle on the surface, and the curiously identical ceremony of manning the bridge and deck gun taking place.

'I can get to the gun,' Leo growled, starting to sidle inboard.

'I thought you wanted to do something really heroic: blow up the King George the Fifth dock,' Rietz retorted. 'You won't stop *that* one putting out a signal to the Tommy Admiralty by playing Cowboys and bloody Indians!'

A loud-hailer crackled from the enemy. 'What ship?'

Rietz cupped his hands and drew breath. Fischer snarled, 'Oh f'r *Christ's* sake – it's my life too, and your English is excruciating.'

He leant over the wing again. '*Java Star*. Independent on Route *Oboe*. Norfolk, Virginia, bound for Southampton.'

'Any casualties, Captain? I can lend you an SBA.'

'What's an SBA?' Rietz muttered blankly.

Leo looked at him. 'Sick Berth Attendant – in the *Royal* Navy . . . Just be damn glad I'm coming with you. Your English is even worse than I thought.'

He turned. 'Negative! No assistance required, thanks.'

'Maybe you should thank him for torpedoing our U-boat as well,' Rietz hissed.

'Maybe YOU should!' Leo snorted.

The hailer splurged again. 'Any Jerries manage to get aboard?'

Rietz giggled nervously, nerves shot to pieces.

'Picked ONE up,' Fischer bellowed. 'He's a good German. He's dead!'

'I'll wish you safe landfall then, Captain . . . I'll report your present position. Warn Southampton to expect a lady who's been slightly ravished!'

An arm waved from the tower and she began to slide ahead. As she did so she put her helm over and began to make a wide turn to starboard. She continued to swing until she was steering a reciprocal course, back the way they had come.

When Rietz's eyes met Fischer's they were bleak: all euphoria abruptly evaporated.

Neither said anything.

But the light would last for another hour: enough to make out detail.

Rietz found himself wondering how long machine-gunned sailors stayed afloat.

And ship's lifeboats. With the name *Java Star* picked out on the bow?

They'd put the survivor in Chief Officer McGregor's old cabin. Leinweber couldn't stand guard any more because he'd lost his hand to Rohde's boat and was keeping casualty Jakobi company in the small ship's hospital aft. But there were plenty of other volunteers.

Not that it was absolutely necessary. The mystery officer had apparently broken his leg which, apart from his lungs being slowly eaten by fuel oil, still wasn't bad for a chap blown out of a conning tower like a cork from a bottle.

Rietz turned the watch over to Landgraf when they were under way and course set firmly for the southern tip of England. Then he went below with Leo Fischer.

The man was trembling: a Tar Baby in advanced shock. But Landgraf had cleaned him up enough to recognize.

'Please . . .' the oil-creature chattered. 'Please *help* me?'

'You've got three choices,' Fischer growled. 'One: you die a German hero in the gates of the Southampton Dock. Two – you survive the explosion, and enjoy the hospitality of your Nazi contemporaries in a prison camp. They'll look forward very much to extending you the courtesies afforded to all who falter in their support of the Third Reich.'

'No, I can't . . . please, what is the third?'

Rietz placed the Luger on the table close to the man's spasmodic hand.

'*Heil* Hitler!' he said.

He thought it neither opportune nor charitable to mention it was the gun which had killed Maschinenobergefreiter Schauroth. And, for that matter, Funkgefreiter Stemmler.

. . . the one armed with a still part-loaded magazine of dumdums.

Even before Doenitz's U-Bootwaffe men left the cabin Fregattenkapitän von Strelow was sobbing.

Trying to pluck up courage enough to put the Luger in his mouth.

Epilogue

The Captain knew, as soon as he sighted the lean grey destroyers breaking through the chill dawn overcast blanketing the Western Approaches, that the British destruction of the *Forme Ecluse* Joubert – the Führer's *Tirpitz* Dock – would never be avenged after all.

He never dreamed that, had it not been for Oberleutnant Rohde's savagery, and Fregattenkapitän von Strelow's treachery, the whole course of history might – *might* – just have been changed. That within months of the *Stralsund*'s bravest voyage of all, strange concrete harbour-like contrivances such as Rietz could never have conceived of, were to begin construction within the great basin of the King George V Graving Dock.

They were to be known by the code name *Mulberry*. They would prove critical to something *else* that Kapitänleutnant Paul Rietz had never permitted the possibility of to enter his loyal head, but which Kapitänleutnant Fischer – and von Strelow – had foreseen even in June of 1942 . . . Operation Overlord: the return of the Allies to Occupied Europe.

Rietz would have extracted some sardonic appreciation from THAT knowledge. His Juggernaut failed: Overlord succeeded all the more surely because of it . . . the greatest and most exquisite irony of Rietz's thoroughly ironic war.

But the Royal Navy wanted Rietz's blood. And all for something he had no part in. He was a proper U-boat man. He killed ships; he didn't kill people. Once you began to think about men instead of ships you were finished . . . Once you began to enjoy it, like Führer-child Rohde, the Third *Reich* was finished!

Damned ironic, really . . .

He watched them for a moment, thinking what beautiful vessels they were compared to submarines. Not as graceful as a nicely turned merchantman though. More savage. Not the same depth of soul.

There were still a few minutes left. No need to lose the Iron Image and rush about.

Leo Fischer came and stood beside him. Rietz opened his mouth to speak, but Leo said, 'I know – Onslow Class. Forty thousand shaft horsepower, thirty-four knots: four-inch guns.'

'You've forgotten the torpedo tubes,' Rietz nit-picked.

'Eight! Twenty-one inch . . .' Leo looked sour. 'I was *trying* to forget them.'

The Captain stirred. Most of the men were on deck now, hunched against the biting wind. Some of them were looking up nervously and Rietz felt sorry about that. But there wasn't much he could do about it. He leaned over.

'Do you want to make a fight of it, boys?'

'Do we have a choice?' one of them grinned. 'With you in command?'

'You're on a charge for missing out the "sir", Uphoff!' Rietz roared fiercely. 'Report to me personally when we get back to Base.'

They all laughed at that, even the most nervous ones.

'Some of you go and help Leinweber and Jakobi on deck and out of the sick bay – wrap them up well. See they're kept out of the wind.'

Rietz went into the wheelhouse and picked up the phone.

'Chief? We've got four Onslow Class coming up fast. Open the throttles as far as they can go, then get up on deck.'

'I'd like to take a few of 'em down with us, Kapitän. Steer us good and true . . .'

Sindermann put his phone down. Rietz heard the *click* and then nothing. He didn't try again. Sindermann wasn't much of a talker, and he hadn't actually refused to obey an order.

The bits of shattered glass hidden in corners of the wheelhouse began to chatter as the revolutions climbed. Rietz saw Landgraf watching, leathery placid as ever, from the wheel.

'Thank you, Bootsmaat. For all the times you've kept me from landing myself in unseamanlike situations.'

'Sir?'

'Your teeth, Landgraf.' He thought bleakly of Stemmler, then dismissed him as if he'd never been. 'They are given to making noises whenever I propose the wrong thing ... We could, of course, go about: put our stern to the Tommies and use the gun.'

Landgraf's teeth went into spasm.

'It's a bloody *good* gun,' the Captain argued frostily. 'It sinks things without even firing!'

'Show the bastards our tail an' they'll think we're running, sir. With respect, that is.'

Fischer stepped into the wheelhouse and said, 'It's bloody cold out there. British weather.'

'I'm going to try ramming,' Rietz advised him. 'I've had my orders.'

Kapitänleutnant Fischer grinned.

'I'll bet you miss.'

'Beg pardon, Herr Kaleunt. What odds are you offerin'?' the Bosun asked.

Rietz swallowed hard and walked out to the wing, a little bit too sharply for a man who'd earned his Cross of Iron.

But ... well, he'd suddenly found conversation very difficult.

There weren't any warning shots across the bow. Not even a brief notice of execution by flashing lamp. Rietz knew for certain then that he was going to die, not for the crime of killing ships even though he loved them, but for something not even the Führer could have made him do.

When the four warships suddenly swung into line astern and placed their broadsides to him, he knew he wasn't even going to be given the opportunity to make one last gesture for Germany.

He was still roaring 'Hard to STARBOARD, BOOTS-MAA ... !' when the shells arrived on a railway train of displacing air.

He felt the *Java Star* reeling, exploding in disbelief at being done to death by her own kind. An excruciating pain seared down the Captain's side, his eyes stared in shock as the wheelhouse blew clean away. Parts of Bootsmaat Landgraf were still adhering to the wheel but Fischer – debonair, story-telling Leo Fischer – had already gone into the grey sea on his very last adventure.

Rietz saw a leather sea-booted leg . . . not a leather leg with a SEABOOT on it! An ordinary leg – no, a damned extraordinary leg with a LEATHER SEABOOT on it . . . anyway, it was lying a long way away, and Rietz knew it couldn't be Maschinenobergefreiter Schauroth's this time, because Schauroth wore engine-room boots and was already watchkeeping aboard the drowned *Stralsund*.

. . . and then Rietz recognized the leg as being his own leg, and felt all the happier for that.

There were two thousand tons of ammunition in the tween deck of number one. The next broadside would end it quickly.

That's why the Captain felt so happy. Joyous in fact. Because without TWO legs he couldn't possibly run away in the time they had left, and let himself down in front of U-boat men.

Better still: if he *didn't* run away – didn't hide down below in the bottom of the ship – he couldn't ever die in the manner of his nightmare. Never be trapped and go screaming to the bottom of the sea like the poor devil in the *Obero* . . . !

U-Bootwaffe Kapitänleutnant Paul Rietz, who had tried so hard to serve his Fatherland and Führer even though he'd only wanted to sail ships of peace, heard the next express coming and lay back.

Smiling, ever so contentedly, up at the grey sky.